*Harle* ⋯

### And the
### Disruptors of the Wish Maker

# JOHN WISCONSIN

EBOOK ISBN 978-1036921835
Paperback ISBN 979-8293712311

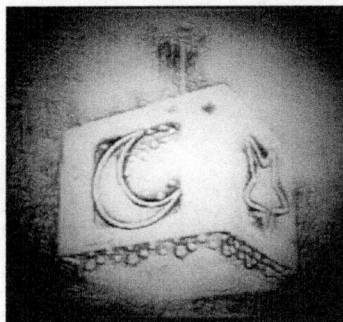

*For Will, Vinny and Dennis*

# CONTENTS

CHAPTER ONE      1
Harlem and the Stars

CHAPTER TWO      16
Day Trippers

CHAPTER THREE      34
The Secret Beyond Pressing Matters Lane

CHAPTER FOUR      50
The Life of Herrifurus

CHAPTER FIVE      66
The Story of the Boy in the School

CHAPTER SIX      84
Witchwratht and Mirrors

CHAPTER SEVEN      103
The Path to the Whitewash Woodland

CHAPTER EIGHT      119
The Calace of Judgement

CHAPTER NINE      139
The Lantern

CHAPTER TEN         151
Meeting Johnathan North

CHAPTER ELEVEN         172
The Countdown

CHAPTER TWELVE         194
The Landlord's Plight

CHAPTER THIRTEEN         213
The Zoo

CHAPTER FOURTEEN         228
The Trouble with the Cobbles

CHAPTER FIFTEEN         250
The Grottlers Rise in a World Gone Mad

CHAPTER SIXTEEN         271
Fighting Wrongs

CHAPTER SEVENTEEN         286
The Storming of the Calace

CHAPTER EIGHTEEN         302
The Final Showdown

☆☆
☆

# CHAPTER ONE

## Harlem and the Stars

For Harlem Hodge, a typical teenager who loved his life in the bustling city, to be advised that he was to move far away and say goodbye to his friends, the news wouldn't have been well received.

There would unquestionably be a teenage tantrum along the way, yet here he was in the last minute or two before his life would change forever.

Little did he know that the most astonishing set of developments would commence in moments to come, including an unexpected encounter with a figure he had only read about in stories.

The conspiring events and Harlem's fate were twisted within the ticking of the clocks, for destiny walks on unfaltering paths.

Harlem was vehemently against the idea of moving.

He patrolled his room repeatedly, dreading the impending day when the removal men would arrive, and the inevitable began.

Harlem longed for his parents to change their minds and yearned for his bedroom door to open, hoping Mum and Dad would enter with the much-welcomed news.

'Harlem, there has been a change of plan. We've discussed the move and its potential impact on you... a new school and having to find new friends… We don't think it's fair, so we've decided to continue living here!'

If only that could be, but it wouldn't happen, no way, not a chance! Mum had made it indisputable earlier.

'Harlem, we have some news. Don't overreact, and no silly behaviour, please! We're moving house at the end of the school year. We're going to Wishwisely.'

'WHERE?!' Harlem's voice was filled with frustration and disbelief.

'Wishwisely – it's a village in the centre of the middle of nowhere, out in the countryside. It's not even on the map. You could say it's the time that land forgot,' Mum expressed nervously.

Harlem wished with all his might that this was just a bad joke.

Mum never made jokes. Don't start now, he thought, and don't get the punchline wrong! Harlem turned to face Dad - good old Dougie. Dougie was the ultimate yes man, who always did what Mum demanded. He was never one to stand up for himself, and he was always one to back down from confrontation.

Harlem was confident Dad never even owned an opinion, and certainly not since meeting Mum. Dougie wasn't allowed to speak; it was a superb ventriloquist act. Harlem understood Dad was being dragged along for the ride, ensnared in Mum's selfish chase for promotion. A pursuit ended with Mum smugly confirming her new position as Headmaster at Wishwisley

School. Harlem scowled at his dad. 'Grow a spine, Douglas!' he muttered.

'HOW DARE YOU, YOUNG MAN!'

Mum was furious, but even she knew Harlem had a right to be mad, although she would never outwardly condone such behaviour nor admit it. Mum continued to make her point, still reeling from the disrespect and the audacity of Harlem to answer back.

'You'll have the summer holidays to make friends and familiarise yourself with Wishwisely. Get used to the idea; it *is* happening! It'll be a wonderful adventure!' she insisted.

Harlem had little doubt about what would happen on the day of the move. Harlem's mother, whom he often called 'Colonel Mum' due to her strict and organised nature, would stare at her watch; everything had to be planned to military timing.

Harlem knew it wouldn't go as scheduled. The delivery drivers would be behind time, tossing Colonel Mum's timetable out of the window.

She would supervise all furniture from the room to the van, witnessing damaged appliances. The dining table would probably lose a leg.

'*Be careful - that's expensive, and you've broken it!*' Mum would berate.

Colonel Mum was terrible at galvanising the troops. Dougie would be hiding well out of the way, most likely cowering in the car.

The last four hours had been a daze since hearing the unwelcome news. Harlem was adamant that his parents still thought of him as an infant and that it wouldn't be a big deal to him, but it was a big deal. Harlem switched off the light and dropped onto his bed.

The darkened room was interspersed with hundreds of bright yellow stars and two crescent moons that shone lustrously on the walls and ceiling. Despite asking on multiple occasions to have his ceiling lampshade changed, Dad had never gotten around to it, and as a fourteen-year-old, such a light shade keeping the room aglow was embarrassing!

The square light contained fluorescent stars and crescent moons projected onto the walls and ceiling in the dark for up to twenty minutes. It was designed to look 3D; the problem was that it was intended for three-year-olds.

'I wish it *would* be an adventure!'

Instantly, as Harlem mumbled those words, the stars and crescent moons began to glint. Harlem hadn't noticed at first, as he had closed his eyes, hoping that his situation was just a pretend production in his mind. The blinking, which had become more rapid and dramatic, caught Harlem's attention. Even with his eyes closed, Harlem sensed the light pulsating. He opened his left eye, raising the eyebrow to force a glimpse, pulling an unconventional face as he did so.

A few seconds later, his right eye opened to observe the stars and crescent moons flaring out of control. The shapes began to revolve on the walls and ceiling, whizzing round and round, spinning erratically. Harlem focused on the light shade, which remained perfectly motionless. Harlem was dumbfounded by what caused the patterns to dance along with the scintillating winks, as the light shade should be moving in tandem.

The flickering abruptly ceased, as did the whirling stars on the walls and ceiling. Then, the next unconventional event commenced. While Harlem composed himself, unsure if what he had just witnessed had indeed occurred, the ceiling light shade began to sway; however, the shapes on the walls and above remained stationary and did not pulsate.

Harlem had not remained at ease for long; he was now in a state of panic. He jumped from his bed, and the very second his feet hit the floor, the lightbulb came to life; the stars and crescent moons had vanished. Harlem produced the most significant gasp; he stood against the wall, staring at the light switch ten feet away. As he gazed up, the light shade was still swinging with no thought of pause.

'Oh golly, I think I'm going to be sick!'

The voice emanated from within the light shade, a low, croaky voice with an irate tone. Harlem stared in disbelief, a sense of doubt clouding his mind at the unimaginable sight before him.

This was not the usual schedule Harlem kept for a Thursday.

'A little help if you would be so kind! Harlem Hodge, I know you're there... *a little help, please!*' croaked the voice.

Harlem was utterly confused, unable to comprehend what was happening. With cautious steps, he approached the light, his head slightly bowed. Standing directly underneath, he slowly raised his eyes, a mix of fear and excitement in his gaze.

'I really would hate to be sick on you, Harlem, now help me down! It isn't every day I do this!' Two hands revealed themselves from within the light shade. 'Pull me down, boy!' insisted the irritated voice.

Harlem grabbed both hands and yanked with all his might; finally, a small head popped out.

'What took you so long? Come on now, PULL!' the voice demanded with impatience.

With the mightiest of heaves, the strange being concealed within the light fixture was now stooped on the floor, looking lightheaded.

'It's about time… now let me look at you, boy!'

Harlem towered above this peculiar creature, so the stranger clambered onto the bed to make his footing more even. The odd fellow reached out, gently pushing Harlem's head down so the two were eye to eye.

The diminutive creature resembled a little old man with deep wrinkles, sunken cheeks and exhausted grey eyes. The strange being was three and a half feet tall. He owned long, curly, wispy, black hair and an enormous, sooty, bushy beard, and he wore a dusky silk robe that covered his feet.

A black scythe was tucked within the robe and belt, which the man pulled out with his right hand. Harlem was taken aback by this unexpected sight.

'Who are you?' asked a flabbergasted Harlem.

'My name is Vincent Garrison, you will have heard of me, for that, I'm sure!'

'I'm sorry, but I don't have a clue; I've never heard of you.'

'Vincent Garrison is my true identity; you will know me by my given moniker, by my more famous name - Father Time.'

'One moment, please,' demanded Harlem, 'hold on, give me a minute!' Harlem grasped his phone and hastily searched for images of Father Time. 'Father Time is ancient with white hair and a wavy beard; he wears a white robe and carries a white scythe and hourglass...'

'*Oh, really?*' snapped Father Time. 'Well... *look here...* I've dyed my hair and beard. I'm going for a new, younger look if it's all the same to you! How do you or any of your beings know what I look like? None of your kind has ever come across me before, yet here stands a boy lecturing me on my appearance... very rude indeed!'

The irritable man opened his robe to reveal numerous clocks and watches fastened to the inside of the fabric.

Vincent Garrison was becoming crotchety, hurling all types of timekeeping gadgets onto the floor, from old eighteenth-century pocket watches to modern digital alarm clocks; he even tossed a sundial onto the floor, followed by hourglasses, pendulums, smartwatches, and stopwatches - much to Harlem's astonishment.

'Now listen to what is told, Harlem Hodge! There are those beyond the reaches of this world who would stop at nothing to know my whereabouts. I am a wanted man on the run with very few whom I trust. Who is more powerful than he who is time itself? Even the creators did not create me, not even in the subconscious or with a sound of thought. *Come!* Time flies, and I endanger myself with every second that passes... Imagine, for a moment, a phone line that's been tapped. I undoubtedly will have someone attempting to track my location in the system as we talk. You must not speak of my arrival to anyone, be it of your world or not! You must keep this a secret, for soon I make haste!'

Although he believed the man's ramblings, Harlem found it hard to keep quiet. He wanted to ask questions, but Vincent Garrison had no intention of holding an audience much longer.

'Harlem! Monsters, aliens, witches... demons... it is time to ask yourself what you believe in. How far will you go? *Come! Make haste!* I have been hastily despatched to present this world-shaking information to you.'

After patting, probing, and inspecting his pockets, which took considerably longer than necessary and with great befuddlement, Father Time presented a tattered note containing perfect handwriting, which Harlem immediately read out loud:

*'Wishwisely*

*Do you daydream of living in a fantasy of a village? Is it a delusion, or do you have the imagination to see ALL that is around you? From the Pining Forest to the Cobbles of Hankering. Make the desire a reality. The invitation is yours only. See it to believe it. No dream is involuntary. Harlem means vanquisher; that means you!'*

'What does this imply?' asked the curious and confused Harlem, who read the note twice more before repeating his question. There was no one in the room to answer him.

As Harlem came to his senses, he concluded that Father Time had disappeared, as had all his discarded timekeepers.

The light extinguished; the childlike reflections of the stars and moons were again shining, fully ingrained on the walls and ceiling as they had been for the many years Harlem could remember.

Later that night, Harlem couldn't sleep after slipping into bed. He peeped at his phone; the time was five to eleven.

'Is the ceiling moving?' he mumbled.

Harlem sat up and stared fixedly above. Even though the room was deathly-black and his hand in front of his face seemed absent, he was adamant he could make out movement on the ceiling as if it were alive.

A mercurial night-time dance routine was underway. This lasted for around thirty seconds before the dancing shadows above quickly scurried into the corners before disappearing.

Harlem sensed an unpleasant portent; he was aware that the shadows with piercing blue eyes were alive and harboured danger within them.

There had been peculiar and unearthly activity overhead, although to be reassured, Harlem tried to convince himself it wasn't real. He was restless a while longer before finally drifting off, but it is often the case that when the mind weighs heavily, sleep quantity and quality suffer. It couldn't have been truer here in Harlem's bedroom.

A room where nothing significant ever happened; that was, until a few hours earlier.

Less than an hour after nodding off, Harlem woke up; he sat up urgently with a heavy sweat across his forehead. He had been woken, disturbed from his slumber.

Harlem had the instant need to reread the note passed to him by Father Time, or as he now knew him, Vincent Garrison.

As Harlem snatched at the paper containing those words and their mysterious meaning, he was in for another shock. The tattered paper remained, but the peculiar, ideal handwriting had vanished. Confused, he stared at the blank sheet, blinking as a new subject began to appear:

*Wishes, what wishes? For they are no more!*

'Someone's playing games with me!' exclaimed Harlem, his determination to unravel the mystery evident in his voice. He knew he wasn't imagining the strange happenings, having just witnessed the words appearing on the recent blank piece of paper. He also understood he wasn't going mad, so what in the name of all things sane was happening?

Due to tiredness, Harlem concluded that someone had been playing tricks on him. A superb hoax, well-designed and very intricate, but by whom?

He began to compile a list of suspects; his mind set on finding the truth.

The first name on the list was Grandma; she was remarkable at performing magic tricks. She had gotten Harlem interested in magic from an early age, and for his eighth birthday, she had purchased him his first magic set. As a young boy, he would be mesmerised by some of the tricks she would show him. Harlem remembered the finger-in-the-guillotine illusion, but the one that made him sit up and take note was when Grandma flummoxed him with the fake thumb trick.

The fake thumb trick is where the magician, using a pretend thumb tip, claims to make small objects, such as silk handkerchiefs, disappear - *'I will now make this handkerchief vanish into thin air!'*

The audience is unaware that the illusionist already has a fake thumb hidden inside their clenched left fist.

The crowd watches as the handkerchief is pressed into the fist and secretly inserted into the phoney thumb using the real thumb of the magician's right hand. The thumb is then pressed into the pretend tip, completing the trick. All that remains is for the conjurer to raise both hands and, *'Hey presto!'* the handkerchief has vanished. The crowd, therefore, doesn't notice the fake thumb over the real one.

Now, this trick has been performed all over the globe for many years and is well known, so much so that it comes as part of most beginner's magic sets.

Grandma had taught Harlem simple tricks and had encouraged him to learn and wow his friends; this he had done and continued to do.

He was a huge fan of magicians and great illusionists who performed the impossible. Though he didn't know how some deceptions worked, Harlem firmly believed in rational explanations for everything, or so he thought.

'No, it can't be Grandma. Grandma doesn't know the first thing about technology. She struggles with a calculator; how could she pull this off?' Harlem chuckled to himself. 'Nope, *no way* she could fool me!'

Believing Grandma was capable of such a miracle was amusing. Grandma wasn't the culprit, but who could be guilty of such an outlandish act?

The second person on Harlem's list was Dad, but he was quickly dismissed. Dad didn't have the sense of humour to do something like this, nor was he so elaborate. Boring Dad, the accountant, accountants don't have fun; get a life, Dougie! Suspect number three was Mum, but like Dad, she was immediately struck off the list. All the boss did was work, work, and when she finished work, she started work again. Whether the boss was at home or work, she was always face down reviewing educational curriculum updates.

His friends were in fourth place, but then Harlem quickly remembered he hadn't had time to tell them he was moving to Wishwisely. His list was growing tired.

'That concludes that, then!' bemoaned Harlem, who had been acting a little out of his mind, compiling lists of suspects, paranoidly thinking that he must be on the receiving end of a trick. This wasn't like him, but he knew something inexplicable had occurred. No straightforward answer made Harlem increasingly uncomfortable - what unknown forces were in operation?

Just before midnight, it struck him that the school year would end one week tomorrow - eight days and counting.

For the finer part, Friday came and went without further incident, and as much as he wanted to inform someone of the strange events of the evening before, he knew he must not. Vincent Garrison had instructed Harlem to keep the encounter a secret, and he would honour that.

It was late on Friday evening when Harlem began making his journey home.

The Sun was out in full force, and as he made his way down Shifty Shiver Avenue, the sunlight suddenly began setting at an alarming rate; he could see the shrinking directly in front of his very eyes. Before long, the darkly ambience had jostled in and triggered an immediate turn for the worse.

Shifty Shiver Avenue: an unremorseful and seldom-used cut-through, a long, narrow, pebbled track with grand old English oak trees on either side. It looked jarringly out of place next to its immediate surroundings and had always imposed itself with an unearthly atmosphere. A terrible past event seemed trapped within the avenue, unwilling to fade away, a feeling only magnified by the abrupt evaporation of sunlight.

As Harlem passed through, a hostile aura filtered down from up above. Harlem raised his head, and to his horror, even in the unsettled shades and rays of premature moonlight, he glared at witches sitting on the upper tree branches—two witches per branch, two branches per tree hosting these horrid hags.

The witches were of the gruesome, stereotypical Halloween sort – they had green skin, pointed noses, warts on their lips, and hair on their chins, wore green smocks, black capes, leggings, and pointed black hats.

They were gesturing their brooms towards Harlem menacingly. The witches began cackling, becoming increasingly clamorous whilst their black cats hissed balefully. Witches glared down at Harlem eerily from both sides of Shifty Shiver Avenue.

'Nope, *not real*, they're not real,' groaned Harlem in a state of shock.

Harlem shook his head and scampered as fast as he could. The moment he exited Shifty Shiver Avenue, the Sun greeted him warmly. Upon looking back towards the avenue, to his relief, there were no witches to be seen. However, the oddity was not yet complete as four steel dustbins suddenly began to crash from high up in each tree.

Faster and faster, they fell until a powerful gust of wind knocked them all over as if someone were playing a bulky game of Skittles. As soon as the bins toppled, they vanished. Harlem sprinted the rest of the way home, gripping his completed homework tightly to his chest as he ran.

The hour was now nine o'clock, time for Harlem's favourite programme of the week – *Dirk Hader and His Excess Baggage*.

'Never missed it yet,' remarked a jovial Harlem, who, in his moment of relaxation, had somehow managed to push the earlier incident of witches to one side in his mind.

Harlem settled on the large, comfy three-seater sofa. Dad was slumped in the armchair, pretending to finish his crossword. Harlem knew it was a decoy as he would often catch Dad looking at the TV, trying to understand what was happening in the world of Dirk Hader. All the time, Mum was at the table, buried in her work as usual, with no time for rest.

Harlem was riveted to the screen; every action and sentence from the show gave him a grin. Dirk Hader indeed led an extraordinary life. 'Brilliant writing!' yelled Harlem, who had not stopped chuckling from minute one. Unfortunately, the show had been rudely interrupted by the first round of TV adverts.

'Mum, please, can we go to Wishwisely tomorrow?'

'Absolutely not!' scoffed a busy but exhausted Mum.

# CHAPTER TWO

## Day Trippers

At last, and not a moment too soon; the prolonged and unpleasant journey was at an end. The car screeched hastily outside the new house at Wishwisely. Mum had been correct: Wishwisely certainly was in the middle of nowhere.

A nearly four-hour drive, fraught with tension and ill-silence, was an uncomfortable trip for all three involved. It had been boiling and bubbling the whole way.

The moment Grandma sat in the car, she glared at Mum. 'Oh, put your face straight, Geraldine!' Grandma sensed Mum's frustration. Mum had no desire to visit Wishwisely today, and she did not keep it a secret.

'Let's just do this, *shall we*, and don't you dare talk to me!' Those snappy and infuriated words from Mum would be the last that were muttered the whole sorry way.

After Mum had said no to Harlem's request last evening to visit Wishwisely tomorrow, which was today, Harlem hadn't taken no for an answer. He had bypassed Dad; there was little point in approaching him, so Harlem had contacted the one person he knew could swing it in his favour - good old Grandma.

In a hurry, Harlem dashed upstairs, striding over three steps at a time until, in his joyous but careless ecstasy, it was one step too far. His feet felled, and his chin smacked the top step edge.

He was dragged back down half the flight of stairs, and for a moment, Harlem pondered if an invisible enemy was intent on preventing him from achieving his mission.

He called out a pitiful, self-sorrowed groan before rigidly concluding his aim back up the remaining stairs.

He impatiently phoned his grandma, instructing her to call Mum and demand that Harlem visit his new home the following day.

Mum was a strong character, but Grandma was craftier and sharper-tongued. Whenever the two disagreed on a matter, there was only ever one winner, and that was Grandma.

After hanging up the phone with Harlem, Grandma set to work. Immediately, the mobile rang, and Mum answered.

Harlem sneaked back downstairs to eavesdrop. Mum put the conversation on speaker to continue her work whilst bickering.

'Geraldine, I'm not begging you; I'm ordering you! That boy is going to Wishwisely tomorrow, mark my words! He *is* seeing Wishwisely! You can pick me up at seven o'clock; I'm coming for a nosey too, see you in the morning!'

Harlem sniggered. 'Get in, Grandma!' he whispered, but loud enough for Dad to hear. Dad knew what was coming - someone was going to get it in the neck, most probably him.

Dad looked up, offering a vast sigh followed by a shaking head; he disappeared behind his newspaper. Mum left the room in a less-than-calm manner.

Several minutes later, Mum returned looking flustered with visibly red cheeks. Her face filled with hollow annoyance.

'HOW DARE YOU!' she bellowed at Harlem, in a thunderous voice.

'How dare I what?'

'Ring your grandmother after I said no!'

'Are we going tomorrow then?' asked Harlem sarcastically.

'Yes, you know we are. You haven't heard the last of this, *not a chance*, young man!' threatened Mum.

Grandma had pulled it out of the hat, having delivered just as Harlem knew she would. Grandma: forever Harlem's champion.

Back in the present time, the car had come to a shameful standstill outside the new house. Mum exited the car, slamming the door behind her with generous force. She fiercely opened the garden gate and marched up the steps and along the path. She bitterly inserted the door key, turned it, and swiftly disappeared inside the house. Mum didn't say a word; her foul attitude was enduring.

Harlem and Grandma slowly exited the car, stretching languidly after being cooped up for so long. That was the price they had to pay, as they had schemed together; now they stretched together.

'Wow, Harlem, this is your new house - it's huge!' exclaimed an astonished Grandma.

Harlem lifted his head, gaping at the house. 'It sure is,' he replied, 'I wasn't expecting anything *this* big.'

The house was detached and completely isolated, with no other nearby houses in sight. Harlem's new home had an immaculate cream exterior and a well-to-do thatched roof.

The house was built on a mound. There was a steep and challenging stairway to negotiate after the entrance gate. Although it consisted of five steps, walking up was awkward due to the incline. Harlem took his grandma's elbow to guide her up the steps.

A narrow, cobbled path ran through the middle of the garden, leading to the impressive, red front door at the centre of the home. A large Palladian window was situated on either side and two above. Harlem eased the front door forward, allowing Grandma to enter before following her in.

The old lady closed her eyes and inhaled an almighty deep breath. Holding out her arms, she nervously exclaimed, '*Aaahhhh!*' doing a slow turn, a full three hundred and sixty degrees.

'Are you okay, Grandma?' Harlem asked worriedly.

Grandma smiled. 'I love the aura of a new house, the energy of the past and what is yet to be. What secrets and mysteries does this house hide, I wonder?'

With no curtains, the Sun shone directly in, highlighting little specks of dust floating aimlessly in the light. A glimmer of brightness in a bleak, frosty atmosphere - thanks to Mum. They left her alone in the kitchen to calm down, as the two set off to explore the house immediately. The two wandered, spending much time touring Harlem's new home: there was so much to discover.

Room by room, they drifted. So far, they had encountered two living rooms, a dining room, the kitchen, the laundry closet, a vast cellar, two spacious bathrooms, an office, and three bedrooms. Strolling down the landing, they arrived at the fourth bedroom. Harlem jovially opened the door and entered; this was the most enormous room.

'This is my bedroom!' Harlem proclaimed both giddily and enthusiastically.

Harlem stared at the view into the back garden. Looking straight down, he glanced at a prosperous patio area with steps leading to the lawn. As Harlem leaned forward, with two hands resting on the window and the now squashed tip of his nose against the glass, his eyes again alighted on a peculiar sight.

The timekeepers that Vincent Garrison (or, if you prefer, Father Time) had flung to the floor in Harlem's room were now incongruously lying on the patio. The old eighteenth-century pocket watches, digital alarm clocks, the sundial, hourglasses, pendulums, smartwatches, and stopwatches. They were joined by a colossal church bell that seemed out of place alongside an eclectic collection of timepieces.

With the house tour complete, Harlem and Grandma returned to the kitchen, encountering an eternally bad-tempered Mum.

'Oh, *you're not, are you*, Geraldine?' asked Grandma sarcastically.

Mum was standing at the breakfast bar performing work duties. All in the name of education. She couldn't help but bring vast sums of paperwork with her.

Mum, who was still frustrated with levels of irritation, sharply retaliated, 'Now listen here! I told you I was busy, so why don't you two get lost and walk around the village?'

'We shall then, we will take our time. Come along, Harlem!'

Harlem and his grandmother speedily departed the house and viewed the immediate surroundings. Over the road, the two gazed at a green wooden bench and a good old-fashioned, red British telephone box. A narrow gravel track separated a break in the trees, which seemed to run the length of the road on which they had arrived. That road seemed to last forever, and the route ended right outside the house.

'Which way do you reckon, Grandma?' enquired Harlem eagerly.

'Over there,' replied an excited Grandma, gesturing at the gravel track, as they had seen nothing of note on the inbound journey.

Sauntering down the track, full of twists and turns, they came upon an old, moss-covered church to the right of the path. Harlem peered into the churchyard; it was in a sorry state, with long, shadowy, overgrown grass towering over and covering many gravestones. Eventually, the trail ended, and Harlem got his first glimpse of Wishwisely as the trees gave way.

A gigantic field stretched as far as the eye could see. One stupendously large, solitary, and unknown species of tree proudly held its position in the centre of the field. It was a monumental round field, easily a few miles in diameter.

Turning left, they began their tour, venturing onto the dusty high street.

Thatched cottages, each painted in a different pastel shade, lined the street in a charmingly unique manner. The repetition of the colour scheme added to the village's distinctiveness, making it a truly remarkable sight.

Throughout their walk, the main road continued to curve sinuously.

Upon arriving outside the village pub, one extraordinarily tall and bizarrely dressed country bumpkin wearing a fading poncho acknowledged the two strangers.

'Don't get many visitors round 'ere, day tripping is thee? We've had no… had no newcomers 'ere for a long time; what brings thee 'ere today? Tell me, you… you must!'

Grandma hurriedly dragged Harlem away, waving politely at the man as they proceeded. 'Ignore him, Harlem; he's probably drunk or befuddled!'

On they went about their business, but it hadn't gone unnoticed by Harlem that four teenagers on bikes were following them, scurrying, and hiding behind the rows of cottages, poking out their heads to get a sneaky glimpse.

The group looked like they belonged to another era; their clothing and bikes wouldn't be out of place in the 1960s.

Grandma was so enchanted with Wishwisely that she hadn't noticed the snoopers - one girl and three boys. If their game was to stay out of sight, they were terrible at it.

Marching onwards, they reached a quaint quintet of white windmills. Harlem had never seen a real-life working windmill before; he was in awe as he watched the four black propeller blades slowly rotating on each windmill.

'Do people still use these in this day and age?' asked Harlem dubiously.

'Looks like they do here... *very strange*,' answered Grandma whilst pointing to an additional set of horizontal blades on top of the windmills, precisely like the ones on a helicopter.

No other windmill in the world possessed propellers like these.

The road continued to curve, and the day trippers stumbled upon the village school. The school could easily be overlooked, nightmarishly imprisoned by a lofty wall and railings, with towering, thick oak trees imposing down on the school ground from all directions, seemingly encroaching on the school's personal space. The somewhat medieval gates were locked and appeared almost sinister, even in the daylight.

Harlem peered through the railings. The school was considerably larger than he had imagined, but it appeared as austere, derelict, and ominous as he had feared, and that was without Colonel Mum's presence.

'Let's be gone, Harlem; this place gives me the creeps!'

Grandma gestured to Harlem to come along immediately; she wanted to distance herself from the dreadful school. Until now, it had been nothing but sunny, calm blue skies.

Without warning, a monstrous, forbidding, darkened cloud had materialised purposefully over the school. Claps of intense thunder began disturbing the previously peaceful atmosphere.

A dour, grey energy had manifested itself solely above the education centre. As far as the eye could see, magnificent, pleasant, splendid weather was all around.

What was happening aloft the school? Harlem and his grandmother did not wish to dwell on it.

After twenty seconds of hurrying onwards, Harlem stared back, sensing evil-looking company. His eyes landed upon a boy standing inside the school grounds, gripping the gate. The boy waved menacingly at Harlem. The impudent rascal then proceeded to usher Harlem away; his threatening gestures with his fingers left Harlem with no doubt that he must go urgently. Harlem dashed and caught up to Grandma, not mentioning a word about the boy.

Several minutes later, the journey led to the village shop. Upon entering, they found knick-knacks and trinkets everywhere. Ducking and weaving between and under the clutter, they met a little old lady sitting at the counter who engaged them in conversation.

'I bet you're the ones who've bought the old, empty North house; *why else* would you be here? Not since the North's upped and left has anyone settled in that house. They left sixty years ago after the North boy disappeared in the woods. The villagers searched and searched, but he was never found. No one knows what occurred… perhaps… other-worldly hands were loitering in Wishwisely! A most baffling and peculiar event… and for all that time, the house belonging to them has remained empty. Some say it's cursed,' croaked the old crone.

'We'll be leaving now,' insisted Grandma.

They hastily left the shop without purchasing any items; Grandma certainly wasn't buying the old lady's yarn. Passing five more windmills and one reservoir, the tour of the high street was all but complete. Harlem once again eyed the four teenagers following him. He pointed them out to Grandma.

'I don't see anyone, Harlem, *don't be silly,*' she said dismissively.

Typical! The one time that Grandma looked, they remained out of sight. Returning to the gravel track, the two understood that they had strolled for several miles around the village high street; both were aware that Mum would impatiently be waiting for them at the house. The two unhurriedly made their way back.

The week bolted by, and it was soon time for Harlem's first night in his new bedroom. He was content that it was all over; the move was finally complete, having gone exactly as he had envisioned. The removal men were indeed late, and furniture was dropped, with several items damaged beyond repair. Quarrels had occurred between Colonel Mum and the furniture handlers, with Dad sitting in the car, avoiding all the troubles.

Now, at Wishwisely, Harlem knew there was a secret to uncover relating to the information handed to him by Father Time. Harlem rewrote those words on a piece of scrap paper. He read it aloud:

'*Wishwisely*
*Do you daydream of living in a fantasy of a village? Is it a delusion, or do you have the imagination to see ALL that is around you? From the Pining Forest to the Cobbles of Hankering. Make the desire a reality. The invitation is yours only. See it to believe it. No dream is involuntary. Harlem means vanquisher; that means you!*'

Harlem pored over the words repeatedly. He nestled on the bed, scrutinising them. Later, he walked his room like a thespian reading a script aloud, with the screenplay in hand. He could not decipher its meaning, regardless of his posture or expression. Harlem was exhausted from overthinking, but just as he drifted off, an idea came to him.

'OF COURSE!' yelled Harlem. The word ALL was the only one in capital letters. Harlem knew where he would be heading in the morning.

The alarm clock was beeping its way into life at half past five. Harlem was up, ready, and downstairs in a flash. He sneakily exited the house and bolted across the road and down the gravel track. He didn't stop galloping until he reached the ginormous tree in the middle of the colossal field, right at the centre of the village.

It had struck Harlem that to see ALL around you, he had to be in the very centre of the village, precisely where the one tree gracefully stood. Harlem pressed his hand hard against the trunk and closed his eyes as he recalled Father Times' message out loud. Instantly, Harlem was greeted with an immediate, bothersome itching all over his hands and arms - the tall grass was intolerably scraping against him.

This distinctive grass was purple and at least four feet tall. Harlem had the peculiar but correct sentiment that he was no longer in the village of Wishwisely. The tree had vanished; not only that, but the grass at the village centre had recently been mowed and still offered that fresh-cut smell and texture. Besides, that grass was green.

Bewildered, he glared hard at a mystifying aluminium signpost floating purposefully over the purple meadow; the words printed in plum read *"THAT WAY"*, accompanied by an arrow below.

The mauve scenery above depicted a setting of a permanent, premature sunset, but with dozens of aimlessly drifting puce asteroids passing by at an unrushed pace. Harlem was shocked but stepped forward without a pause.

At the edge of the field, a farmyard gate covered in purple crushed velvet separated Harlem from whatever lurked beyond. Harlem could see nothing on the other side, as if staring at a blank universal screen. He leaned forward for a closer peek at the miniature words imprinted into the velvet:

*'No need to lock the gate behind you!'*

More confusing still was that there was no fence around the field's perimeter, just the gate and two posts. Harlem thrust the gate forward and dutifully locked it behind him, thus ignoring the instruction printed on the gate.

He was now standing at the beginning of a cobbled path, with two cobbles set side by side comprising the width of the walkway, followed by two more in front, and so on, all in line and connected.

The cobbles followed a gaudy comic book colour scheme of orange and blue, forming a criss-cross pattern.

As Harlem took a step forward, the walkway began shaking timidly. Focusing hard on the cobbles, Harlem witnessed, with shock, a word materialising under his feet. The word was painted in black and spelt out across the width of the path.

WOOSH! The word was gone - it had whizzed away. More words followed, travelling at supersonic speed.

Harlem concluded that it was best for him not to stay stationary, so he ventured onwards. As he did, more words hurtled onwards. This peculiar action continued throughout the entire strange journey he was undertaking. A thick, humming, unearthly smog accompanied Harlem. An unusual fog that did not hinder his view of the cobbles but strangely prevented him from knowing what was on either side and above the walkway. Harlem paid little attention to the smog as he concentrated on the task: walking along a quaking path was tricky and complicated.

After five minutes of ambling on the cobbles, Harlem heard a booming, violent and fearsome voice.

'YOU, FROM THAT HUMAN LOT, GO BACK!'

Despite the threatening nature of the disembodied voice, Harlem somehow found the courage to continue on his way. The smog slowly dissipated, allowing Harlem to catch a glimpse of an unpleasant and frightening sight ahead. He was approaching what appeared to be two clowns standing face-to-face on opposite sides of the cobblestones, both waving manically and laughing.

To the left was a male clown, just over six feet tall, dressed in a bizarre costume, even for a clown. On his feet were black, oversized shoes with gold coins stitched into the leather. Accompanying this, he wore green and black baggy trousers with five-pound notes printed on the fabric. The clown was overly portly; his bright, red shirt did not fit him well, nor did it completely cover his rotund stomach, as some of his gut was partially exposed.

The words "I HAVE MORE MONEY THAN YOU" were embroidered on his shirt in bright, white letters. The clown wore a tall, black, shiny top hat and a red tailcoat. The tailcoat had a much more faded red hue than his shirt.

Pinned to the tailcoat were hundreds, if not thousands, of twenty-pound notes. Sizeable red gloves covered his giant-sized hands.

As for his face, it was masterfully painted, far from the classic smiling clown design intended to make children cheerful; the makeup seemed to match the money theme of the rest of the ensemble. A fifty-pound note was perfectly painted on his face with rich detail. Harlem noticed one strange anomaly - the nose was not a clown's nose, not a standard, red-painted circle. It wasn't even a human nose but instead a tiny pig's snout. To the right of the cobbles stood a much shorter lady clown standing precisely five feet.

She closely resembled her male counterpart, wearing a matching outfit. She was simply a smaller, mirror image of him; she was also overweight, and her shirt was far too small for Harlem's taste.

Oddly, the clowns began oinking feverishly at one another, followed by jovial squeals and shrieks. Harlem cautiously approached, never taking his eyes off the grotesque beings standing before him.

The male clown removed his top hat, revealing a head of balding, luminous curly hair. He pulled out an enormous cream cake from the depths of his top hat, like a magician revealing a rabbit. The lady clown started clapping at the show somewhat excessively. He returned his hat to his head before shoving the cream cake into his mouth. The cake was gone, not including a dribble of cream that had escaped on his chin. Both clowns applauded enthusiastically, and the larger clown tore off a twenty-pound note from the tailcoat and wiped away the cream residue from his chin. He next took it upon himself to fiendishly devour the money.

The clown opposite found the show hilarious; she quickly tore away several twenty-pound notes from her tailcoat, munching away gleefully. The oinking noises returned, accompanied by much salivating and licking of their lips.

The clowns looked at Harlem for the first time, as he had been standing all but next to them during the bizarre performance. Both clowns suddenly became agitated, gesturing at him menacingly.

The male now gripped, with both hands, a broken golf club with a missing clubhead. As Harlem passed, the clown lunged forward, swinging the fractured golf club towards him.

Thankfully, Harlem had youthful speed on his side, whilst the clown was overweight and slow. The youngster ducked and shuffled his way forward. Fortunately, the golf club missed the intended target. The clown remained rooted on the spot, admonishing himself for failing to whack Harlem.

The clown shouted irately, 'DO YOU KNOW WHO I AM, DO YOU?!'

Harlem had the good sense not to hang around; he was already making his way further along the path, distancing himself from the despicable duo.

A minute later, the smog again dissipated. Harlem had arrived at a wooden signpost - *"Pressing Matters Lane"*. The cobbled path had abruptly ended, cut short by a whopping, rugged, darkened, slate rock that had positioned itself immediately in front of Harlem.

He had come all this way, but what was next… was this the end of the adventure?

'Excuse me, young man; I am not old! I am sixty-four hundred and two years… and two years of your time. My predecessor handled the job for ten thousand years before retiring!'

The voice belonged to an incredibly bizarre man standing on the rock. It was the same man loitering outside the pub last week. The man leapt from the rock, elegantly floating to the ground. He was splendidly tall, standing at seven feet seven inches. Although impressive, he was spindly and carried no fearsome qualities.

The stranger had thick, blazingly white hair pulled back in a ponytail, but his remarkable feature was his incredibly long, white, bushy handlebar moustache. He wore a fading stripey orange and blue poncho, exposing two gaunt-looking wrists. Visible underneath the poncho was a dull orange pair of safari-styled shorts that came down to just above the ankles, paired with dirty white socks. He wore sandals on his feet that were dirtier still, his big left toe sticking out of both sock and shoe.

The man carried the biggest, darkest, puffiest bags under his eyes that Harlem had ever seen. His hygiene was questionable; a damp, fusty smell accompanied him, and his teeth were a stale brown colour. His fingernails needed a trim, if only to remove the dirt that had accumulated.

'Forgive me for my outburst; I'm sensitive about... about my age... maybe a pre-pre midlife crisis, who knows... *who...* knows? Do you know?'

Despite his wacky appearance, Harlem couldn't help but instantly like the man. The stranger had difficulty communicating effectively due to his apparent inability to control the volume of his husky voice.

He would speak with a regular cadence, then all at once very slowly. Intermittently, the slowness would be replaced with sudden bursts of rapid-fire speech.

When speaking, the volume would rise high and then drop back down. Additionally, the man had a habit of repeating words, often between pauses...

*'Harlem Hodge; I'd say you are... you are... yes, you are!* I know, for I've been keeping an eye... an eye on you... My name is Herrifurus! You stand presently on Pressing Matters Lane! To come thus far, you have entered a class of just eight children of Human who once stood where you stand now.'

'Where am I again?' asked the bewildered boy.

'Harlem Hodge, you stand on... you stand on Pressing Matters Lane... You have walked upon the Cobbles of Hankering. *Come... come...* we have work... have work to do!

Through this rock, a world lies hidden... *hidden*... from humankind. A world created for hope, prosperity, and enlightenment. For the well-being of your kind, it must be kept... kept secret. Hope must flourish; without hope, you are lost... lost... forever!'

Herrifurus pushed his hand hard into the rock; it appeared to be quite a struggle. It did not have the desired outcome. Herrifurus then put his back to the rock and pushed and heaved with all his might. With his backside against the rock, he heaved with one last massive strain of effort. A wavy, misty, black doorway with a white chalk outline appeared within the rock.

Come on, Harlem; there's nothing to be afraid of, come ... come, let us step... *step forward together.*'

# CHAPTER THREE

## The Secrets Beyond Pressing Matters Lane

After proceeding through the doorway, Harlem found himself standing in a room that barely resembled an office. It should be noted that the office was a tragic and messy space, with a large timber desk situated in the left corner.

Harlem wouldn't be surprised if the desk hadn't been used for many years, possibly decades, as it was now covered with yellowed, scattered paperwork. The documents were engulfed in dust, not just one layer but multiple levels that had accumulated over what must have once been an ornate and purposeful desk.

The desk chair, at one time or another, had probably been upholstered in expensive, green leather. Over the years, the green had faded, and the chair had suffered several rips and tears, which had been crudely patched up with tape. The chair had also become obscured with a noticeable level of dust.

Next to the desk towered a large oak bookshelf consisting of eight shelves—a bookshelf with no books.

Crumpled pieces of paper crowded each shelf; the papers were coated with a layer of grime that had accumulated over many years. The dust was rife; if you weren't cautious, you could easily clog and choke on it.

Wood chip wallpaper had been pasted on the walls a long time ago, and over the years, someone had made a decent attempt at picking out the wood chip pieces.

Of the remaining pictures on the walls, all were hanging lopsided. It was obvious to Harlem that many pictures had fallen off and remained lying face down on the grubby floor.

Footprints were interspersed across the tattered, dusty, and faint remains of the once-ruby carpet. One tall coat rack, minus any coats, leaned crookedly against the back wall.

The woodworm had found its home in the coat rack, and evidently, the damage was already done.

Stacks of books had been positioned precariously throughout the room, all haphazardly piled upon the carpet. Some heaps had to have been between forty and fifty books high. The stacks were not organised systematically but were erratically strewn in random spots. Harlem wondered if, at some stage, individual piles of books had toppled over and had long since been forgotten. The casualties still lay where they had found themselves.

In the right-hand corner, a superbly constructed solar system model was propped up, and it was an authentic replica. It contained the eight planets, the five dwarf planets, the Sun, the moons, belts, rings, dust clouds, centaurs, and comets.

'Herrifurus, *did you* build this model?' wondered Harlem, with awe.

'Indeed, I did... *I did*... Many... many moons ago, when time was kinder to me. In the days past, when the job wasn't so... wasn't... so... demanding, I had much more free time to myself... *Now it is impossible... impossible to find luxury in one's hobbies...* The world has become so toilsome... *so...* toilsome...'

Herrifurus expelled a massive sigh before solemnly gazing at the roof whilst shaking his head.

Harlem blew heavily on the model scale of Planet Earth, causing dust to scatter; the entire model was swamped in dust - layers of grime ingrained within more layers of dirt.

The office hadn't been cleaned in a long time. Harlem wondered if it had ever received a cleanse.

'Herrifurus, do you have a cleaner who could give this place a once-over?' he asked.

'Oh, there is no call for that! The tidying of an office does not affect the work I do here. *Pristine or disorderly...* the role I have been entrusted with does, as always... as always, come first. *Top of the list, number one on my agenda...* I like my office as it is... as... it... is... Mokwug is always on my case, demanding that she be allowed to tidy up in here.'

'Who?' enquired Harlem.

'Mokwug is my number two, my secretary, charlady, and all-round ear grinder... *Everything must be so serious... so serious! All done by the book, the sanctimonious so and so...* The deputy to my Sheriff, but come outside... *outside...* for I have so much to tell, and you require so much... so much to learn...'

Harlem and the eccentric departed the room, entering a pleasant, golden field. Harlem glanced back, realising that the office they had exited had been inside a red and white painted circus marquee. Harlem would never have guessed it while standing inside.

Harlem next observed a crooked wooden table next to the entrance. Staring at the table, he glanced at eight globes on top. One globe was smashed; they reminded Harlem of the snow globes he loved to entertain himself with during Christmas.

'Walk with me… *walk*… with me!' instructed Herrifurus as the two cheerfully sauntered over to the single tree within the field.

'Herrifurus, I've never seen a tree this size!' exclaimed Harlem.

'Absolutely not… absolutely… not,' replied Herrifurus gleefully. 'This is the biggest tree to have ever lived on the known planets… and the oldest… and… the oldest. Clear the mind… the mind of any doubt, for the following words will undoubtedly reveal impossibilities and extraordinariness which no child of Human could have envisaged. Open yourself to the impossibilities… in doing so, you will see… you will see past the boundaries of logic. *From the impossible to the probable… for the ludicrous becomes the standard, make the unexpected the conventional…* What you are about to hear has only been uttered six times in the past! Regardless of how you listen… you must listen! The fate of Enduring Crave rests on you, Harlem Hodge!'

Harlem had been listening and absorbing every word with immense intent. Whatever he had found himself mixed up in, he knew it was serious.

After all, he had just been informed that the fate of Enduring Crave now rested upon him, even though Harlem had no idea what that meant.

Herrifurus motioned at the tree and began talking chaotically once more.

'What you stare upon is known as the Motherhood Tree - the only one of its kind, breathing effortlessly for over twenty thousand years. I wouldn't be showing enough respect if I only mentioned her age; the height of this beauty stands majestically at five hundred feet. *The width... the width is fifty feet...* with leaves beyond golden than the greatest treasures of Egypt and as wholesome and light as the fairest beach ball. Motherhood provides life to Enduring Crave. A world in which all its prosperities and substance are produced within the confines of the colossal centre of the terracotta trunk. At the dawn of Enduring Crave, she was planted in what would be the very centre... the very centre of this world... All activity flow stems from here; our world survives through her. *Motherhood gives us life... planted in the morning, standing triumphant... triumphant by evening.*'

Harlem had urgent, pressing questions that he immediately put to Herrifurus; they came at him exceedingly fast and without pauses.

'Where is Wishwisely? What happened to Pressing Matters Lane? How can I be here, and what is Enduring Crave?'

'Harlem, my dear boy... *my... dear boy...* I would ask for your complicity and patience... and patience. This is all coming at you very fast, and there is much to take on, but take on you must... *you must!* If you allow me to explain all that must unfold without interruption... *without...* interruption... then you will understand. If you permit me, there will be a time for questions at the end; now, may we agree... *may we...* agree?' asked an animated Herrifurus.

'Herrifurus, can I ask just one question before you begin?' pleaded Harlem. 'Just one, that's all. No more, I promise!'

'*Very well, you may question... you may question...*' replied Herrifurus gleefully.

'Herrifurus, soon after we met on Pressing Matters Lane... you said I was the eighth... *what was it...* err, yes, the eighth child of Human to have stood where I was. But just a minute ago, you told me I was about to hear something that had only been heard six times before. How can that be with seven humans here before me?'

Herrifurus was visibly dumbfounded, his face showing a severely disconcerted expression. 'What... what was that?' he replied frantically. 'Forgive my scatterbrain. Of course... of... course ... that doesn't make any sense. Seven children of Human and seven times before... I have forgotten to carry my facts correctly. *So bumblesome... I am so bumblesome!* Be attentive to what follows, Harlem. *Ears to the ground...* ears... to... the... ground; it is imperative you internalise what is spoken... of what... is... spoken...'

Harlem smiled at Herrifurus. He couldn't help feeling that Herrifurus was a little absent-minded at times - and not just due to how he spoke. Herrifurus was kind-hearted, good-natured, if maybe frequently prone to blunders, and somewhat scatter-brained. Harlem would pay attention to the information within his grasp; for now, there would be no intrusions.

*The Awful Account of Man*

'It had become obvious to the Eight Curators that mankind is flawed. Mankind, the name given to humans by humans... If ever an epithet did not carry an accurate representation to describe a flock, this was it... Long before this moniker was widely adopted, the Eight Curators labelled them 'Sapiens'. The Eight Curators had never seen a species filled with hate and anger. Self-destruction is programmed and rooted firmly within. A sort who, without hesitation... *without hesitation*... would willingly kill, harm, maim and disfigure... A group that allows children to become orphans. Creatures waging war for greed... Scoundrels loot treasure and make slaves of conquered armies whilst decimating foreign cities. Beings who willingly allow their fellow man to endure famine! It is not only today that those suffering from poverty are ignored... are ignored and cast aside as the disease of society. It is common practise to walk past those whose homes are the streets in cities and towns... and towns, as it has been for millennia over and over! From the convincing of the... of the smallest of lies to those closest, the theft from family and friends, and the cheating on loved ones, Human Beings act on immorality as a means; it is their natural behaviour. Man's fundamental flaw is self-obliteration; *why else* build weapons of mass... of mass destruction but to destroy...but to destroy himself? Why I ask, why?'

Herrifurus ceased talking momentarily. He frowned at the ceiling, shaking his hands dramatically in vexation.

'The Eight Curators viewed in... *viewed in with distress*... The Curators clutching responsibility for the functioning of the eight largest planets. A Curator fashioned one orb, but it was deemed inappropriate for the creator of that planet to be the Curator... In the beginning, the Curators marvelled at the prodigiousness of their creations, new worlds hatching the existence of life. This was the dream... the determination accomplished. Actuality isn't always as humans imagine; just because you cannot see it doesn't mean it cannot be... it... cannot be! The quiddity of Alien beings is not only flesh and bone! Harlem, there is life on Mars; the question has long been answered, if not by man. Man... who knows all... *no... not at all*... not... at all... and not at all, how to live responsibly! *Life on Mars, I do titter... the Marsipanians loved Ziggy for that one...*'

Herrifurus chuckled to himself and began caressing his moustache in joviality; he approached the model of the Solar System and carefully wiped away a deep line of dust from Planet Earth.

'...An assembly was held to discuss and remedy the Sapien concern. An outcome had to be constructed and without delay... *without...* delay... The Eight Curators present, as were the Five Principles of the Outer planets. Merkle, the mastermind of Mars, called for the destruction and the end of humanity, whom she described as having given up... given up the right to harvest the most vibrant of planets. Merkle despised the gall and contempt that Sapiens exhibited. The most hospitable orb was inhabited mainly by the most undeserving... *undeserving of beasts...* Earth contains the lavishness and prosperity that its contemporaries lack. Despite Merkle's prosecution... the end of humankind was not ratified. Though with the power of planet creation, this did not involve meddling... meddling with the demise of a species. Grief inherent, poverty customary, and all the vulgarities of war, I have spoken thus far. Good was an oasis in a desert world... a desert world of wickedness! The Curators voted seven to one to approve a second motion...'

Herrifurus paused yet again, his mannerisms indicating he found the story too demanding to work through without a break. He smiled at Harlem, played with his moustache once more and then jerked his ponytail several times...

'...Planet Earth had become an insupportable cesspit, colonised by the most monstrous monsters. The solution was to instil humankind with the power of wish. *To wish is not a right; it is a gift from the Curators.* **Wishes: a reason to believe, a purpose to follow, and the bestowment of hope in human hearts...** Without wishes, there is no aspiration, only evil iron tickers! Although the Curators are not allowed to involve themselves in Sapiens' business, the gift of a wish was the one exception. The Curators created a new world, hidden in conjunction with the human world. The one pitfall was that... was that this all had to be regulated attentively, as there had to be rules to govern; not every wish could come true. Can you imagine what would happen if humanity found out where in their world wishes were approved... approved... or rejected? *No, no, no, it had to be a concealed unknown, set within a secret world... a... secret world...* The world of Enduring Crave *is* that secret world! A dimensionally engineered triumph, where we must go back over twenty thousand years! The human world and Enduring Crave inhabit the same planet, but those two worlds never commingle, except for the occasional anomaly, which is why you are here, Harlem. There had to be a gateway between worlds so that wishes could be received here... in Enduring Crave - from one world to another... That portal is Pressing Matters Lane - a space-time corridor - through the Meadow of Purple Purpose, then on to the Cobbles of Hankering. Instantaneously, a wish, when made, arrives at Pressing Matters Lane; once it materialises on the Cobbles of Hankering, it hurtles onwards, entering Enduring Crave and arriving at the Calace of Judgement. Seconds after a wish is produced, it arrives at the Calace. *Not bad, eh, Harlem? Talk about speedy service.* Your world... your world to ours in three seconds... three seconds! We are proud of this feat. *Three-two-one* - from anywhere in the world to the Calace in three seconds. *One-two-three...* Those... those vocables you witnessed on the Cobbles of Hankering represent the wishes of the citizens of Earth. We receive millions every day from people desperately probing hope. As the centuries pass, more and more wishes come our way. *A powder keg... a powder keg I say!'*

Herrifurus abruptly ceased talking. He repeated his vexation this time by waving his arms about and staring fixedly at the model of the Solar System.

Harlem sensed that Herrifurus had lost concentration, having become befuddled.

'...Where was I? Ah, yes, *yes*, back to the gateway. It was supposed to be a one-way affair, with only the Ambassador of

Enduring Crave, *that is, me*, permitted to pass between worlds. However, five hundred years ago or so, we witnessed the first Human Being arrive on Pressing Matters Lane. *I was too late... too... late...* to intercept him... A circumstance no one had foreseen thus transpired. Not even the Curators had made contingencies. The first man to leave his world behind and acknowledge ours. It had been nigh on one hundred and ninety-five centuries, and we had masked ourselves for all that time. The portal had, at last, been breached. Godfrey, what a pleasant man; he and his family settled where Wishwisely would flourish. One morning, Godfrey wandered into a field, and right at the very centre of that meadow, he planted seeds. *A coincidence? No, it couldn't be... it couldn't be...* A direct connection occurred as those seeds instantly sprouted into life, interweaving within the roots... within the roots of Motherhood. The Childhood Tree in Wishwisely grew... grew instantaneously... on the spot... to the size it stands today. This opened the gateway for Godfrey. With his time of Enduring Crave complete, he promised never to relate his visit to another, and he never did... Many years later, Godfrey's ancestors were allowed access to Enduring Crave after consultation with Motherhood. Harlem, my boy, yes, in case you're wondering, the seven priors are Godfrey and his successors. You are the first to come here without the surname North...'

'You mean he was called Godfrey NORTH!' expressed Harlem with great excitement and a shrill voice.

Herrifurus peered down at Harlem with an inquisitive and questioning frown.

'Harlem, my new... *my*... new friend... is everything okay? You seem a little... a... little... taken aback?'

'*No*, I just remembered a story someone advised me. It brought back a memory; it doesn't matter. Please continue!' Harlem recalled the tale of the missing North boy that the old lady in the shop had retold to him.

'Harlem, my friend, memories can never... can never escape. They are a part of who we are. Though bygone eras have given up on their time, they live on... they live on inside in the form of memories. The last of Godfrey's descendants journeyed here sixty years ago. We haven't greeted another North child since... Over time, the Meadow of Purple Purpose was installed, featuring purple grass that deliberately reduces oxygen, causing temporary confusion of short-term memory. To overcome that with a full sense of mind... should not be probable... This isn't magic, of course; none of what you see is magic; it is simply two worlds colliding. Touch the tree and believe... you *must* believe!'

Even after everything Harlem had witnessed and discovered thus far, he still couldn't comprehend how two worlds on one planet could function without affecting the other. It made no sense. Herrifurus could feel the confusion within him.

'We do not question the Moon and its existence in daylight. Nor do we... nor do we ask if the Sun lives when the nights reign. We acknowledge that the stars are always present. We cannot see the wind, but we know it leaves its calling with the breeze and shaking of the trees. You believe in your favourite picture-vision-box programme, don't you? *That holds two worlds, but when I give you guidance on fact...* you find it implausible... *you find it... implausible...'*

Herrifurus referenced Harlem's favourite television programme, Dirk Hader and His Excess Baggage.

Harlem adored this show -Dirk Hader, a retired international astronaut and a hero on planet Earth. Having endured too much fame, Dirk had retired to an obscure village to run a local pub. His only customers were the ghosts of the dead. Aliens had invaded the spirit world, and the dead left their world through a portal, seeking refuge and Dirk's help. The series centred around Dirk Hader as the hero, defeating the aliens in the spirit world.

Harlem acknowledged that Herrifurus was correct; here, the impossible was probable. Herrifurus had opened Harlem's eyes with the parable of the unapparent. Two worlds could, of course, share Planet Earth.

'Harlem, let us return to the stories; the tales... the tales of humankind from millennia many times... *many times over.* I concede how darkly the world had mutated; no words could justify the terror that ruled. A pandemic... a pandemic of fear, misery, panic, depravity and trepidation; *complete insanity!* The rising of a new dawn could not... could not diminish the hideousness of night. Only in the day of light were nightmares real. The greater humanity's fears, the closer they became to reality; man had stepped within a whisper of self-destruction. The world's population had diminished to the last one hundred thousand... Historians have no suspicion... *no* suspicion that man has been marching the world over for so long through time;

the evidence has been obliterated! Without hope, the blemish… the blemish rooted within was triggered—a long-embedded flaw, the flaw to eradicate one's species. To detach the ability to wish would bring about the return… the return to the darkest of man's days. To deny aspirations and be in a circumstance of no… of no positive outcomes is not worth contemplating; Enduring Crave must… must flourish!'

It had been an extraordinary day, filled with unprecedented and intriguing information that had found its way to Harlem. He had just experienced his first encounter with Enduring Crave, which would mark the beginning of his bewildering journey. Harlem had learned that to wish was not born at the beginning of humankind's tenure on Earth. This had, at a later stage, been incorporated into daily life.

To see the abandonment of wishes would usher in the rise of the ultimate dark age; a considerable debt was owed to the Eight Curators.

Harlem and Herrifurus entered the circus marquee and returned to the disorderly office. Harlem sat on the green, swivelling chair and was immediately assaulted by the cloying dust. He gazed at the unkempt sight before him; it was a sorry, grubby state.

'Harlem, it must soon be time to end our first day together,' expressed Herrifurus. *This is only the beginning… the beginning…* Much learning awaits… awaits you… We cannot and will not let too much too soon weigh upon the mind. We shall resume tomorrow, and then our tour of Enduring Crave will begin.'

After exiting the office, the two again found themselves beside the whopping, rugged, darkened, slated rock on Pressing Matters Lane.

'Follow the cobbles home. To tell others is to close your door… your door of return!'

Herrifurus, for the first time, was stoney-faced and serious; Harlem noted this.

'*Why me*, Herrifurus?' Harlem's curiosity was piqued, and he couldn't help but ask. He was eager to understand his role in this unfolding adventure.

'Because you desired it, didn't you? You wished for an adventure—and here you are. You are not like the others. You do what is right; I speak of truth, of your studiousness. The man who does not follow the flock cannot be a sheep… The wise man walks alone; the fool hides in the crowd.'

Harlem bid his farewell and set off on the cobbles, heading in the opposite direction from which he came. The Pig Clowns were nowhere to be seen on his return journey, which was reassuring. He approached the gate, closing it behind him, before striding purposefully across the Meadow of Purple Purpose. Harlem did not emerge at the tree; he had returned to his world to find himself standing on the gravel track.

Harlem had the peculiar notion that he was being watched. As he turned around, staring back towards the Childhood Tree, he realised he was now ominously facing over thirty black cats. Cats with overgrown claws and whiskers in dire need of a trim.

The mystery of these cats added to the intrigue of Harlem's journey.

At once, every cat began hissing and spitting at him balefully. Harlem hurried home; the cats followed. Despite his certainty that the mangy felines would maul him, they did not launch an attack.

The clowder of cats kept pace with Harlem, leaving a five-foot gap between them and him as they pursued. Harlem panicked and hastily turned left into the churchyard. He waited and waited, his heart beating a tattoo in the darkness, and when he thought it was finally safe to go home, he sprinted the rest of the way.

Checking the clock, Harlem realised the time was only half past eight. What happened to time flying when you're having fun? Harlem had mistakenly believed it was afternoon. Mum and Dad remained in bed. He would spend the rest of the day revisiting the incredulous information he had gleaned from his strange new companion.

# CHAPTER FOUR

## The Life of Herrifurus

It would have made no difference had Harlem exhausted himself jumping up and down on a trampoline all night.

The hours that should have been spent sleeping were instead filled with restlessness.

His eagerness to return to Pressing Matters Lane and what he now knew lay beyond was utterly overwhelming.

Once again, Harlem was bright-eyed at the unsociable hour of half past five. The alarm clock was carrying out its duty, although it need not have bothered; Harlem had been wide awake all night. He dressed, washed, and crept slowly downstairs and out of the house.

His parents would be suspicious of his activities at this early morning hour.

Harlem was in excellent spirits, carrying a grand grin as he raced to the Childhood Tree. He would have still dashed the journey if the tree had been ten times farther away.

Before reaching out to connect with the trunk, Harlem's eyes slowly observed the area, ensuring no one else was around to witness his act. In the distance, he caught sight of the four teenagers who had been following him on his very first visit to Wishwisely. They were riding their bikes once again. What were they doing up this bright and early, merrily riding along? And why did they look like they would be better placed in a period six decades ago than now?

Harlem was sure they hadn't seen him, but as an extra precaution, he hastily moved around to the other side of the tree to remain safely out of sight.

Placing his palm on the trunk, he read the message from Father Time. Instantaneously, Harlem was whisked away to the Meadow of Purple Purpose, with the tall grass annoyingly scuffing against him.

As Herrifurus had explained, this purple grass was planted to simulate short-term memory confusion.

Harlem had forgotten this; however, as the grass had quickly achieved its purpose. He confusedly stared at the wandering asteroids for several minutes before consciously following the floating sign and heading in the instructed direction.

A new statement appeared on the purple, crushed velvet gate. Harlem read it aloud. *'Go around if it is easier?'*

Harlem decided to ignore the suggestion and open the gate before closing it properly after passing by; in doing so, he found himself back at the start of the Cobbles of Hankering. The path appeared to be shaking much more aggressively than it had yesterday. New words were hurtling off ahead of him, recent new wishes making their supersonic way to the Calace of Judgement.

A familiar, booming voice resounded sinisterly above the smog.

'YOU DON'T LEARN, BOY! YOU, FROM THAT HUMAN LOT, GO HOME!'

Harlem dismissed the voice and skilfully navigated his way onwards despite the inconvenience of the quaking cobbles beneath his feet. His only sight was the cobbles directly ahead due to the thick, unnatural, humming smog. That was, until the haze cleared, and the horrifically familiar sight of the dreaded Pig Clowns came into his view.

Both clowns remained on either side of the cobbles. Today, they were crouched on all fours, each clown devouring food within a deep metal trough. The two troughs were full to the brim with a disgusting amount of unhealthy fare: pizzas, chips, burgers, beans, jam tarts, custard, cakes, biscuits and fifty-pound notes.

The clowns were not using their hands, only their mouths and snouts; they were face down and devouring everything in sight.

As Harlem went to pass, both clowns lifted their eyes from the mountains of food before them to glare at him ominously.

The Pig Clowns acted crazy with rage and began manically pointing and squealing at Harlem. The male clown pulled out his trusty broken golf club, attempting to strike Harlem with it as he scuttled onwards. Fortunately, he missed his intended target once more.

'DO YOU KNOW WHO I AM, DO YOU?' he screamed before angrily waving his useless golf club and oinking hysterically.

Seemingly to relieve himself of misery, he dipped his head back into the trough and was soon imitated by his female counterpart.

Harlem could hear the grotesque oinking and gulping noises way in the distance. Continuously, more words continued zooming and whooshing by beneath him.

The smog cleared again, and the wooden signpost became visible, quickly followed by the massive, rugged, darkened slate rock that had appeared in front of Harlem.

Today, a note was attached to the rock – 'Be back in five minutes, let yourself in'.

Harlem observed Herrifurus' frantic and comical attempts to open the rock the day before. He didn't want to repeat the chaos he had witnessed. He was determined to find a more convenient way to access Enduring Crave than the one Herrifurus had struggled with. Harlem carefully studied the rock for any signs or clues of a secret entryway. His focused eyes landed on a small circle - the size of a ten-pence coin - chiselled into the rock amongst all the jagged and snaggy protrusions.

Harlem pressed the circle with his thumb. Of course, it was a button. The wavy, misty, black doorway with a white chalk outline appeared. Taking a deep breath, Harlem passed through.

'What… a… hideous… mess!' spat Harlem upon stepping inside and taking in the familiar, chaotic view.

Despite the disordered nature of Herrifurus' office, Harlem accepted it as it was. Herrifurus, with his unique ways, seemed to like it this way. Harlem had embraced his new friend, quirks and all, including his less-than-hygienic office.

Harlem impatiently approached the replica model of the ten-foot-high by fifteen-foot-wide solar system. He blew on the coating of grime and giggled as he created his own dust cloud.

Today, he reflected on all that he had learned thus far.

Before yesterday, it would have been inconceivable to believe, but now, Harlem marvelled at the Eight Curators' creations.

'Harlem, my dear boy. *You made it*... you... made it!'

Herrifurus' sudden entrance startled Harlem, who leapt with surprise, disrupting masses of dust.

'*Ah, the Solar System, I see you take... take interest.* Glorious doings... *glorious*... doings. Sorry, I say... I apologise for not being present when you arrived. Every which way I turn, the wishes of humans require my attention. My business has thus far been my obligation. But come now... come forward... come forward. We have lots to see... *lots*... to see... of the world of Enduring Crave! What transpires herein? *Step forward... step forward to believe.*'

With a wide grin, Harlem was ready to believe in the wonders of Enduring Crave.

As he and Herrifurus left the office, they entered the field of the magnificent Motherhood Tree.

Harlem was filled with a mix of emotions – amazement, disbelief, shock, bemusement, and joy.

'*Oh, Motherhood... oh, Motherhood... Bewitch us once again this day,*' shrieked Herrifurus. '*We have here an alien in human form. A tourist, a sightseer... a sightseer.* Here to seek the very fabric of your world. Please spare no allowance... no... allowance... Permit access to all the degrees... all the degrees, for this boy, unknown to him, holds the key... the key to the withstanding of Enduring Crave. If he fails, all we live for is gone... is gone forevermore! You see, Harlem, the

Motherhood Tree is not just any tree. It is the heart of Enduring Crave, the source of all life in this world.'

On completing his soliloquy, Herrifurus ushered Harlem thirty feet away from the magnificent tree, making great efforts to lower his voice.

Still, it did not come easily to one such as him.

'Harlem, I keep distance from Motherhood, so she cannot… cannot hear. For a normal tree would not understand, but not Motherhood… *not*… Motherhood! My love and respect… and respect are too great. I have spoken gently to Motherhood every morning for over two thousand years. Praise be… praise be given… Creator of life; purveyor of existence. I cannot help but stop… but stop and talk, to tell of all that is happening in her world. Harlem, feel free… feel free to mock… I know it is strange to converse with the everlasting perennial, who cannot return… cannot return the exchange… *As they say in your world – a sign of madness… of madness… Then I must be of madness!* So long have I been here in my position that to express one's feelings is burdensome, for we are all too absorbed in our work. I take comfort in knowing I can converse with her without being interrupted or ridiculed. Whatever the mind consumes, I can unshackle… unshackle with the freeing of conversation; she will always listen… yes, she will always listen to my cares and worries.'

Harlem felt a sense of sorrow for his new companion. He had come to understand that Herrifurus was not human. Outwards, he appeared human, but he was - what was it again — sixty-four-hundred and two years old?

Furthermore, Herrifurus was the Ambassador of Enduring Crave, but with whom did he communicate?

Herrifurus must report to the ones responsible for the creation of the planets.

He had to be in contact with the Eight Curators, the obscure, ancient beings who had overseen the birth of the planets and continued to guide their existence.

'Not all eight, Harlem. Just the one... *just*... the one... We are on Planet Earth. If there is anything of note, I report only to... only to Camerok, Earth's curator. *Why would I bother the rest, why I ask, why?*' shouted the frustrated Herrifurus.

'Herrifurus, can you read my mind?' replied the bewildered Harlem.

'*Absolutely not,*' answered Herrifurus, 'no life form within this system can flick through another's thoughts. To contaminate free will is to deny... is to deny living... If one is to disengage from one's faculty of mind procession, then one cannot... cannot consider or reckon for oneself... Can you imagine how terrible... how terrible that would be? Of course, you do... of course, you do... You can cogitate.'

'Herrifurus, how did you know what I was thinking just now? *Tell me that then!*' exclaimed Harlem.

'It is simple, Harlem, you were thinking out loud... out... loud... talking loudly enough for me to hear. No psychic deceitful monkey business, no abducting of the mind... *Quiz away, my young chum; for queries, head this way.* Your questions you must free... Go ahead... *go ahead*... inquisitive you must be. Ask much, be answered more... *be answered... more!'*

Harlem was visibly nervous despite the reassurances given. His articulateness quickly dissipated as he blurted everything out with great acceleration.

'Where are you from, Herrifurus? How did you get to be on Earth? Are you over six thousand years old? Please tell me everything, *oh,* please tell me everything, please, I am so confused!'

Herrifurus gently guided Harlem back into the office.

'Relax... relax; sit down and calm... and... calm. With a chalice of relaxation tea tonic, I will inform you of all you desire... desire to know. *I will be returning in... in an instant.'*

It was a good job that Herrifurus had offered refreshments; Harlem's mouth had suddenly run exceedingly dry.

As he sat on the dusty, grimy swivel chair, Harlem wondered where Herrifurus could have possibly gone to prepare something to drink. He certainly hadn't seen anywhere in the field to make a refreshment, and what exactly was relaxation tea tonic?

The pondering abruptly ended with Herrifurus' sudden return. He gently placed a laden wooden tray down on the cluttered desk.

The tray contained two silver and gold chalices embedded with red sapphires and a plain, white China saucer with what looked like four suspiciously pre-used dirty tea bags heaped upon it.

'What do you think of my relaxation tea tonic... *my*... tea... tonic?' asked Herrifurus.

Harlem closed his eyes and bravely swallowed a mouthful of the dubious liquid. As he had expected, it wasn't very nice.

There was nothing pleasant to say about any of it. It was lukewarm, clearly not boiled. As suspected, the teabags had been used many times previously. The worst part was the sensation of feeling the lumps in the milk make their way sickeningly down his throat.

Harlem just about prevented himself from being sick, although he did wretch twice. It seemed that Herrifurus had stirred pickle juice to sweeten the drink.

'Herrifurus, your tea tonic is lovely. But *how* did you make tea out in the *field*? Where did you get the tray and chalices from?'

Herrifurus replied, 'Harlem, my friend, I procured it all from the kitchen... the kitchen... *where else?*'

This only brought on more puzzling thoughts for Harlem, as he knew there was no kitchen in the field. There certainly was no kitchen in the office or the circus marquee. Harlem couldn't fathom where Herrifurus had got it from, adding to the mystery of Herrifurus' actions.

### *The world of Herrifurus*

'Mankind, *ha*, excuse me... excuse me as I shake my head at the very idea. According to the prevailing theory, I belong to a planet that is now a dwarf planet... A hypothesis of the greatest minds of Sapiens. However, I am displeased with this major incorrect assumption about my home planet, Pluto. We are... we are, I let it be known, Plutonians, standing at an average height of seven feet and seven inches in human measures, and Humans have the nerve... the nerve to call Plutonians dwarfs, such brazen cheek... My home is over three billion miles from Earth, and what flummoxes me is man's arrogance... man's arrogance on the matter! I cannot quite put my finger on it, but we have been labelled as dwarfs, yet humanity's quest to find life in the system continues. *It has muddled me... muddled me... so it has!*' Herrifurus was passionate about the defence of his native planet.

It was evident to Harlem, who just about stopped himself from giggling, that Herrifurus did not understand the term 'dwarf planet'.

Herrifurus had taken this slur personally. It was, after all, his home sphere.

'Sapiens,' continued Herrifurus, 'for all their faults, do possess... do possess an incredible gift – the human brain! Venturing into space is no easy feat. For thousands of years, humankind dreamed of travelling to the stars and beyond... and... beyond...*To reach out and learn the truth... the truth; for the truth is out there...* To come so far in such a short time. From horse and cart... horse... and cart... to 'one giant leap' in sixty-nine years... It is truly remarkable; more achievements were made in that time than ever in the preceding fifty millennia. However, humans must understand that their operations are still primitive and in their infancy. Man will hunt for extraterrestrial life, and extraterrestrial life will likely remain hidden. Centuries will pass before you even begin to catch up with the technology existing in the system today. We must permit... permit humankind to continue believing that the Solar System was formed with the supernova's explosion. They must never learn... *never*... learn of the Eight Curators' involvement, but I sincerely hope one day notions of Plutonians being dwarfs will cease!'

Harlem burst into laughter. He knew it was inappropriate, but he couldn't control himself. He found the 'dwarf' comment too amusing.

'When you are quite finished, may I... *may I continue?*' asked a vexed Herrifurus, who stood with his arms firmly crossed.

'Please do,' replied Harlem, wiping a tear from his eye.

'...My appearance is human; do not be deceived... *do not...* be deceived! You see my outer image. Inside, I am my true form. Before my role here, I was, of course, my born identity. Pluto is not Planet Earth; my selfhood, as I mentioned to you yesterday, is not flesh and bones; we are a mixture... a mixture of heavy water and inconceivable volatile gases. Plutonians are members of the 'Solar Unification Board'. The belief is that Earth can never be on board due to man's evil actions... *Moving swiftly on*, after it was agreed that humans could wish, Enduring Crave was created. The first Ambassador appointed here was Lanus, hailing from Saturn. For eight thousand years, Lanus's incumbency lasted. To follow... to follow in her footsteps appeared Epochlion of Jupiter... Ten thousand years elapsed, the most enduring undertaking ever! Eventually, time and humans wore Epochlion out. Wore him out, they did! The day job we uphold is overbearingly draining. Ten thousand years is a testament to Epochlion and Lanus before... *My* career was expanding communications beyond our system. I had established contact as far as Planet Balcron, deep... deep within the second universe. The Curators came calling. I was to be the next Ambassador of Enduring Crave. My Plutonian name is Kuiper, but Mokwug, and her unmatchable unsense of humour, thought it apt to christen me Herrifurus. In English, it means 'hurry for us', her slur towards greedy humans. Say it rapidly, and it becomes Herrifurus. Over time, it has stuck. I must admit... I must admit... *I don't mind... don't mind at all.* Throughout the centuries, the world's population has grown, and as the number of people intensifies, the wish rates have increased. The wishes of humankind are relentless. The more populated the world becomes, the harder it is for hope to survive - the two collide!'

Unexpectedly, the conversation was rudely interrupted by a strange beeping noise from Herrifurus.

*'No rest for the wicked, for the wicked, as they say,'* sighed Herrifurus, who presented a small, bleeping gadget from his short pockets.

It appeared to Harlem like one of those obsolete pagers from the 1990s. Harlem had only ever seen them in movies and had never actually believed they once existed. Is that how people communicated before mobile phones?

'Forgive me, Harlem, but business calls... business... calls... *Unforeseen circumstances have transpired...* Our plans are to be put on hold. *It was not my intention.* Our schedule is henceforth delayed. *A scatterbrain, I am a scatterbrain.* If this rude disruption of mine does not deter you, will you permit me to give you the tour tomorrow?'

'Absolutely, I'll be back tomorrow and every day after that!' Harlem responded with unwavering enthusiasm.

Further apologies from Herrifurus followed, and after that, it was time for Harlem to head back to Wishwisely. Once more, he went through the strange experience of exiting the office and finding himself standing at the rock rather than in the field. Herrifurus apologised a final time; the two shook hands and bid farewell. Harlem set about heading home. He arrived beyond the start of the Cobbles of Hankering and into the Meadow of Purple Purpose. He found himself in familiar territory in a trice, standing in the middle of the gravel path.

'*Hey*, where did you come from?' asked an unknown voice.

Spooked, Harlem turned around quicker than a startled gazelle.

He stood facing the four mysterious teenagers who had trailed him on the village high street. The same group had been on their bikes today from at least five o'clock.

Harlem couldn't help but be intrigued by this strange bunch. Where did they come from? They seemed out of place, not from this day and age, adding to the mystique of the situation.

'Where did you come from?' the girl asked abruptly, her tone cutting through the air.

'What do you mean?' answered Harlem both coyly and nervously.

'You just appeared here, we've just come from that way, and you *weren't* there when we passed. I turned around, and you were there. *So* where did you come from?' she repeated, her voice tinged with a hint of mystery.

Thinking quickly, Harlem replied, 'I jumped down from that tree!'

The four strangers stared at the top of the tree from which Harlem claimed to have jumped, their surprise evident, adding an unexpected twist to the encounter.

'I *don't* believe you!' replied the girl. 'And where did you go this morning? We saw you at that tree in the village centre. You disappeared after that; did you climb *that* tree, too?'

'Maybe I did,' Harlem answered, his voice betraying his nervousness, which added to the confusion and tension in the air.

The boy with the hat joined in the conversation. 'He sure is an odd one, Margo. He'll fit right in with us,' he commented.

'I believe he'll do just that, Phillip,' remarked Margo. 'What's your name?'

'Harlem Hodge,' he answered. 'I live at the house at the end of this track. This is my third day in Wishwisely.'

'Third day, you say... what year is it?' enquired Margo.

'Are you making fun of me?' asked Harlem.

Margo insisted she was not mocking him before dropping her question. The four teenagers introduced themselves: Margo Nutmeg, Phillip Day, James "Steiney" Wilkins, and Tubbs McLard.

Appearance-wise, Phillip Day was in a league of his own, wearing light blue denim flares with an outrageously oversized belt buckle. On his feet were brown cowboy boots, and up top, he wore a predominantly pink shirt with hundreds of little white polka dots. Several of the top buttons remained unfastened. A pink neckerchief was positioned around his neck. Sunglasses and a brown cowboy hat completed his look.

Harlem could see that Phillip Day had the worst case of earwax he had ever known.

James "Steiney" Wilkins and Tubbs McLard resembled two of the Beatles on the Ed Sullivan Show, with their Paul and Ringo mop tops and 1960s tailored black suits. White shirts with black ties and black shoes complemented their style.

Margo Nutmeg kept the dream and legacy of the decade of love alive. Her hair was styled in a messy, blonde beehive. She wore a sixties yellow baby-doll dress with a white stripe down the middle and a further white stripe around the waist. Margo wore thick, white tights with yellow Mary Janes. All of this was finished off with a yellow leather handbag.

As for their bicycles, Margo had what would now be considered a vintage, yellow Elswick Hopper. Margo's was not vintage, though - it looked brand new. Harlem knew that this bicycle model was no longer in production.

Phillip, Tubbs and Steiney rode 1960s black and silver Raleigh Police Bikes. All three bikes were immaculate and well-maintained.

'HARLEM HODGE, GET HOME NOW!'

Harlem and his new friends were alarmed at this shrill and piercing voice. It was, of course, Colonel Mum, looking ready for war.

'I SAID HOME, NOW! HURRY ALONG!' yelled Mum.

How embarrassing for her to react this way, especially in front of his new pals. As usual, she was oblivious.

# CHAPTER FIVE

## The Story of the Boy in The School

The anguishes became unbearable; the waiting never seemed to end. It had only been one day since Harlem had set foot in Enduring Crave, but it felt like a whole year to him. He yearned so deeply to leave the house and head for the secret world he now knew.

He wasn't allowed to until Mum determined the punishment for the crime.

Dad answered 'the call of nature' early yesterday morning and heard Harlem leaving the house just after half past five. Dad peered out the window, watching Harlem dashing towards the gravel track.

His parents were worried and concerned - what reason did Harlem have for being up and out of the house so early? He had kept his plans quiet and failed to inform them of what he was up to. So yes, his folks were not thrilled. They had gone on a frantic search for Harlem, spending two hours looking for him, until Mum found him on the gravel track.

Of course, Harlem couldn't tell them the truth, so he concocted a story of exploring the neighbourhood. Mum scolded him repeatedly. Dad, for the most part, kept quiet - only speaking on the rare occasion when he dared to get a word in edgeways, and of course, he would perpetually repeat what Mum had already stated. This always won Mum's approval.

Harlem felt guilty about abandoning Herrifurus; he would have expected Harlem's arrival. Harlem wasn't coming, and Herrifurus would doubtless be disappointed. Would Harlem's new fellowship know why Harlem could not attend today?

Today was Tuesday, and Mum had returned to the city to collect some books for work; she wouldn't be back until evening. It was, therefore, well-earned peacetime for Dougie and Harlem, with Dougie falling asleep on the couch while Harlem lay on his bed, wallowing and lamenting in self-pity.

KNOCK, KNOCK, KNOCK
KNOCK, KNOCK, KNOCK

'Dad, the door - somebody's at the door!' shouted Harlem.

Dad, who was groggy and exhausted, stirred from his almost slumber. Upon opening the door, drowsy Dad could see no one standing there. He expelled a yawn and rubbed his tired eyes before a second yawn completed its short lifespan.

'There's no one here, Harlem; I don't know what you think you heard. No more games, *please*, Son!' groaned Dad wearily.

KNOCK, KNOCK, KNOCK
BANG, BANG, BANG

What was Dad playing at? Harlem knew he had heard the door. Somebody was banging and knocking on the door before Dad checked. Harlem raced downstairs and bucked open the grand, red door. To his astonishment, he found his four new friends standing there – Margo, Tubbs, Phillip, and Steiney.

'Do you want to come for a bike ride, Harlem?' asked Margo.

'*shhh!*' whispered Harlem, placing a finger over his lips, signalling everyone to be quiet. 'I'll go and ask my dad. My mum is still annoyed about yesterday.'

Harlem pulled the door closed. He tiptoed towards Dad, who had all but hit the land of nod.

'Dad, please, can I go out? I'll be back before Mum gets home!' begged Harlem.

Dad, who hadn't listened to Harlem's question, gave his usual response, except this time he wasn't responding to Mum.

'Yes, dear,' Dad mumbled softly.

Although Harlem knew Dad believed he was replying to Mum, it was good enough for him. Dad had said yes! This was Harlem's free pass to go out.

Harlem hurriedly grabbed his bike from the front garden; the five were off on their travels.

Harlem and his four new friends toured parts of the village and the surrounding woods and forests. The four were eager to hear what city life was like and were enraptured as they listened to Harlem's tales.

'We've only ever known life in this village,' moaned Margo. 'Possibly decades of this dull, old village!'

Hearing this strange admission from Margo, Harlem quickly looked up and made eye contact with Steiney.

Steiney shook his head, placing his right hand on his temple and twirling his index finger in a circular motion. This was his way of expressing that Margo was crazy and that Harlem should pay no attention to her.

Harlem averted his eyes and caught Phillip Day eating his earwax. Phillip would constantly stick his fingers in both ears and gulp down any portion of wax he managed to dislodge.

Phillip would regularly do this when he believed no one was looking, much to the disgust of others. Harlem turned away, repulsed.

'Tubbs and Steiney, why do they call you *that*?' asked Harlem, eager to think about anything other than earwax.

'I'll tell you *why*,' chuckled Margo. 'It's because Tubbs never stops munching, and Steiney, he would have us believe it's because he's a genius like Albert Einstein, but it's *really* because his head is as big as Frankenstein's monster's head!'

Margo and the three others fell into a giggling heap.

Steiney placed one hand on his head with the other resting below his chin. He then positioned both hands on either side of his face, attempting to measure the size of his head. 'It's not *that* big!' he moaned.

Harlem wanted to change the subject to that of the 'North boy'. He wondered if his four new pals had ever encountered the mysterious story of the boy who had disappeared in the woods.

'Don't laugh!' began Harlem, 'but the old croak in the shop told me a tale of a boy who went missing in the woods sixty years ago. She mentioned that he used to live where I do now, and the house has been abandoned for all that time. He was never found, and ever since... the house has remained empty... *cursed*...'

The group stared at Harlem, astonished and open-mouthed.

A chilling, tense silence echoed all around.

'Is that *really* how long it's been - sixty years?' remarked Tubbs, ending the awkward hush.

'Well, I never... who would have thought it?' added Phillip Day.

'Thought what?' inquired Harlem.

'Sixty years, confirmed, that is a long time in the past... a long time... it doesn't seem that long at all,' expressed Phillip. 'I can recall that monster's face, but he still gives me headaches when I think of him, and I try so hard not to think of him! A sinister presence was embedded deep within him. Just before he left, something wicked had taken over; something had gripped him with a wrongful purpose. He was distant and closed off from the outside world. One morning, he was seen bolting into the trees.'

'Sixty years have gone by, you say!' added Margo. 'Those of us old enough to remember have diminished over the years. The trees still clutch onto the secret and yield an unforgiving apology... *vanished... swallowed...*'

Margo appeared to be suffering from a spiteful headache, causing her to hold her head as she squinted and grimaced in agony. Despite the genuine struggle and pain, she somehow continued telling the story. 'For all that time, your house has been left empty. No comings, no goings... cursed... left abandoned until his return. *Well*, that was until you moved in, Harlem.'

Harlem stood up swiftly. 'I'm off now, Margo. I knew you lot were making fun of me!' he huffed.

Steiney also found his feet, pretending to jab Harlem twice in the arm, albeit very softly. 'Don't go, don't go!' he insisted.

'No one's making fun of you, Harlem!' assured Phillip Day.

'Well, what was that story all about then, Margo?' asked a slightly calmer Harlem, although he was sure the others were deliberately teasing him. It was, after all, a strange tale.

'Read into it what you like - *it's all true*. That boy vanished, and he lived where you do now,' insisted Margo.

Harlem was starting to form the idea that Margo was the unofficial leader of this unconventional group, who kept the others in check. All four new friends were severely squinting with their eyes, seemingly suffering from throbbing migraines.

'Margo, I think Harlem should know about the school...' began Phillip Day.

'What about the school?' asked the inquisitive Hodge.

Phillip Day stood on his soapbox, the migraine having diminished.

'Our school's haunted by a boy trapped within the grounds. The boy, devoid of friends, has found comfort and refuge within the school. He never leaves, only wanders, counting the hours until the school reopens. It is said that the legend must be kept confined to the kids who attend our school. When the final day of your last school year is up, it must never be mentioned to anyone, ever! It's forbidden to speak of the boy after you move on. For if you do, a plague of immeasurable wickedness will consume you-'

'-He's often been seen sitting in class amongst the living,' interrupted Steiney, 'but he never attempts to communicate with the other pupils directly, as if he carried a distasteful disdain for them. When the teacher asks a question, the boy raises his hand but never gets to answer. Adults can't see him. Sullenly, he gets up and exits through the walls. Others have witnessed him peering in at the windows, watching as they study. Sooty handprints hold out on the glass as evidence of his presence. On occasion and without warning, he'll meander from room to room. As expressed, the bricks are no deterrent for him. The educators mustn't be told... *and note*... the curse applies to any kid who runs to a teacher.'

Harlem didn't know what to make of it all. 'Have you seen him?' he queried after a long pause.

'We do our best not to!' exclaimed Margo.

'*I must say*, we haven't said hello to any new pupils at school for many years, have we, folks?' stated Tubbs jocularly.

Harlem glanced at his watch; it was time to go home. He had to be back before Mum returned and realised he'd broken the rules again. Dad was most likely still asleep. The poor fellow was completely drained and fatigued by Mum's never-ending distribution of tasks to complete.

A narrow gap in the overgrown pasture allowed for cycling; however, cycling had to be done in a single file. Margo led from the front with Harlem at the rear. Harlem sensed a tingling and peculiar feeling that he was being spied on, and as he peeked over his shoulder, he was shocked to witness a dark, shadowy being with piercing blue eyes staring at him. It had sharp-edged limbs, long, thin, spikey fingers, and what appeared to be horns on its head.

The shadow would expand until extremely thin or stretched out, then draw back into itself at intervals. The oddity was hovering twenty feet above the ground. Without warning, it charged towards Harlem, who hit a groove in the dirt with his front wheel as he wasn't looking in the direction he was pedalling.

Harlem was forcefully thrown from his bike and found himself lying face down on the dusty, dry floor. After dazedly getting back on his feet, Harlem determined that he had somehow, miraculously escaped uninjured from the fall. He swiftly jumped back on his bike, pedalling furiously to catch up to the others.

That evening, Harlem was feeling rather pleased with himself. He had managed to hoodwink his dad into allowing him out. As he had predicted, Dad was still asleep when Harlem returned home.

Harlem had an enthralling time with his four eccentric new pals. Best of all, he had made it back before Mum. Neither of his parents understood he had been out and about earlier that day.

It went without saying that Enduring Crave never escaped his mind, but right now, it was time for Dirk Hader and His Excess Baggage. Now that the satellite dish had finally been installed, Harlem could watch last Friday's episode. He had taken command of the sofa.

'Brilliant… just brilliant,' he yelled at the TV.

This episode showed Dirk making supercharged rocket jet packs for the dead to use in the spirit world. Except, of course, things were not turning out as planned. The ghouls, comically, could not get to grips with the weapons designed for them.

Harlem was futilely shouting at the television, 'THEY WON'T WORK IN THE REAL WORLD; YOU HAVE TO OPERATE THEM IN THE DEAD WORLD. IT'S COMMON SENSE!'

As it turned out, Harlem was correct. The dead could only use the rocket jet packs in the spirit world. The programme ended, the credits rolled, and Harlem laughed. 'What a cracking show!' he exclaimed gleefully.

Wednesday morning arrived, bringing an unapologetically overcast and despairing atmosphere, almost as if it were deliberately summoned to Wishwisely by the deity of inclement weather. The rain had been persistent for the last six hours, never once retreating in all that time, encouraged further by bullying, dark clouds poised precariously above.

The rain drummed violently against the windows so loudly that one could easily mistake raindrops for golf balls.

As Harlem dared to peer through the living room window, his view was obscured by rising mist; it was impossible to see beyond the garden's reach.

This morning, at the beginning of August, it appeared more like a cold, wet November evening.

Mum had gone out, and Dad was at work, no doubt coerced into fiddling with someone's taxes and expenses. Mum finally relented and allowed Harlem to leave the house, as there was no point in him staying home all summer. She encouraged him to go off and make friends.

However, that was only if the weather was sunny and dry, which it certainly wasn't today.

While busy preparing some magic tricks for his friends, there was a knock at the door. On opening the front door, Harlem began laughing at the sorry sight. His four friends were loitering by the door, soaked and drenched by the merciless deluge; their outfits were unsuitable for the downpour.

'Come in quickly!' begged Harlem.

He and the four at the door hurried upstairs to the sanctuary of Harlem's warm, dry room. Harlem kindly distributed towels to allow his friends to dry off more quickly.

'I'm famished, Harlem. Do you have any goodies?' asked Tubbs, whose stomach was already beginning to rumble.

After rummaging in the cupboards, Harlem returned with two packets of biscuits. Tubbs scoffed at the lot.

'What can we do now? I hate the rain!' complained Margo.

'We can go on our bikes! *Margo, you aren't a wicked witch; you won't melt!*' Phillip Day dared to remark brazenly.

'Shush, Phillip, just because you've got that hat to keep those never-ending candle factories you call ears dry,' snapped Margo.

Harlem once again felt sick at the thought of Phillip eating the seemingly unlimited supply of earwax.

'*I know*, let's go to the school and sneak in!' suggested an excited Steiney.

Harlem was reluctant but had an overwhelming desire to see inside the school. Aware that he wasn't allowed out in the rain, he bravely put on his coat, and remembering he wanted to show his friends some magic tricks, he placed a few tricks into his deep coat pockets, intending to perform those illusions at school.

It did not take long for the five to arrive at the school; it turned out that pedal power in this dreadful weather made for great determination. Harlem glared at the school through the gates. The building was indeed old and dilapidated; in Harlem's mind, it could have been built at any stage between medieval and Victorian times.

Harlem squinted, desperately trying to imagine what it would have been like to be a pupil here in the past. It looked austere now; who knew what might have occurred here in bygone eras? The school was made of stone; it certainly cast an imposing presence on its attendees. Harlem glanced up at the roof; just below the eaves, small, gargoyle-like figures perched. His eyes alighted on a smaller-than-usual steeple tower and the obligatory stained-glass windows.

The school was a converted church, with extensions added and constructed over the years, surrounded by thick stone walls and railings made from cast iron, interspersed with tall, imposing trees.

From the gate, Harlem could make out a tight, narrow alley to the left of the school, with trees looming over it. Harlem couldn't figure out what was to the right of the school, as a seemingly never-ending mass of trees obscured his view.

'The gates are locked; how do we get in?' asked the nervous Harlem.

'Come this way, *follow me!*' responded Margo, taking the lead once again.

They slowly navigated their bikes through the trees to the right of the school premises before abandoning them.

Margo deftly reached up and began to rotate the last three rails on the wall, which loosened as she expertly pulled them out of their former position. With the rails removed, the gap was wide enough for the average school child to squeeze through.

Margo gleefully explained that every kid in school had known about the story of the movable rails for at least a hundred years. Wayward children were always careful to replace the rails immediately; therefore, the teachers never discovered this little secret.

The five friends worked together as a team to pull and assist one another through the gap. Harlem jumped and landed on one of two large, felled tree trunks. The trunks were now used as makeshift benches in the playground's corner.

'How do we get inside the school?' whispered Harlem.

'Why are you whispering?' asked Steiney.

'I'm not sure,' sniggered Harlem.

Harlem had no idea how they would access the building. His doubt soon ended, however, when he saw Margo remove a set of assorted keys from her yellow bag. She carefully searched them, eventually opting for a long, sparkling silver key. Margo carefully inserted the key into the enormous blue door on the back wall. The door creaked open, and the five entered the school kitchen.

'I liberated that key from Mrs Wormpick after she detained me one time… that old battle-axe! I thought she'd never hang up her headmistress's cane.'

The kitchen wasn't dirty, but it resembled a Victorian workhouse kitchen. Harlem couldn't help imagining gruel being served at lunchtime and, if lucky, a slice of mouldy bread!

This room belonged in the past. It still had a cast-iron fireplace, stove, and a humongous wooden table. A large, grey cooking pot was positioned centrally on the table.

Tubbs, of course, couldn't help but eat the various sweet treats he had found after rooting through the cupboards. Just as they were about to leave the kitchen and venture into the school, they heard a loud, thunderous crash.

The cooking pot in the centre of the table was now unexplainably on the floor, smashed into a thousand pieces. A second noise began to instil fear within the mischievous children. The echo of footsteps gradually became louder as they approached the kitchen. Harlem recognised those footsteps. His four friends quickly scampered behind the table just as the door hurled open. There she was! There, right before Harlem, growled Mum.

She was the new Headmaster. Of course, Harlem already knew this, but he had no idea Mum would be working at school today; it *was* the summer holidays. Mum was outraged. She accused Harlem of 'breaking into the school in the rain', as she described it.

She was so engrossed in her moment of fury that she failed to notice the other four children hiding behind the table.

She swiftly marched Harlem through the school to the front door. The gate was unlocked; Mum ordered him home immediately. Before returning home, where he was sure to be grounded again, Harlem turned right and went back through the trees to collect his bike. He found Margo, Tubbs, Phillip Day, and Steiney waiting for him there. Mum had luckily forgotten to lock the kitchen door before sending Harlem on his way, allowing the others to sneak out unseen. Just as they had replaced the third rail and jumped down from the wall and off school property, Mum had come steaming out of the kitchen door and had marched into the schoolyard. She scanned the surroundings, ensuring no one else was up to no good.

'It will be a long time before I'm allowed out again. You may not see me for a few years with the mood *she's* in!' moaned Harlem.

'We'll wait for you... But don't go, please don't go!' begged Steiney.

Nevertheless, it was time to go home; the three boys sped off on their bicycles. Harlem decided to accompany Margo to her house; she lived in a beautiful white bungalow opposite the reservoir. The bungalow was the old village police station. The old blue police lantern with white lettering was fading. Was there ever any crime in Wishwisely?

'That's far enough, Harlem. If my dad sees you, he'll go crazy! He hates people coming here. Sergeant Nutmeg is *not* a man to cross!' warned Margo.

After that, it was just Harlem alone as he slowly pedalled back towards home. He wanted the lonely return to last as long as possible. He missed his grandma; how could he use her help right now? As he passed the churchyard entrance at a snail's pace, Harlem suddenly wanted to get off his bike and sit on a church bench. It was the same church bench that Harlem and Grandma had sat on during the first trip to Wishwisely.

After completing the tour of the high street, Grandma wanted to stop and chat with Harlem, possibly to aggravate Mum a little more.

They had discussed the new house, the village sights, and the story the old lady in the shop told them. Grandma had been somewhat upset and wanted to tell Harlem about her brother. Harlem recalled everything that Grandma had uttered:

'Harlem, the crone's story about that boy disappearing. I once told you that I had a brother named Donny. I failed to mention at the time that he went off to war and sadly never returned. I was furious with Donny and never got to say goodbye to him properly. Even after he'd gone, I felt betrayed and hurt for a long time. We'd lost both our parents less than a year before, and now I was losing Donny. Donny chose to go off and fight, despite my efforts to talk him out of it and get him to see sense. I begged and pleaded... fighting never solved anything! War wasn't the answer, but he made up his mind.'

A tear glistened in Grandma's eye. This startled Harlem; he had never seen her this upset before.

Harlem was alone on the bench today; Grandma wasn't beside him to offer advice or wisdom.

Mum was still at school, so at least he would be home before the suffering bombardment commenced. He wouldn't have to walk through the door and suddenly be shot down in the firing line. Mum accused him of breaking into the school; a significant punishment would be looming...

He was right; Harlem had been grounded since Wednesday, the day he inexcusably broke into the school. Today was Sunday, and all his optimism had long since dissipated. He was starting to believe he would never again enter the secret world. He would never walk the Cobbles of Hankering nor find himself in the untidy, cluttered office. The worry of perhaps never returning weighed heavily on Harlem. The desperate urge to sneak out of the house and visit Herrifurus began to creep up. Harlem came to his senses; he couldn't disobey his parents again. Especially not now; if he did, he would likely end up at boarding school or worse.

The time was a quarter past eight on a Sunday evening in summer. It was usually bright, warm, and serene this time of year. Due to the endless rain and increasingly permanent darkened clouds, it felt like a January night: cold, wet, gloomy, and miserable.

The winds howled like a wolf alone in the woods in the dark of night.

The positive thing was that his parents were away for the night, staying in the city to attend one of Dad's clients' parties. Harlem lay in bed, watching the telly. At least he was snug and warm.

Due to the tempestuousness outside, the best thing was to be safe and comfortable indoors.

Whilst glued to the idiot box, Harlem's attention was suddenly diverted by the noise of something hitting his bedroom window. Seconds later, it happened again. Harlem jumped up, wrenched his curtains open and pushed his window forward. To his astonishment, Herrifurus stood on the patio in the pouring rain, holding an enormous blue and orange umbrella.

The sounds that Harlem had heard were the pebbles that Herrifurus had tossed at the windowpane to attract Harlem's attention.

'Come to the front door, Herrifurus!' urged Harlem.

Harlem set off downstairs, taking two steps at a time; he opened the front door and waited. Herrifurus was not so light on his feet; he was slower and more cumbersome.

At last, the old man reached the front door, entered the house, and closed his umbrella, which was saturated and dripping.

*'Gee whiz, it's like cats and dogs… it's like cats and dogs out there!'* groaned Herrifurus. 'Where have you… have you been? I was… I was concerned.'

Harlem ushered Herrifurus into the living room. He graciously offered the old man a seat whilst making a good, old-fashioned cup of tea. On Harlem returning to the living room, the two drank the tea as Harlem explained the reasons why he had not set foot in Enduring Crave since Monday - from initially being confined to the house to hanging out with his new friends up to being grounded because of his antics at the school, as well as disobeying Mum's wet weather policy.

'I see… I… see… Now is the time to come with me… to… come with me… we should go! A fountain of information is to come your way. I must show you in a wink… *in a wink, I say…* Your place in Enduring Crave is… is now!'

Harlem once again explained to his friend that he was grounded.

Herrifurus stared around the room before rising stiffly from the chair and walking to the door. He leaned his head outside and listened.

*'No parents here... no... no parents here...* So why not come with me?'

Harlem knew that Herrifurus was correct. 'I'll get my coat!' he replied.

The two embarked, hurriedly walking towards the centre of Wishwisely.

'Herrifurus, why is there a need to throw stones? Surely you have the power to get into my house?'

'I am not a criminal. I do not break into folk's homes, nor do I ring... do I ring... the doorbell. Imagine what would happen if another opened the door to me? *What would they think... what would they think?'*

Both chuckled as they continued.

# CHAPTER SIX

## Witchwratht and Mirrors

Upon arriving at the lonesome Childhood tree, Herrifurus' umbrella was, without mercy, whisked away by the unforgiving wind.

The deluge and stormy torrent had kept everyone indoors. Not a soul could be caught sight of out and about in Wishwisely.

'Come on now, Harlem, come on! Do your thing, boy… do your thing! *Hurry now, the rain… the rain soaks me.* My umbrella is gone… lost and out there all alone. Scared and alone… scared… and alone! We have not got all night! *Let's be off, I say!'*

Harlem prodded the tree trunk and recalled those words, just as he had on the two previous occasions. Herrifurus and Harlem quickly found themselves idling in the Meadow of Purple Purpose, staring fixedly at the peculiar aluminium floating sign hovering overhead.

*'I know the way. Come on, Harlem, it's this way… it's this way.* Follow me… follow me,' insisted Herrifurus dreamily.

'No, Herrifurus, it's *that* way! The sign indicates *that* way,' demanded Harlem, pointing in what he knew *was* the right direction.

The Ambassador of Enduring Crave appeared to be suffering from short-term memory confusion. Harlem, however, was not showing any symptoms. He was unfaltering as they set forth on the correct route.

Rambling across the field whilst being inconvenienced by the intolerable, scraping purple grass, the gate slowly neared.

There was a vacant space as no message had been imprinted in the velvet today. Herrifurus opened the gate and advised Harlem that it didn't need locking this time, as Herrifurus was by his side.

'*Regular rules are not obligatory with me around.* Feel free... feel... free... to leave the gate open.'

'That's okay, Herrifurus,' replied Harlem, 'I'll lock it anyway, just to be safe.'

Upon closing the gate, they found themselves standing at the start of the Cobbles of Hankering.

'*Excellent, Harlem.* Very good indeed... very good... *indeed!* You paid no heed... no heed to my tests. Of course, the gate needs to be locked. *Hats off to you... hats off to you, Harlem!* Always do what is right... what... is right, up here! Heading in the direction you know suits you better.'

The path began to shake and tremble violently beneath their feet. New words fizzed across the cobbles, whizzing ahead far faster than Harlem recalled from his previous visits. The heightened number of wishes hitting the path strengthened the shakes and the haste with which those wishes travelled.

Harlem had difficulty maintaining his balance as he carefully placed one foot in front of the other. Navigating the cobbles with increased fluctuations could best be described as attempting to walk in a straight line on a bouncy castle whilst fifty people jump all around you!

Herrifurus insisted that Harlem walk in front and instructed him not to step backwards on the cobbles.

'Harlem, you see, today is Sunday, and come Sunday, the wishes of Sapiens increase forty-fold... *What is the reason... what... is the reason?* Could it be that humankind believes their wishes will be heard more on the day of rest? That their deity is generous enough to grant them on his day? Well, fools... fools... may believe what fools want to believe! *But what is tomorrow... what is... tomorrow*? It is a rarely known but accurate fact that the worst stage of the Monday blues occurs between ten o'clock and one minute to midnight on a Sunday night. No Sapien of wishing age is exempt from this feeling. Back to the woes... the woes of school or the turmoil of returning to work. Oh, the endless rat race of life. An influx of introspection is most certainly experienced during these times. The juveniles wish to see their teacher call in sick or their school burned down. We often receive wishes calling for a snow day, for the school to remain closed, more times than you could count. You wouldn't believe how many types of these wishes and more we receive here... here on a Sunday. As for adults, the strain of another five days at work makes wish levels go through the roof and out the chimney - "I wish I had another job" - "I wish it were Saturday" - "I wish I were on holiday" and "I wish I didn't have to go to work tomorrow". I lose count of how many of these wishes end up... end up at the Calace on a

Sunday. Of course, there are more ominous wishes, such as imagining something unpleasant happening to a superior or co-worker. It can get very unpleasant... *very*... unpleasant indeed on a Sunday night.'

The pig clowns were far from menacing during this current expedition on the cobbles. Though still positioned on either side of the path, both pig clowns seemed busy working. The larger clown was exercising his broken golf club as a pointer, bizarrely summarising what appeared to be business analytics on a pie chart. The lady clown was oinking and offering suggestions to him, licking her lips at the thought of pie. They were seemingly utterly unaware that Harlem and Herrifurus had passed by.

Herrifurus once again re-enacted his comedy sketch while attempting to open the rock, despite Harlem calling attention to the chiselled button and its purpose.

Herrifurus went through the same rigmarole as last Sunday morning.

Harlem impatiently nudged the button himself in the end, deciding to save time and put an end to the madness.

The wavy, misty, black doorway with a white chalk outline glistened into view, and the two hastily entered beyond.

Harlem welcomed the grubby sight that befell him. He had ached for the untidiness of the office; he was thankful to be back.

Herrifurus began spluttering terribly, pulling an exaggerated, outlandish, pitiful face as he did so. It was the look you might present while sucking on a double sour lemon.

Herrifurus crookedly leaned forward, blowing forcefully out of his mouth, his hands gripping his knees.

'What's wrong, Herrifurus?' enquired Harlem.

'Now don't take offence... *don't*... take offence! The cup of tea you made me was this your first time... *was this your first time making tea*? It just... it just tasted rather ghastly... I recommend you use a chalice next time. Drinking tea from a cup is just... just unsavoury! *Fresh milk indeed... indeed, how disgusting!* Did you know that making a good cup of tea requires the bags to have been used at least twenty times? *Anyway... anyway... hang your coat on the rack, my boy. It is not needed... not needed here.*'

Harlem placed his coat on the coat rack; it would be perfectly safe, as he reasoned that the woodworm posed no threat to fabric, but could the decaying rack withstand the weight of its guest?

'Let's be off! *I wish to show you the sights... the sights of this world!* Before we do, let's go outside and gaze... and gaze upon Motherhood.'

Harlem suddenly wanted to dash around the marquee when the two departed the office.

With excitement, he hurriedly completed his quest. Herrifurus seemed baffled by Harlem's antics.

'What the blazes... *what*... the blazes... were you running for?' he asked.

'I was just checking for something,' answered Harlem, who had been searching for a hidden room or compartment.

Harlem was still puzzled about where Herrifurus had gotten the tea and chalices from on his last visit.

*'Come, I say… come… I say, let's head to Mucky Waters! Goodbye… goodbye, Motherhood.'*

Herrifurus guided Harlem back into the office and straight out again. They now stood, inexplicably, at the start of the most unwelcoming, formidable, unlit, imposing jungle – this must be Mucky Waters.

Herrifurus dutifully informed Harlem that nobody wanted to visit here; corruption, misery and depravity were omnipresent. Setting foot in the jungle, Harlem became nauseatingly aware that the ground had quickly become sullied and slimy, with bubbles splurging and popping through the mucus.

The harsh wilderness reeked, emitting putrid, sulphuric fetors that tried but failed to overwhelm and suppress today's visitors.

Harlem glared at the savage, long-forgotten, overgrown vegetation, surrounded and interspersed with bogs, joined with sporadic patches of golden quicksand and pockets of green, sticky, treacherous swampland.

The trees remained upright and compact, although it was clear that most had drawn their last breaths many years ago, slowly rotting and decaying over time.

A trillion decomposing leaves littered the ground, presenting hazards to any brave pedestrians as it became impossible to decipher what lurked beneath.

Rusty, serrated iron stalagmites thrust upwards from below the leaves, adding to the potential risk of peril. A long-forgotten presence of destruction and catastrophe had frightened away the sunlight above.

Manoeuvring cautiously down the overgrown, tangled path, hopping over and weaving under the razor-sharp vegetation, they narrowly avoided slipping into bogs and quicksand.

It felt like entities from within were crying out for new victims, reaching out to swipe them off their feet. The path precipitously ended at a large, unwelcoming, and perilous swamp.

As far as Harlem could see, the only way across was via a very unsecure and worn-out rope bridge. The fatigued bridge appeared to have given up, having had enough of its predicament here in this most horrible of places.

Harlem summoned all his courage; he was going to go first.

The bridge was extraordinarily rickety and unstable, swinging haphazardly from side to side with every forward step.

Harlem stopped halfway across, not to steady himself, but because he had just set his eyes on a rather unusual sight. To his right, in the swamp, was a silver metal dustbin, three and a half feet high.

The bin was lying on its side, barely keeping afloat on the muddy, slimy, and sticky surface.

Poking out of the bin, bizarrely, was a witch: a stereotypical-looking crone that would not be out of place roaming the streets on Halloween. She had green skin, warts on her nose and hair on her chin. Her head was crowned with a black, pointed hat, and even an archetypal broom poked out of the bin beside her.

Fortunately for Harlem, the witch had been dead for some time. Her black cat was pouncing on thousands of strange, flying insects that had amassed around the deceased hag. Harlem frowned at the insects - each one the size of a golf ball, perfectly round and headless, forming just one round, odd blob. Each blob was a sickly, brown shade. Each flapping insect had four enormous eyes, a small pink nose, a minute mouth and two barely visible hands. The creatures were equipped with four wings but were unlike any insect Harlem had seen in his world, as each wing was shaped like a question mark. It was most absurd.

'The bridge… *the bridge, hurry, Harlem!* It looks ready to collapse… it will soon go under, quickly now, quickly,' urged Herrifurus frantically.

Harlem just made it across to safety. As he reached the far side, the bridge seemed to accept that it had performed its last duty. It made a final farewell groan, then collapsed into the swamp below. Thankfully, Herrifurus hadn't slipped in along with it. He was miraculously standing on top of the swamp, somehow managing to stop himself from being sucked under.

To Harlem's horror, Herrifurus began shaking the witch aggressively, trying desperately to establish communication with her. She wasn't moving; what was he thinking? Herrifurus lifted the bin upright; it suddenly dawned on Harlem that the old hag was melded to the bin. The shaking from Herrifurus became even more violent. In a fit of temper, he intentionally kicked the bin over.

Herrifurus yelled out in anger. 'VERY WELL THEN, PLAY YOUR GAMES, YOU VILE HAG! Go to the bottom... the bottom for eternity. That's where you're heading!'

Herrifurus was outwardly seething as he paced towards Harlem. He did not stop; he only continued striding whilst chuntering under his breath. He appeared to be having a tantrum, displaying a foul temper.

The path inexplicably split ahead of them, branching into three separate routes. All three ways were obstructed by overgrown and treacherous-looking jagged vegetation. Harlem and Herrifurus opted to take the path which led straight ahead. Harlem wondered what monsters lived in here. '*Here be monsters,*' he thought aloud.

'Harlem, forgive my behaviour... my behaviour earlier... That witch wasn't dead as such. She was going out of her way to ignore me... to ignore... me!' muttered Herrifurus.

Continuing their journey, they encountered hundreds, possibly thousands, of the peculiar, flying insects they had seen buzzing around the witch. They looked sickly, malnourished, and were in a desperate search for sustenance, foraging for whatever scraps of food they could uncover.

They glared at Herrifurus disdainfully when he drew near to them. The insects made it clear that they wanted nothing to do with him by keeping their distance and buzzing away. Of course, Herrifurus was oblivious to this slight.

## *Witchwraith*

Progressing into an area of dense, decaying trees with several pockets of swampland, the two stumbled upon a vast, pewter cauldron. The cauldron rested on what must have been the only dry patch of grass in the whole of Mucky Waters. Harlem peered inside; the cauldron was without content. It was the most absurd item one would ever expect to find in such a place.

'Herrifurus, *what on Earth* is a cauldron doing here in Mucky Waters?' he asked.

'It belongs... belongs... to them... to them!' replied Herrifurus.

Harlem followed Herrifurus' gesture with his gaze. He was pointing to three witches thirty feet away. They were also melded to metal bins. As soon as they set eyes on Herrifurus, the witches turned their heads away. They were strictly intent on not looking him in the eye. Herrifurus got closer and seemingly took great delight in antagonising the hags.

'Good morning, BinBags. Such a pleasant day... *such*... a pleasant day... I enquire as to what you have planned for today. Do you have anywhere special to visit, or do you intend to stand around here and watch the day go by?' he asked sarcastically.

The witches held their heads high; they would not entertain Herrifurus as if deliberately stubborn. Herrifurus grinned, satisfied with provoking them, before smirking at Harlem.

'Don't hold any fears... any fears for these BinBags; they're harmless... *harmless!* The time when they could impose their terror has long since ended. Ancient crones and she-devils...

and… she-devils! Throughout history, at various stages, we have experienced periods and resurgences of Witchwratht! Beginning over twenty-five thousand years ago in the long-lost city of Gradun. Women of all ages were willingly corrupted by a, still to this day, mysterious demon. The purpose of Witchwratht was to conquer the planet and exterminate humanity. Those who so freely… *so*… freely… boarded this ride became hybrids - one-third human and two-thirds witch, having the ability to force… to force their new potency on their victims! They would lose… lose sense of whatever little human morals remained. Their evil ways and actions would send… would send many innocents to see their maker. The more kills, the more influential the witches became, eventually allowing them to obtain the capacity to hex and curse… hex… and curse… Witchwratht, or, as it is mistakenly known today, witchcraft, was supposed to have limits… Fifteen hundred witches maximum. Each was sold the pitch… the pitch that the planet would be theirs, for it would! Being two-thirds witch would mean seeing appearances and convictions… and convictions radically mutate. The pigmentation of their skin altered to this disgusting green you see here before you, with warts and hairs and all. Their voices changed… changed… to a deeper, more malevolent tone, accompanied by hysterical cackling. Their fashion became ridiculous: a pointy black hat and cape, green smock, black leggings, and boots. Don't forget the black cat and broom, of course! Designed to instil fear, it certainly had the desired … the desired effect as planned.'

As Herrifurus narrated the tale, the witches loosened their stubbornness, no longer staring at the sky. Instead, they had taken a chilling interest in the yarn. Harlem noticed that the witches appeared proud of their past wicked ways; the witches had comfortably nestled back down in the bins, all displaying evil, satisfied grins.

When Herrifurus made eye contact, the BinBags stretched and gawked at the sky, unwilling to take Herrifurus on in a staring competition.

'...The witches gripped delight in carrying out the calling without discrimination. Friends, family, strangers – everyone was a target. All because... all because of the selfish ways of these crones. For the world would be theirs. What the demon and the witches had miscalculated, however, was that while the world fought itself, a standstill would be agreed upon. A truce... *a truce...* where the world's four corners would unite in war with the she-devils. Too many sapiens had cruelly been delivered six feet under, but ultimately, the witches were defeated by their more incensed enemy. The crones were destroyed... *or so* it was believed. Five thousand years later, the rise began again; this time, newborn witches took up arms on every continent to wipe out humanity. Like five millennia prior, they commenced their hideous... hideous murderous spree. Man was still performing his best act of waging war. Don't forget, Harlem, that today's weapons and transportation were unheard of. It took years to circumnavigate the known world—bad timing for the witches but good fortune for humans. The Eight Curators had implemented the gift of a wish. Pressing Matters Lane began seeing more activity than previously known. In the end, the wishes of the world were heard. Humankind once again… once… again… overcame the threat and held out. The new rise of the witch was defeated, but eighteen centuries ago, the green-faced, old bats resurfaced. They had quadrupled… *quadrupled*… in number. One aspect had changed; the ratio of human to crone had altered; they were no longer merely one-third human. They were now split fifty-fifty… split… fifty-fifty. *What did this signify?* It meant… *it meant*… that somehow the right to wish became accessible to these monstrous, warty bags! Those horrible, sad excuses for ladies began to vie for complete control to become the ultimate Chief Witch. They began to plot and scheme underhandedly - in secret covens; they conspired to eliminate rival factions in other lands. They wished them dead and worse. Then, behind closed doors, witches unbelievably began to wish death upon the very same witches they had recently collaborated with - once humanity was destroyed, of course! A slow and excruciating death, where the suffering would long endure, even six feet under… I made several amendments, with some tweaking of my own. I could not stand idly by for humans to be no more. One by one, the witches fell. I granted their wishes, *but* with additional changes. I manipulated the wishes by adding my *own* concessions so that the old bats had inadvertently wished this horrific, long-lasting death upon themselves. Witchwrath is good for one place and one place only… the dustbin! I have ensured that the witches' memories remain within their minds. I allow… I allow them to remember their sinister aspirations. I brought them here, and now they are no more than half bin, fused with half witch. Only the top portion of their past form now remains. Cast aside and forgotten, with an eternity... an eternity to be racked with pain for their misdeeds. I have licensed them to live on in death. A perpetuity of hopelessness... of... hopelessness! The BinBags are skilled at avoiding eye contact but are better at issuing threats and recriminations my way! They tell me that the day of revenge... of revenge, will come. The BinBags hope to overthrow me and turn the tide of incarceration tenfold... I believe that, for one day, a new generation will walk amongst men, as they have done on numerous occasions. During the Middle Ages, they abandoned their haggard appearance, infiltrating everyday life and, to the untrained eye, looking like humans. Their one flaw was that they could never conceal the wart on their upper lip. The wart formed... the wart formed when entering Witchwratht...'

Harlem correctly sensed that the wicked ones were indeed resurfacing. After all, he had already encountered these loathsome and appalling hags. This was their warning to him – a sign of things to come. Their day of terror would one day rise.

Continuing through Mucky Waters, the duo encountered and passed many stubborn BinBags.

Herrifurus informed Harlem that, over time, he had punished many witches by tossing them into the swamps, where eventually they would sink to the depths, spending every day living out their deaths in unremorseful darkness.

'Oh, over time, I must have cast three thousand witches into these swamps. It is what they deserve. I assumed it would be a deterrent for the rest to keep the threats they screech at me to themselves. It wasn't... it wasn't... Who knows when I will next decide to fling another... another from my sight?'

Upon passing the very last BinBag, the howling and screeching commenced immediately. The BinBags had squawked as one:

'Our day will ensue; we will come for you, Herrifurus, and for all you hold dear. New depths of evil, depths you do not even know are possible!' they croaked in unison.

Herrifurus was enraged. 'Right, that is it! Harlem, forgive me... Wait one minute; I must do... I must do what is necessary...'

Harlem was merely a spectator as Herrifurus aimed at the nearest BinBag, kicking it over in his moment of infuriation. He began rolling the hag towards the closest patch of swampland, using his feet to push it along. The BinBag loudly screamed out in pain every time her face hit the ground hard as she rolled around and around. As the bin toppled into the swamp, a long-protracted yell and cry of 'NOOOOOOOOO' was heard, followed by bubbles bursting on the slimy surface.

'I suddenly feel a lot better... a lot... better... Come, we are done here... done here!' affirmed Herrifurus gleefully.

### The end of Witchwratht

The wretched, despicable and dispirited sight of Mucky Waters fell behind them in the distance. The two now found themselves strolling on a gleaming limestone pavement. The Sun had returned, as had the favourable, calm and serene feeling that Harlem had lost somewhere within Mucky Waters.

Harlem's attention was now diverted towards the path's edge as he gazed upon a magical and exceptionally dazzling sight not too far away.

Herrifurus couldn't help but have his say.

'Harlem, yes, that is the horizon you stare upon. We are indeed... *indeed*... close to the edge... the edge of this world.'

To the right of the pavement lay a twenty-foot grass perimeter, and nothing else. There was simply a horizon of land and sky—such a breathtaking sight, a splendour of tantalising blue and green pulsating flashes.

Harlem was immediately drawn to this most peculiar sight, stepping and striding across the grass but seemingly making no progress in reaching the mystical and dazzling horizon.

'Harlem, you can stroll ahead as far as you like, but the world's end will remain... will remain at the same distance as if you had stayed... stayed on the path. Just take it in... *take it in... Marvel at Motherhood's magnificence.* For a sight... a... sight... like this will never be repeated in your world. Not a chance... *not... a... chance!* Let's make way... make way... on the Path of the Life.'

The pavement was stupendously reflective. Harlem chuckled at his reflection; it reminded him of being in the hall of mirrors at a fairground. The images of him on the pavement shifted from tall and skinny to short and fat. His arms enlarged, but his legs shrank. His head expanded, yet his body did not. Harlem's mirror self was constantly distorted as he proceeded onwards.

The skewed reflections and the horizon continued to accompany the two as they progressed. This part of the splendid expedition had been a welcome distraction for Harlem—a pleasant, temporary diversion from the forthcoming and far-reaching consequences of events.

The walking ceased upon the sudden arrival of a break in the path. The discontinuity of the pavement was caused by a slightly sunken stream running across and cleaving the path in two.

The brook was twelve feet wide, and nothing positive could be said about this foul waterway; it was not one of beauty.

There was no fresh, clear water flowing here. No picturesque waterfall mixing in with little rocks on the water's way. No little swimming fishes to marvel at.

This stream was a repulsive sight. It had to have been polluted. It was a stream containing a thick, black, tar-like, gloopy substance with what looked like human waste mixed in, although Harlem sincerely hoped it wasn't.

The contents of the stream were slowly drifting forward. It was so slow that its movement was hardly noticeable to the trained eye, possibly due to the thick and stagnant consistency of the liquid. The course seemed to lack energy, but it did emit a nauseating and stomach-turning stench.

Whatever its purpose, the stream ended abruptly at the horizon. Harlem stared upon a remarkable waterfall beyond the realm of Enduring Crave.

A vertical drop of thick, black, viscous liquid was somehow visible through the marvellous light of the horizon. The sound was unique - tonnes of unnatural black noise crashing into whatever lay beneath.

'Herrifurus, what on Earth is that eyesore? *It stinks, it's horrible!* I feel sick; it looks polluted!' exclaimed Harlem.

'*Polluted*? No, my dear boy, not polluted... but... contaminated... *Defiled from the squander of human neediness and sorrow...* The source of this brook is found at the Calace of Judgement, running beyond Enduring Crave and relieving us of its filth... *its filth...* and excrement. The dung I speak of is the wishes unworthy to pass the boundaries of the Hogsty,' answered Herrifurus.

'I beg your pardon?' interrupted Harlem.

'The Hogsty, where the many... the many... stir up a concoction of vile self-want and selfishness, with no care... no... care for the effect of abuse or suffering it has on others. When these wishes are made, the maker is talking out of his backside... *his...* backside! The Hogsty is constantly being filtered and rinsed to cleanse away the faeces and discharge. It is then drained and poured back into the atmosphere of the human world through the waterfall. It will be recycled and dispersed across the globe with the aid of the propellers from the windmills, sending the vileness back towards where it came from. I will not have Enduring Crave covered in... covered in human excrement! I have named this brook - The Stream of Mean Dreams Returned to Human Beings! *What do you think, eh? Very catchy, isn't it*? Yes, it is... *yes, it is...* I am proud of that one,' confirmed Herrifurus, chuckling at his creativity.

Harlem also found it amusing, but he recognised that it had a more serious purpose – to clear the filth out of Enduring Crave and return it to its sender.

# CHAPTER SEVEN

## The Path to the Whitewash Woodland

Harlem scowled at the Stream of Mean Dreams Returned to Human Beings. Leaning over, he inadvertently inhaled a gulp of the vileness emanating from below.

'Whoa!' grumbled Harlem dazedly.

The whiff had made him temporarily dizzy; however, it had the effect of clearing his mind of all other distractions. His thoughts now turned to crossing the indecorous brook. Four miniature circular-shaped stepping stones were positioned throughout the stream, presumably intended for making one's safe passage over the abominable stretch of water. However, their placement would make it difficult to do so. The stones were separated at great lengths from one another, and they were also positioned far to the left and right.

Harlem studied the stones, pondering deeply about the practical way to do this - slowly, with due care and concentration, or quickly, hoping for the best? He had no appetite to bathe in the rotting cesspool below. The stench would never wash off his body.

Someone caught Harlem's attention just as he was ready to vault to the first stone. From the corner of his left eye, he glimpsed a curious little man sitting on a blue and black striped deckchair. The diminutive, peculiar fellow appeared to be fishing in the stream.

Herrifurus twisted towards the man in question, 'I say... I... say... *Larry Cornelius, what are you doing...* what... are you doing, you mad Marsipanian?' asked Herrifurus, seeming at the same time happy and irritated.

'*Larry Cornelius, I say again...* I... say... again! *What are you doing?*'

The repetition of the question awakened Larry to his senses. He bounced up, startled, accidentally dropping his fishing rod into the stream.

'*Argh*, I've been fishing here all day, not caught a thing, and now the stream has hooked my rod!' he groaned.

Larry did not answer Herrifurus' question; instead, he raced to Harlem and eagerly shook his hand. Larry peered down at the stream, gesturing and nodding towards the stepping stones. As he did, he grimaced.

'Rather you than me, matey!' exclaimed Larry whilst winking at Harlem.

There was something about Larry Cornelius that meant you instantly liked him. Perhaps it was his welcoming and pleasant character. He was humorous and good-natured, but his appearance possibly made him even more appealing.

Larry was a sight to behold. His black and silver hair was styled like a court jester's coxcomb, with little bells tied at the end of the three spikes. Harlem assumed that Larry must use a tub of gel daily to get his hair to stick up that way. Larry's full attire resembled that of a medieval court jester.

His long-sleeved tunic was adorned with blue and white patches, their black stitching visible. His upper garment stopped just before the waist, giving the impression that it was too small, even for him. The hem of the cuffs was ruffled, slightly worn, and had a tear. His short trousers mirrored his tunic, with the same pattern and stitches.

He wore little winklepicker shoes with white laces and the most immaculate white socks and gloves. Just barely clinging to the tip of his long, thin, pointy nose were incredibly thick-lensed glasses with blue and white frames. Larry spoke with an excessively high-pitched voice. Had any dogs been present within a ten-mile radius, they would have been sent into a barking frenzy.

Larry was four feet and two inches tall. His small stature appeared exaggerated when standing with Herrifurus, although, in fairness, everyone was small compared to the giant Plutonian.

'Larry Cornelius, have you... have you been hitting the bottle? *What are you doing... what are you doing here?*' asked the increasingly annoyed Herrifurus.

'Herrifurus, you are too tense, my behemoth chum,' expressed Larry. 'Working too hard without a holiday for so long: it's not good for you. You'll do yourself a permanent injury if you aren't careful. Your occupation so burdens you that it weighs you down; it consumes you! So eager to appease the humans, but at what cost? It's merely an ailment to you now, but when will it become an infection?'

This speech made Herrifurus outwardly agitated, becoming increasingly incensed by the second.

'*Now listen here, Larry Cornelius!* You will never overstay... never overstay your welcome. But humankind has reached… has reached… unprecedented levels of hope… of hope… these last few years. I must not rescind my dedication to the cause. *We will have no further chitter-chatter on the matter!* Now is that clear… *is that…* clear?'

For all responses, Larry stuck a finger in each ear, indicating that he wasn't listening to Herrifurus, shaking his head in defiance.

Larry then raised his right hand, snapping his thumb and forefinger together. Larry hastily repositioned the deck chair away from the streambank and insisted that Herrifurus sit down. It was apparent that Herrifurus was finding Larry to be increasingly irksome.

'*I am too busy…* too busy… to play these imbecilic games. Larry, I do not have the time… the time to go along with these antics. *Not today… not… today!*' insisted Herrifurus.

'Sit down, you big bag of gas and wind and listen to me for once!' argued Larry.

Herrifurus slumped into the deckchair, defeated, crossing his hands whilst grumbling to himself under his breath. He was having another little sulk, thought Harlem.

Remembering Harlem didn't have a seat, Larry searched and delved through his pockets. He miraculously pulled out a second deckchair from their depths.

Next, he procured a 1970s vinyl record player from his seemingly bottomless pockets, followed by a giant speaker.

This was too big and heavy for Larry to lift by himself. Harlem jumped up to assist Larry with the load before the weight and size of the amplifier could crush him.

Bizarrely, one speaker wasn't practical, so Larry presented a second one. After connecting both speakers to the record player, Larry finally produced a vinyl record from within his pocket.

All the while, Herrifurus was muttering and becoming increasingly annoyed.

'Be quiet, Herrifurus; now you sit there and take your medicine!' demanded Larry.

Larry urgently placed the record on the turntable and lifted the needle, which began spinning the record. As the needle struck the vinyl, the melody and lyrics began to emanate from the old machine.

'When this old world starts…'

Harlem immediately recognised the song as one of the long-time classics: 'Up on the Roof'. He had listened to it on many happy occasions at Grandma's house. Herrifurus appeared to be unwinding slightly. He was nodding his head and tapping his feet to the rhythm of the music.

Harlem began to acknowledge the reason for this song as he reflected on the meaning of the words, with Larry implying that Herrifurus needed to go up on the roof and release his troubles right into space. Indeed, Herrifurus, too, needed sanctuary, a place to visit and be free of it all, if only temporarily.

'That song was dedicated to my long-time friend, Herrifurus. Take the advice; you stubborn so and so! Herrifurus, be a good chap and do a spot of fishing while I chat with young Harlem here. It'll do you the world of good!' demanded Larry.

'*Chat about what… about what?*' replied Herrifurus, whose relaxation had been short-lived.

'Not for your eyes or ears, my giant friend. Here's another fishing rod – make good use of it!'

Larry presented a new rod from his bottomless pockets and flung it towards Herrifurus, who was once again chuntering to himself.

Larry gently guided Harlem away from the grumpy Ambassador…

'You see, Harlem, long ago, I received an urgent request from Herrifurus, who was reaching out to his friends. A terrible event of immense magnitude had occurred, sending shockwaves across both worlds. The Eight Curators conducted their investigation. What had happened? How could Herrifurus have allowed it? Was it preventable, and most alarmingly, was he the right chap for the job? Herrifurus received encouragement from all over the Solar System, a boost that would deliver the outcome deserved. Many advocates, including myself, visited Enduring Crave to express our gratitude and endorse Herrifurus. I never returned home to Mars after that. You see, Herrifurus has an unenviable job… the most demanding and challenging profession in the galaxy… in *this* universe! Herrifurus is not impervious to emotions - sorrow, despair, or aggravation. Humans drain the very fabric of this world; he's not a machine; Herrifurus is being worn down and gradually eroding over time. The cracks are beginning to widen. Herrifurus cannot continue like this. Eventually, a gasket will blow. *He won't stop.* Humankind: his focus is to save them… to make their world prosperous, even if it's at the cost of his well-being. Therefore, I stuck around, knowing that as time counted down to when the truce would end, Herrifurus' stress levels would rise to a crescendo. The days rapidly recede, and soon, the two will face each other again, except now you have been drawn into the chaos. Tick - tock, tick - tock, the time ever dwindles; Sixty years is all but upon us.'

Harlem focused on Herrifurus pointlessly fishing in the stream, sorrowing for his newfound alien acquaintance.

Herrifurus' job was not for the faint-hearted or weak-minded; it was taking a mighty toll on him.

'Herrifurus didn't have to answer for what happened, of course. He couldn't have known what would transpire; let's be honest, no other species thinks or acts like man. Fortunately, no professional disciplinary action was levelled at him. There could, and most likely would have been, a different result had Merkle orchestrated the investigation as she had demanded. Merkle loathes mankind and would be glad to see the back of them. Thank the skies that she was not in charge. Aspiga of Venus held control instead. "Not guilty," she proclaimed.'

'Yes, but what happened? You still haven't told me, Mr Cornelius,' pleaded Harlem.

'Please, Harlem, call me Larry. I am wise to the events that occurred sixty years ago. It now lies with you and Herrifurus. Right the wrongs, however grim it is… fix it!' demanded Larry.

Herrifurus had had enough of aimlessly fishing in the stream.

He indeed held no desire to humour Larry Cornelius any longer.

'Right, you two! *Are you ready to finish… to finish gossiping*? There is so much to do… so much… to… do… We cannot stay here all day prattling on. Larry, you are as bumblesome today as you always have been! You waste your day away fishing here. *You know this… you know this is true…* You require a level head… you drink too much! We shall leave you now; we have important matters to attend to. Oh, and Larry, I heard every word you said just now. You speak excessively loudly, far too loudly. Larry, thank you, you are a dear friend. It means a lot… it means a lot,' rambled Herrifurus.

Larry abruptly faded into thin air, as did the deck chairs, speakers, and record player. It was a most astonishing sight.

'Where did he go?' asked the baffled Harlem.

'Most likely to a watering hole, such a shame… *such…* a shame,' replied Herrifurus.

'Herrifurus, *I mean*, he vanished right in front of us! Just disappeared… *gone…* what just happened?' wondered Harlem.

'*Now*, I understand… I understand your question… Larry has teleported to his next destination. He is using his Marsipanian teleportation ability.'

It was now back to the matter at hand – crossing the hideous stream.

'Harlem, the path… the path you take in life is one of age. The man you become is linked with your actions at the outset - the foundations - the bricks, and walls… and walls will follow. What will a man become, a skyscraper or a bungalow? Never let it be said that a person's path takes a turn… *a turn…* somewhere along the way. Poppycock… *poppy… cock…* utter unfounded nonsense! The path *is* the Path of the Life. Harlem, your walk is set; its course prepared. Are you committed to what your calling has in store for you? The next stage involves the upcoming chapter and subsequent calls. The quest is waiting for you to step over these stones. It is your destiny to save Enduring Crave!'

Harlem inhaled a deep breath and lunged to the first step. The precise moment his feet hit the stone, it vibrated beneath him so much that Harlem began experiencing a build-up of static shocks in his feet due to the aggressive and powerful vibrations emanating from the stone.

The pain was increasing, and his feet were becoming severely numb, but he survived somehow to hop over to the second stone successfully. This stone began rapidly rising six feet in the air and coming back down twice as quickly.

The up-and-down motion made Harlem's stomach turn. Amazingly, he kept his balance as the stepping stone rose and fell repeatedly.

After the fourth instance of the stone shifting up and down, Harlem seized the opportunity to cross over to the third stone. Like the two that came before, the stone, on sensing Harlem, launched into chaotic action.

It became very evident that the stepping stones were not to make his journey across the stream an easy one, far from it.

The third stone instantly began rotating anticlockwise, starting fast, then slowing, accelerating, then decelerating.

The swirling movement meant that it was just about impossible for Harlem to get his bearings and make it safely to the last stone.

Harlem spun, searching frantically for the concluding stone's location. It was now or never, although it was highly likely that he would end up in the putrid stream. Harlem leapt into mid-air and fixed his eyes on the last stone.

To Harlem, it all happened in slow motion as he neared the penultimate challenge.

His left foot hit the stepping stone, but he knew immediately that his equilibrium was off, his right leg teetering precariously over the excrement below.

Harlem fought hard to keep his balance, struggling with all his might to avoid taking a dip in the abhorrent water. Just when it seemed that his journey was at an end, his composure won out; both of his feet were just about at last solidly planted on the final stone.

Harlem breathed a sigh of relief; there was one more jump.

The ultimate stepping stone was positioned four feet away from the bank of the stream. Harlem didn't wish to assume that it would be an easy task, given the twists and turns his crossing had taken up to now, but he was confident he could make it.

After all, unlike the others, this stone had remained stationary when he landed.

Harlem stared at the far bank; he was almost home and dry, but just as he was to leap over, the last stone began to tilt, rising at the back and causing the front to subside into the filthy stream.

He had no time to waste, so he bounded towards the bank. His leverage was insignificant, but he landed painfully on his right knee. His left foot narrowly avoided skimming the quagmire by a whisker. Harlem rolled forward and sighed with relief; he had made it.

Herrifurus was somehow already present to greet and congratulate Harlem, who stared back towards the stream; the menacing stepping stones he had just risked his life on were strangely nowhere to be seen.

He did, however, spot Larry Cornelius standing on the opposite side. Larry gave a two-thumbs-up salute and then vanished again. Harlem and Herrifurus spun and recommenced strolling along the path.

'Harlem, it was *not* true... was... *not*...true... what I informed you before you stepped over those stones. A person's path can change at any time through the actions they choose to take. Perhaps a conscience or a speck of guilt and remorse can turn one's direction. Eventually, they make pivotal choices. They may see the errors of their way and come full circle. A new outlook on life - to make things better and put right the wrongs... the wrongs of the past... Our path will certainly affect us the most, as well as those close to us. Harlem, decisions, and actions of yours alone... yours alone saw you beyond those stones. When tested... *when*... tested... you did not waver. No one would have pointed the finger at you had you objected. *But you didn't... you didn't...* You have been handed a kismet that was bestowed upon you before you were born. Harlem Hodge, your name is written in the Doomsday Scribble, after all,' announced Herrifurus.

'The... *what*... scribble?' replied an astounded Harlem.

'Harlem, the Doomsday Scribble is the foretelling… the foretelling of the demise of Enduring Crave. This, in turn, shall lead to the destruction… the destruction of Planet Earth and all humankind. Between warnings, there is a victor who will be the vanquisher of destruction. The vanquisher is, of course, you, Harlem Hodge… *yes*… it is you!'

Harlem didn't know what to make of that last statement, but it did sound like an important prophecy.

'Herrifurus, who wrote the Doomsday Scribble?' wondered Harlem with excitement and intrigue.

'*Why, the Motherhood Tree, of course!* Chapters of the Scribble have come to pass… been and gone. *There is more to be revealed… to be revealed in the future…* Motherhood will reveal when she is ready. Come on, time is not our ally… *not*… our ally,' urged Herrifurus desperately.

All the time they had been strolling along the path, Harlem had been talking to Herrifurus; not once had he taken his eyes off him.

For the first time, Harlem turned to gaze forward in the direction they were heading. They were approaching a tunnel.

The path that they were taking entered through the tunnel, so Herrifurus and Harlem continued to follow it.

Once inside, the tunnel was as dark as a miser's pocket. Harlem couldn't even see Herrifurus through the gloom, although he knew he was standing beside him. After only a few seconds, the two exited the tunnel. Harlem wondered how such a short tunnel could have been so dark inside while the daylight was just behind them.

He didn't have time to dwell on it too much, for his eyes began to focus, and what he was gazing at now was indeed a unique and spectacular sight.

'Harlem, welcome... *welcome*... to the Whitewash Woodland.'

Harlem gawked around in awe; the woodland was blazingly white, as if someone had painted every square inch with several coats of thick paint. The trees, from the roots to the trunks and the tiniest twigs and leaves, were entirely white.

The lack of pigment spread to the birds singing in the branches, the galloping deer, the sly foxes, the rabbits, and the badgers.

Harlem couldn't see the sky through the canopy of trees; was the sky white, too?

The duo skirted around an enormous milky lake, with spectacular fish cresting the water to greet them.

Soon, the two stumbled upon a hidden garden, set deep within the woods, surrounded by a pallid, eight-foot circular wall with an archway allowing ingress inside. The garden displayed an immaculately cut, round, white grass lawn encircled by a stone walkway.

Four ivory marble benches were positioned symmetrically on the walkway. At the centre of the lawn, a natural fountain proudly stood tall and firm, carved with engravings of woodland animals, emitting gentle spurts of pale water.

Herrifurus headed towards the fountain; rabbits appeared on the grass, followed by deer, strolling badgers and excited foxes. The last to enter were birds that flew down from the trees.

Herrifurus washed his hands in the fountain and then held out his arms, welcoming the animals to approach.

Herrifurus relished the opportunity to pet and stroke each animal by hand. At once, the visiting birds gently alighted upon Herrifurus' fingertips. Herrifurus pecked each bird gently on the head before slowly kneeling in front of the animals.

'Go and tell your kind that all shall be well… all shall be well. The Whitewash Woodland shall live on. Do not… do… not… be afraid! The boy will prevail. *Go forth with the knowledge… with the knowledge.*'

The birds again took flight, and the deer, rabbits, badgers, and foxes quickly scampered away.

To Harlem, the woodland brought back snow-covered memories of winter strolls, but it wasn't winter, and it wasn't snow. The white was not paint but nature itself, confined to the forest.

'The Whitewash Woodland is home… is home to the soldiers of Enduring Crave. Relax, Harlem, not any army… any army… that you know of. These soldiers defend this world in another way. *They are the Grottlers… the Grottlers…* All day and night, fast asleep in the forest, awaiting battle and to play their part for this… for… this world… Grottlers will not charge in numbers, of course. They stomp… they stomp alone. If a wish has been granted in error or a turn of wickedness is used as part of a granted wish, a Grottler is sent to smash that wish. *To smash and destroy…* and… destroy! That is the duty… the duty of our military. Regrettably, it is a one-way assault into the human domain. The battle won; the wish defeated! The Grottler will sadly not live to see a new day; his bravery is his legacy…'

Continuing to explore the vast woodland, they came upon tens of thousands of little white statues, no bigger than garden gnomes. That is what they looked like, in fact – little gnomes. Grottlers were resting on the ground with their eyes closed, wearing a uniform of white boots, trousers, a belt, gloves, and a polo-neck jumper with a tiny pin badge engraved with the letters EC: Enduring Crave.

Their ensembles were complemented with small berets atop their heads. None had beards, but each wore a thick, bushy moustache.

Harlem, of course, believed what Herrifurus had told him about the Grottlers, but it was hard to accept at this moment; after all, they were little statue-like figures, fast asleep in a world where they may never wake up.

It was difficult to imagine them charging into battle in their current state. The tour of the woods continued, and they encountered thousands more Grottlers along the way.

'Harlem, we have over five billion Grottlers in this forest. Most may never be called… may never be called into duty… Hopefully, only a few, if necessary, will be enlisted in battle. They all reside here in this woodland, whether up in the trees, high up with the leaves, on the ground, or inside the trunks, sleeping and hibernating. No cares or worries… or worries in the world.'

Sauntering on through the breathtaking woodland, Harlem began to relax in the calming atmosphere; for a moment, it temporarily escaped his mind that the forest was part of Enduring Crave.

No matter what extraordinary sights he had seen thus far and what stunning discoveries he had made, the Whitewash Woodland was the most utterly bewildering of them all.

The trees became sparser, and Harlem could now see the entrance to yet another tunnel.

'Say goodbye... *goodbye*... to the Whitewash Woodland. We must press on... we must... we... must,' urged Herrifurus.

Harlem stared at the remarkable woodland he had explored, which was such beautiful, peaceful, and idyllic terrain.

Eventually, they left it behind and entered the tunnel. Like the other, it was dark, but this time, it was as dark as the awful account of man.

Harlem couldn't see his hand, even when it was held up to his face, but within seconds, they had stepped beyond the tunnel and were back on the path.

'How on earth can tunnels that short be so dark? It doesn't make any sense!' exclaimed Harlem.

'Tunnel, Harlem, we have entered and exited... and exited one tunnel... *one tunnel!*' replied Herrifurus.

Harlem was amazed, if not entirely surprised. The rules of Enduring Crave seemed to apply less and less to the laws of reality that he had once known.

# CHAPTER EIGHT

## The Calace of Judgement

Harlem pondered how much longer the journey would take. It seemed they'd been walking for hours thus far. Although he had encountered numerous, unforeseen, and uncovered sights he thought were impossible, Harlem had left Wishwisely before midnight. There was no indication of the current time, and Harlem's legs were beginning to ache.

'Herrifurus, how far do we have to walk?' he asked concerningly.

'Until we reach the Calace of Judgement. Harlem, are you… are… you… ready… for the Calace?' replied Herrifurus.

'Yes, absolutely,' answered Harlem eagerly and excitedly.

'*Very good… very good.* Stupendous… stupendous… well, in that case, here we are… *here we are.*'

Herrifurus held out his left hand, indicating a boulevard that trickled away from the left side of the Path of the Life. The boulevard was splendidly sprinkled with gold dust, which glistened majestically in the Sun, causing the light to refract off the ground and into Harlem's eyes. Ten-foot-tall rose bushes adorned both sides of the boulevard; the roses were tinged in the most magnificent shade of ruby.

'*Hold on, Harlem, hold on…* Bear with me… bear with me… please… If you would allow me to check my pockets… my pockets,' mumbled Herrifurus.

Herrifurus was becoming befuddled again, unable to locate whatever he was searching for, as he checked and pulled at the side and back pockets of his shorts.

Herrifurus frustratedly patted his poncho around the waist to see if he could detect whatever was escaping him.

'Where on Earth did I put them? I know I brought them with me! *Why can't I find them*? Oh, please do not say I left them… I left them in my office. No, I categorically placed them in my pockets… in my… pockets… *Drat, where have they gone*? Blasted Larry Cornelius and his improbable pockets! Why don't I have improbable pockets? *I need improbable pockets, blast it all*… blast… it all!' he complained.

'Herrifurus, what are you looking for?' asked Harlem curiously.

'Sunglasses, Harlem, we need sunglasses! I could have sworn… could have sworn I packed two pairs. We require sunglasses; otherwise, our journey would have been fruitless and utterly unproductive. Someone is playing tricks… playing tricks on me! *Who can have taken them… who*?'

Harlem didn't know what to say or do. Herrifurus was acting indignantly and was once again behaving like a sullen child.

Whilst trying not to make direct eye contact, Harlem noticed twine tied around Herrifurus' neck, with a funny, slight shape protruding underneath his poncho.

'Herrifurus, what's that around your neck? There's something tied to it!' stated Harlem, pointing out the blindingly obvious.

Herrifurus tucked in his chin, peered down, and pulled the poncho away from his neck.

'Ah, here they are... *here they are*... I put them here to remember. It didn't work, in any case. So bumblesome... I am so bumblesome,' grumbled Herrifurus.

Harlem smiled with relief. Herrifurus was absent-minded on occasions, and this was one of those times.

Still flummoxed, Herrifurus attempted to untie the sunglasses from the twine. He struggled, gibbering to himself during the attempt.

Eventually, it was a success; two pairs of sunglasses were ready for use, and Harlem was handed a pair.

'*Put these on, Harlem, put these on*... The Sun is shining, and we must... *we must*... wear them as necessary!' ordered Herrifurus.

The sun had been shining all day, and there had been no need to wear shades thus far, so why now? What was the urgency here? The two stood still, facing the boulevard. Even though the Sun scintillated off the gold dust, Harlem noted that there was nothing to see ahead - just the boulevard and the splendid rose bushes. Two things were puzzling Harlem:

1. Herrifurus had said they were at the Calace of Judgement, but Harlem couldn't see anything of note.
2. Harlem did not understand the big issue regarding the sunglasses. Surely, it couldn't be because of the sunlight reflecting off the gold dust.

'Harlem, I repeat... I repeat... *put on the sunglasses*... the sunglasses... on... *on*... and look ahead!' demanded Herrifurus.

Harlem put on the glasses and had the eye-opener of his life. A stupendous structure, one hundred feet away, towered over the skyline. A building of magnificent proportions had suddenly taken shape in front of him. Harlem removed the sunglasses, and all the magnificence was gone. Replacing them over his eyes, the imposing building re-emerged.

'Harlem, you see before your very eyes... *your very eyes*... the Calace of Judgement. Invisible to the naked eye in daylight; remember, it is always daylight in Enduring Crave. What if... what if, by some diabolical circumstances, man's armies had gotten access and successfully invaded Enduring Crave? Humans are a cunning lot... *a*... cunning lot... constantly searching for the unknown. One day, they may do... they may do... just this... Therefore, the Calace of Judgement must remain hidden, for the trees conceal the woods... Imagine Sapiens knowing the location of the Calace, where wishes are categorised and the outcomes are determined. *No, no, it sends shivers... sends shivers down my spine!* You cover your eyes with the Tinted Goggles of Profundity - like night-vision... *but*... day-vision. Allowing sight of what cannot be seen... *of what*... cannot be seen. No ordinary goggles will suffice. You see before you the Calace of Judgement... *impressive, isn't it?* Not a castle nor a palace, it is... *a*... Calace... Oh, the opulence and lavishness of the place are mostly on the outside. Just for my show... just for my show, as those who toil away here in the name of humankind require no extravagance. To be here daily, to grind and graft, isn't so much a concern as there is no time to do anything but slog… but… slog on… There are those in your world, Harlem, who would deem the term 'Calace of Judgement' as very apt indeed. We cannot fulfil all wishes, and undoubtedly, now we would offend someone… or cause offence. Those who would suggest we show no emotion and are insensitive, that we hold an uncaring disregard for the wants of others. Therefore, we must be callous. *Everyone is offended these days!'*

The Calace of Judgement was, for the most part, beautiful and made of the finest Portland stone. The building was in perfect symmetrical proportion.

A grand stairway leading up to the main entrance was taking centre stage.

At the top of the stairway was an imposing archway with an unnecessarily large door that must have been built for the most gigantic of giants.

The colossal oak door opened inward from both sides, which fit the theme of grandeur and palatial elegance. Harlem believed that the Calace was two storeys high due to the thirty windows, framed with resplendent pillars, running on either side of the entrance, making a total of sixty windows.

This was reciprocated above, so it was only natural to assume that there were two storeys. However, above the main entrance door was a massive balcony with twenty-foot-tall pillars, and higher still was a smaller tier that supported a monumental, red sapphire dome.

It was all very opulent, except for four round brick towers in each corner. These towers appeared out of character with the rest of the building.

The brick towers could quickly have been taken from bruised medieval English castles.

Maybe whoever had built the Calace had run out of funds due to all the lavishness, and the towers were a result of that, economically constructed, a stain on an otherwise unblemished piece of art.

The two set off on the short walk along the boulevard to the Calace.

As they strolled onwards, the rose bushes honoured Herrifurus' and Harlem's presence by courteously presenting rose petals at their feet. Harlem believed it was a guard of honour for all the tireless work Herrifurus did for humankind.

Three steps from the top of the entrance stairway, Herrifurus stopped to converse with Harlem.

'Harlem, no human has ever set foot in the Calace of Judgement. None of the seven priors toured here… for it was constructed… was constructed some years after the final visitor bid us farewell. All have been guests here in this world… all granted permission to access Enduring Crave. All were handpicked, but the cloaks of secrecy lay dormant in secrets so off the record. They remain undisturbed… undisturbed, a hush-hush, confidential, shrouded mystery in an otherwise open enigma. It is only for the eyes… only for the eyes of the chosen one, which is you, Harlem. Are you willing to absorb, digest and imbibe the lessons that await? Those lessons that have been placed on hold... on hold for you: how the operational effects are put in place here. Oh but, Harlem, we have a dilemma... we have a foe... *a foe...*'

'We must stop the North boy; *he's* the enemy!' declared Harlem.

Harlem had realised immediately who they would clash against. It was the story of the North boy from sixty years ago, the same boy who had disappeared in the woods.

Harlem recalled the tale recounted by Larry Cornelius, a truce of which the days remaining were rapidly receding—a truce where Herrifurus and now Harlem were dragged into the conflict.

It could only be about the North boy. Everything coincided with Harlem moving to Wishwisely; it *was* destiny.

The Calace entrance door was thrown open with a mighty crash. The tallest lady that Harlem had ever seen stood snarling down on them.

Whoever she was, she had a strict and terrible demeanour. Unlike Herrifurus, she was imposing and terrifying. She had to be over seven feet tall, not quite as tall as Herrifurus, but not much shorter either.

She wore a makeshift outfit reminiscent of a Victorian housekeeper. She had on a long-sleeved black dress, complete with a black bodice. She had tied a rough apron over the top and wore thick, white leggings on the lower part of her anatomy.

On her head rested a white maid's bonnet that failed to cover hardly any of her hair, as she had long, crimson dreadlocks that reached her waist.

Her biceps were impossibly brawny and muscular, as if she worked out at least three times a day. Her bulk and frame would eclipse any monster who dared to challenge her.

She did not wear gloves, and her worn hands looked like they could throttle any dragon. Those hands had seen much hard work, tireless trouble over the years, and probably many fights.

The woman had the greenest eyes that stared right at you and beyond.

Talking of fighting, she had a flat, squashed nose and two cauliflower ears. Her lip was split, and she had a swollen chin. She bit down hard on her lip, allowing blood to seep out. It was apparent to Harlem that this look of hers was one she had orchestrated herself. She spoke in a noxious and gruff voice.

'It's Jonathan North, actually! The North boy… what kind of guesswork is the North boy? Bully for you… the North boy indeed!' The stranger had brutally scolded Harlem.

'I'm awfully sorry,' replied Harlem, 'really I am.'

'Awful indeed, says I! A boy from that human lot, standing here, now that is an awful sorry sight!' she admonished.

Harlem didn't know how to respond to that. This angry stranger had a chip on her muscular shoulder. Herrifurus intervened, attempting to ease the situation.

'I see… I see you are waving the formalities! *Behave, Mokwug,* show our guest some respect… some… respect!' he warned.

'Unwanted guest, Herrifurus! They're all as bad as each other; you should have closed the door to Enduring Crave years ago rather than let more in. When will you learn? We're heading for a lost cause; mark my words!'

Herrifurus was becoming tetchy. 'That is enough, Mokwug, *that is enough...* enough! This boy is unlike the others; he has a purpose... a... purpose... Allow me to introduce you to Harlem Hodge.'

Mokwug had no intention of being polite towards Harlem, nor was she willing to show it.

'Wow, this boy is Harlem Hodge! *Well*, why didn't you say? I thought you'd dragged a stray in off the street. *Of course*, it's Harlem Hodge; *who else* would it be in dawn's early rise?' she spat sarcastically.

'Harlem, as you can rightly assume, this lump of doom and gloom is Mokwug. She is as subtle as a train wreck. You must not... you... must... not... pay her any heed. *She is in one of her foul moods yet again...* Mokwug is far too long in the tooth... in the... tooth... I did warn you what she was like. The last of the great ear grinders.'

Herrifurus was visibly and regrettably displeased, as well as frustrated, embarrassed, and angered by Mokwug's unpleasant attitude and severe, unwelcoming disposition towards Harlem.

'Behave now, Mokwug, behave! I hope... I hope I make myself... make myself clear! Do you hear me... *do you hear me, I say?*'

Mokwug turned to Harlem and gave him the most insincere smile; she was far from jovial.

She speedily diverted her vexation from Harlem, returning to Herrifurus and berating him instead.

'Herrifurus, do you realise the time? Where have you been? Have you lost what little sense of direction you possess? The countdown is nearing, and you and he from that human lot have been merrily taking in the sights, strolling around like two tourists! Did you take photos and buy souvenirs while you were out and about? Herrifurus, you're so bumblesome! The boy is not on holiday. Now, need I remind you what is important?' she lectured.

'Shoo, woman, shoo... shoo... *go away*... go... away... Whatever words just emanated from your colossal mouthpiece were no more than white noise to me. *I did not understand a word... a word you said...* Now, be a dear and fetch us a drink. You can find us in the... in... the... Calace... I shall be showing this young man around. *Now go, shoo, shoo!*' ordered Herrifurus.

Mokwug trotted off in a foul mood. She mumbled as she stomped, punching the door violently on her way.

'*Harlem, believe it or not...* or not... Mokwug means well. She has been with me since day one... since... day one... She is extremely aware of what awaits. Mokwug works tirelessly every day to aid humankind. She sees the worst they have to offer repeatedly. She, too, feels betrayed by what happened in the past. It is not personal... not... personal,' explained Herrifurus.

'She's a frightful one!' laughed Harlem.

'*Absolutely, she is*! Ah, just a few seconds in her company, and you realise that. She wears many hats... many hats, I might add, cut from a different cloth. Come now... come now... let us enter the Calace of Judgement. After you, Harlem.'

After pacing up the final few steps, Harlem entered through the magnificent doorway.

Someone, it appeared, had turned out the lights. Harlem couldn't see a thing, although he did hear the door close softly behind him.

'Take off the goggles... the goggles, Harlem. *Lose the goggles*,' instructed Herrifurus.

Upon removing the sunglasses, Harlem stood inside a fabulous and extravagant ballroom, so vast that it must have been designed to awe its guests upon entry.

The scarlet, marbled walls were fully encrusted with diamonds, which gave off magical, dancing light displays. Massive, claret-coloured crystal chandeliers dangled from the high, ruby glass ceiling.

A striking vermilion-tiled floor matched the impressive walls and ceiling. It had been masterfully thought out and designed by the architect.

The room was so gargantuan and devoid of the hustle and bustle for which it was created that it was also cold, empty, and lacking life. No matter how big or small, every noise echoed over and over in the cavernous space. The room needed warmth and love; there was far too much emptiness.

It was a considerable walk across the ballroom, and getting to the other side seemed to take an eternity. On the way, Harlem noted a small drinks bar along the wall to his right. It was consistent with the theme and colour scheme of the rest of the ballroom. Six red stools were placed at the bar. Several pumps offered a variety of beers, ciders, and bitters, with numerous bottles of spirits on display.

As Herrifurus and Harlem continued and began nearing the door opposite the main entrance, Harlem observed a strange creature sitting at a circular desk. The desk was fifty feet in diameter, and the middle section had been removed.

One thousand portable TV monitors were positioned on the desk, with the screens facing inwards. Every monitor displayed a news bulletin from a separate news station worldwide.

The reporters spoke a variety of languages and covered a range of incidents and breaking news segments. Perched on a stool, in the middle where that part of the desk had been removed, was a most peculiar-looking lifeform.

He had the body and head of a little green man, around four feet in height - humanity's most definitive vision of an alien body.

However, he had one thousand eyes, strangely positioned right around his head in two rows, one row above the other. Each row consisted of five hundred miniature, bulbous eyes.

The peculiar being had no nose, only two long nostrils. His drooping ears were at the bottom of his head, and his mouth was narrow and wide. He possessed no teeth, and his tongue was yellow.

Herrifurus began the introductions, 'Harlem, this is… this… is… Backeyedjection. *Backeyedjection, meet Harlem Hodge.*'

Backeyedjection spoke in a slow, monotone, robotic voice.

'Pleased to meet you, Harlem Hodge; I've heard so much about you,' he intoned.

Harlem nodded and smiled. He was a little embarrassed. He didn't want to appear spiteful or rude, but he did have to hold back his laughter as this alien was a sight to see.

'Harlem, Backeyedjection takes note of all the doings… *all the doings in the human world.* He processes all the news simultaneously, his thousand eyes spinning… spinning eternally as he absorbs… as he absorbs all information at once,' Herrifurus stated both enthusiastically and proudly.

Herrifurus was correct; the two rows of eyes constantly rotated while the head remained motionless. It was a most peculiar and funny sight.

'He does a complete sweep of all one thousand monitors. After a full rotation, the news channels switch. This process repeats itself constantly, continually monitoring humanity to assess the world's situation. He seeks the unusual and any signs of peril. *Is humanity heading for disaster?* Are the events connected? *Has a trigger… a trigger been unleashed?* My dear Backeyedjection is from Saturn; he is a Saturnlite. Farewell… farewell, my ally… *my… ally. Carry on the good work…* the good work. Be left alone to study man's events,' insisted Herrifurus in a borderline patronising manner.

Harlem waved goodbye to Backeyedjection, who had the entire cold and lonely ballroom to himself. What a solitary, isolated and lonesome work environment.

At long last, Herrifurus and Harlem welcomed the ballroom's far side, now facing two massive red doors.

'Herrifurus, *who is* Jonathan North?' asked Harlem, with a concerned expression both in his tone and on his face.

'Why, Jonathan North is the most... the most... ungregarious character of the ages... of... the... ages!' answered Herrifurus.

'Herrifurus, I don't even know what that means!'

'Harlem Hodge, you do not want to... you do not want to... Forget that rascal... that rascal for now. *This is it now, Harlem, this is it.* Operation Flog a Dead Horse sits beyond... beyond... these doors... Doors of Red Envy: SESAME!'

## *Operation Flog a Dead Horse*

The doors of Red Envy gracefully parted, allowing the two to pass on through. Harlem was overwhelmed to find himself standing at the top of a golden spiral staircase that towered over all the activity below, at least five hundred feet below. Harlem hated and feared heights, making him feel light-headed and his knees wobbly as he timidly looked down. If the ballroom had been impressive in size, it was dwarfed by the sheer magnitude and scope of the room where Operation Flog a Dead Horse was situated. Such was the size that Harlem failed to see the room's far side despite being so dizzyingly high up.

If NASA believed it had a sophisticated network of technology, scientists, and engineers, its operation would be at a third-rate level compared to what was happening here. As the spiral staircase dwindled and Harlem neared the ground, he gazed upon rows and rows of computer desks as far as the eye could see. There had to be billions of desks paired with billions of operators stationed at each one. Billions more workers could be found flying around and passing on information. It was one immense hive of activity.

The workers were billions of tiny, green, insect-like creatures, all the size of a tennis ball. Each one had two left and two right eyes. They also had familiar question-mark-shaped wings, two tiny hands and a pink nose.

Harlem believed these were just like the sickly-looking blobs he had witnessed in Mucky Waters. The only difference was that these critters were green and more prominent than those from earlier.

'*Stop, Harlem!* What you see here before you are the Wantwots... *Welcome... welcome to Operation Flog a Dead Horse!* Upon reaching their twelfth birthday, a human is deemed mature... deemed mature enough... and responsible enough to be granted the gift of a wish. Before then, innocence ruled. A Wantwot is assigned to the birthday boy or girl at age twelve. This Wantwot will shadow the individual for life, listening out for their wishes. The Wantwot is physically at the Calace, but it also has a presence on Earth that accompanies the person wherever... wherever they wander. That is why we see those humans on these screens. An invisible aura that goes unnoticed by man. Have you ever looked back on an event and seen it through someone else's eyes? Of course, everyone has... *everyone has...* as you are seeing it from the point of view of your Wantwot!'

Harlem ogled in awe, approaching a nearby desk and viewing the outdated monitor screen.

He peered at a man; his assigned Wantwot constantly followed and surveyed him, waiting for the words 'I wish' to be uttered.

'Harlem, when one half of the world sleeps, the Wantwots never rest... never... rest... The ones not at the desks perform administrative duties. When the morning risers of the world take charge, the roles swap to begin another shift... another shift of eavesdropping; all cloak and dagger... cloak... and dagger.'

That's what it all was, thought Harlem: The world's most significant espionage and surveillance operation. NASA, as well as the FBI, CIA, and a dash of MI6, supplemented with all the secret government cells across the globe, would still fall some way behind Operation Flog a Dead Horse.

After a lengthy walk across the colossal room, Harlem witnessed wishes plummeting from a black hole in the ceiling. Each wish tagged with the name and address of the creator. The wishes impacted onto a conveyor belt before shooting off into a designated dreamduct. Some wishes would last longer on the conveyor than others (up to twenty-four hours) before being allocated a dreamduct. There were seven dreamducts in total:

1. **The Hogsty**: A flat-out refusal of wishes, as those wishes would involve another person being unhappy. They displayed vile selfishness and a lack of care for others by the wish-maker.

2. **Give us a clue, give us a clue**: Wishes not specific enough – because of this uncertainty, the wishes entered

this dreamduct for nurturing. An example would be "I wish I could win the lottery". When does the person want to win the lottery?

3. **No way, José**: Wishes that cannot be approved. For example, a bald man wishes he still had a full head of his real hair. This cannot be done in the same way that a person five feet five inches tall and who wishes to be six feet tall cannot grow overnight. Although ungranted, these wishes are still given life to allow for hope.

4. **Roger, Roger**: A wish clearly defined, "I wish I could win the lottery tonight". The wish maker has specified a timeframe, allowing the Wantwot to review the individual's file. Are they deserving? Have they behaved well? The wish makers' actions determine the outcome, and a speedy turnaround is required.

5. **Others first**: Consisting of wishes made for the benefit of others. This is the ultimate expression of giving and kindness, but have the beneficiaries been deserving? "I wish my friend Julie would find love," or "I wish my son would get good grades".

6. **Game over**: Unlike the Hogsty, these wishes are made deliberately to hurt other people, or worse still. When an evil wish is made, it is abandoned in Mucky Waters. These wishes would automatically find themselves at the

bottom of the swamps and bogs. That human loses their right to wish in the future; it's game over.

## 7.  Witches

Those were the seven dreamducts. Wishes were not necessarily granted or refused immediately; it could be years before an outcome was finalised. Whilst those wishes remained alive, the wish maker carried hope.

Herrifurus and Harlem scurried over a golden bridge crossing the source of the Stream of Mean Dreams Returned to Human Beings. The stool and splodge from those wishes were relentlessly and unapologetically dripping out of the bottom of the Hogsty dreamduct straight into the stream.

Harlem's and Herrifurus' ultimate destination was a gigantic, yellow, and black mezzanine some distance ahead. After a long-lasting, chaotic walk filled with awe, shock and intrigue, Harlem stared worriedly at the mezzanine. You had to climb a one-hundred-foot yellow ladder without safety equipment to reach the top.

Harlem, as we now know, was not fond of heights in the slightest, but he gingerly and nervously braved the climb, although he was feeling all the uneasier and queasier the higher he went.

Once safely on top of the mezzanine, Harlem was introduced to Monocle Sway, the leader of the Wantwots. Monocle Sway resembled the rest of the Wantwots at the Calace, except he was the size of a basketball. He held a golden monocle over his two right eyes and wore a black Gladstone hat.

He couldn't keep still, constantly fidgeting and swaying about. He was very pompous and spoke like a member of the aristocracy, somehow always holding on to a financial newspaper between his two left wings.

'*I say, Harlem, old boy, splendid to meet you in person.* Jolly good show, but excuse me now, won't you? Toodle-pip!' and with that, Monocle Sway buzzed off back to work.

Scarcely above the mezzanine floor and just in front, dangling, was the most humongous TV screen ever constructed. Somehow, it hung from the ceiling hundreds of feet above. The TV screen showed only a map of the world. Nothing more, nothing less.

'All that will change in the coming weeks. What images does this screen have in store for us? Anyway... anyway... *moving on*... moving... on... Operation Flog a Dead Horse is named so... is... named so... and *why* you ask? *Thanks to Mokwug, that is why!* She had thrown her weight about so much that everyone agreed to the title. Forced to keep... to keep the peace... As the years go by, I feel Mokwug believes it is becoming a waste of time... a waste... of time... *Come now... come now... let us descend,*' stipulated Herrifurus animatedly.

Harlem gripped the ladder tightly and closed his eyes for the frightening descent. He also carried no genuine desire to scale that excessively tall spiral staircase.

'Fear not... fear not, we are not heading backwards. *We go forward, this way... this way!*' exclaimed Herrifurus.

Indeed, they did not return in the way they had entered; instead, Herrifurus guided Harlem in the opposite direction until they stumbled upon a door labelled 'Boiler Room'. Harlem was ushered through, and suddenly, they found themselves standing in the unkempt office.

'I may need... may need access to my office at any time. The Ambassador of Enduring Crave need not walk if he does not... does not fancy it. In my office, I whisper... whisper... my destination, and as I exit, I find myself in my desired place. Anywhere in Enduring Crave, I only have to think about it, and I am there once I depart this room. The same goes... if I open any door anywhere in this world. I imagine or say, 'my office' and here I arrive—only I, Mokwug, and now you know the secret. Only the three of us possess and hold this ability. Never disclose this... disclose this to another!' warned Herrifurus sternly.

'I won't, Herrifurus,' agreed Harlem.

After speedily exiting the office, the two found themselves standing on the Path of the Life, where the path intersected with the boulevard that had led them to the Calace of Judgement.

# CHAPTER NINE

## The Lantern

So, on they continued. Harlem's tour of Enduring Crave was not yet complete. He marvelled at what further awe-inspiring sights and stories he would experience. This world was fantastic in every way, from the sublime to the insane.

'Harlem, what do you... do you think of the Calace... of the Calace of Judgement?' asked Herrifurus.

'*It's terrific, wonderful, truly amazing.* It really is!' answered Harlem joyously. He wasn't simply humouring Herrifurus; he absolutely believed and understood how incredible the Calace of Judgement was.

'*Ah, the Calace, a relatively new addition to this realm.* After Jonathan North was caught, the Calace was constructed. A building of such... of... such... magnificence. A place where we were finally able to complete our duties without being seen. Before that rascals' actions, we had been open... been open in our duty, working with nature outdoors. That all had to change, of course, so we came up with the concept of the Calace of Judgement. The staff of Enduring Crave had endured in the days that followed! Create a building so unnecessarily immense, monumental, and grand. The world's population was on the rise... three billion in 1965... nearly eight billion today. It took two months to construct, which was a fantastic achievement. However, as I paid for it out of my own pocket, my funds began to dry up swiftly. The final towers were built from the only materials I could afford, not quite in keeping with the rest of the Calace, as you may have noticed. *A few tweaks and fine-tuning here and there... here and there, and the wishes soon arrived...* We have evolved our methods over the past few decades, but the mission statement has remained constant: to do what is right by the individual and their wishes. As I explained earlier, the Calace of Judgement cannot be looked upon by just... just... *anyone...* To see is to wear the Tinted Goggles of Profundity. Only three pairs exist, one each for me, Mokwug, and now... and now... you. Keep these shades and never... never hand them to another. Monocle Sway and the Wantwots have no call or desire to leave the Calace before they retire; if they did, they would not find their way back. Larry cannot find his way... drunk or sober. I must go out and fetch him. He has never seen the exterior of the Calace. Future enemies and foes must never... never disclose the location of our headquarters. Another significant factor - the Calace never remains in one place - which I implemented as an extra safety buffer. Every month, I reposition the Calace, and it never... *never* harms the environment. Today, where you see it, next month, the Calace could be hiding in the field of Motherhood. Possibly even standing over the Motherhood Tree itself, but having no... having no environmental impact. The Calace is an invisible and weightless classified enigma...'

Herrifurus expressed a notable jaunty manner whilst proudly relating his tale of the Calace of Judgement. Wearing a big grin like a Cheshire cat, he added, 'We have only skimmed the surface of the Calace, so much more nestles deep down, stories for another... another time!' and with that, Herrifurus let out a Leprechaun kick.

Perhaps there was a speck of truth in what Mokwug had insinuated about the two sightseeing. It had been another thirty minutes of seemingly aimless rambling and idle chatting. This abruptly ended when the two arrived at the edge of a blue, inverted pyramid, easily twice the size of the Great Pyramid of Giza, which was inverted and buried deeply into the ground.

'In life, we have... we have challenging obstacles to negotiate. *Everyone experiences ups and downs... ups... and downs...* They see no way beyond the difficulties. No hope... *no way out...* no... way... out... Not reasoning obstructs the progression of our thought processes. Come now... come now... let us walk the Inverted Blue Pyramid. Harlem, think of a fear before we descend.'

It intimidated Harlem as he cautiously descended the slabs and tiers. It was a lengthy decline and severely steep. It then resonated with Harlem what Herrifurus had said about obstacles in life; this was a difficult task he would need to conquer with no lack of ups and downs. Neither spoke as they made the descent, and Harlem acted philosophically; if he could overcome this test, then his rationale was that he could find a resolution to any situation he found himself in.

It took what felt like forever to reach the bottom; Harlem remained on his feet on the mammoth stone slab at the lowest point, halfway across. Now for the formidable task: climbing up the opposite side.

Level by level, tier by tier, Harlem hauled and dragged himself upwards, never looking downwards. Herrifurus was by his side until he began wheezing and spluttering.

Herrifurus was breathing heavily. After a few moments of slurping in all the air he could, Herrifurus finally had enough breath to speak...

'I... must... say... I must... say... I... am... not... I am not... as fit... as... I... once was... once... was... *How very embarrassing*... very... embarrassing... You continue, Harlem, I need a rest... a rest... don't waste your worries on me... on... me...' he wheezed.

Harlem continued alone; it was a mighty struggle as he stretched and lifted himself onto each tier. The levels dwindled, with only five left, then four, three, two, and one. At last, mission accomplished. Harlem stood up, only to find Herrifurus waiting for him at the top. Herrifurus was leaning over and still panting and breathing heavily. His hands rested on his knees whilst sucking in as much oxygen as possible.

'*Hey*, you bloody cheated!' accused Harlem.

'I'm sorry, Harlem, you would have been... would... have been waiting... till... the cows come home... come... home. By the way... we have no cows... no... cows.... *Not cheating... not cheating... more a bending of the rules*... Anyway, this is supposed to be about you. When you were at the lowest point, rock bottom, the only way was up, wasn't it? This applies in life; when we hit our lowest... it cannot get any grimmer. The only way forward is to tackle the dilemma head-on. By completing the Inverted Blue Pyramid, you overcame your fear of heights. Anything is possible, even when backed… backed into a corner, there is an exit route, never forget… *never*… forget.'

Harlem was ecstatic that he had overcome his fear of heights; one obstacle was now behind him. Herrifurus had let it be known that any deep-rooted apprehensions, be it fear of flying, thunder, or any phobia, could all be banished upon hitting the lowest point of the inverted pyramid. Only at rock bottom, when there was nowhere further down to go, did a way out present itself.

Think of one fear before descending the pyramid, which is overcome upon completion.

'Harlem, we have no time… no time… to conquer any more phobias now!' insisted Herrifurus.

A turquoise cornfield separated the Inverted Blue Pyramid from a magical, glowing forest of oak trees, approximately two hundred feet away. As the two hastily rustled forward with rigorous determination, Harlem was aware that the entire forest was audaciously aglow. The almightiest and yellowest golden light beams relentlessly flickered, splendidly illuminating the whole forest.

Delving into the trees, Harlem heard desperate voices calling and pining for long-forgotten dreams. The voices spoke gently and softly as they drifted from tree to tree, the trees acting as wild beacons of energy.

The further the sightseers journeyed, the more wishes of the past they could hear crying out. The greater the distance marched through the trees, the stronger the light and the more full-throated the buzz of the voices. The forest persisted, flaring determinedly with no intent on resting.

The travellers arrived at the very centre of the woods, where a golden lantern sat alone in the middle of a perfectly formed circle of trees, resting on the ground. The lantern contained three small glass panels on three of the four sides. The fourth side held a small, golden door with the tiniest keyhole at the bottom.

It was impossible to gaze inside the panels, as the lantern's brilliant, beaming light was too dazzling and overpowering. It was the lantern that was transmitting the wondrous yellow-golden glow, and it was the lantern that the voices they could hear were crying out to.

It was not a flame that kept the lantern aglow; it was something more poignant.

'Yes, Harlem, I know… I know you know you stand in the centre of the Pining Forest,' confirmed Herrifurus.

'Herrifurus, these are oak trees, *not* pine trees,' Harlem pointed out whilst frowning at the silly name given to the Pining Forest.

'*Oh, that is a good one… a good one. Wait till I tell Mokwug that one! On the other hand, I'd better not… better not…* Harlem, you gaze upon the Lantern of Infinite Wishes… This lantern hoards every wish that never came true, yet we never gave up on them. Not those of the Hogsty, Game Over, or Witches, but the wishes kept alive to afford… afford hope. The unfulfilled dreams in this lantern are the wishes of the departed, wishes that beat long after the maker's heart does not. At times, the wishes endure beyond… endure beyond us… I cannot tell you how many wishes beat inside that lantern, but it must be in the billions… the billions. The lantern radiates so much energy that this is the indomitable luminosity you see. No wish can escape. The lantern is impenetrable… *impenetrable*… and no human machinery could ever break through. The echoes you hear are the words uttered… uttered by the wish maker long ago, recorded in time and played out periodically through the ages… Harlem, it is soon time to take the lantern -'

Herrifurus failed to complete his sentence as he was startled and distracted almightily by an urgent and desperate voice wailing behind them.

'-HERRIFURUS, WAIT UP, WAIT UP!' Larry Cornelius was scampering to catch up.

'*Larry, what is the urgency? Is there an emergency? What, man, what is it*? Is there a crisis… a crisis… talk to me?' urged Herrifurus desperately.

'Herrifurus, Monocle Sway has asked me to track you down. You've not responded to your pager and have left your phone at the Calace. Monocle has had to ring me to locate you. The boy's parents are no more than thirty minutes from arriving home. You must wrap up your expedition right now! Harlem, you need to be on your way… and fast!' warned Larry.

'For the love of dawn,' yelped Herrifurus. 'The time… the… time… *Oh, how wrapped up in the sights I was*… Herrifurus, you fool… *you fool*… you are so bumblesome! Quickly now, Harlem, we need to get to my office… my office, and fast!'

The three began dashing through the luminous rays and past the remaining energetic trees in the Pining Forest.

As they came to the edge of the woodland, Harlem caught a glimpse of the marquee way off in the distance, although entirely dwarfed by the stupendous size of the Motherhood Tree. Herrifurus started huffing and puffing, slowing right down until he stopped altogether. Harlem and Larry grabbed an arm and forced Herrifurus to continue, albeit at a much slower pace.

On arriving at the marquee, Herrifurus sagged into the desk chair fully depleted.

Larry went about his business, most likely planning to waste the rest of his day.

Mokwug came bursting into the office, ill-tempered and enraged, even worse than she was when she first introduced herself.

'*Oi*, you two ungrateful sods, you ask me to make you a drink and then disappear on more galivanting adventures! Don't take the mickey out of me. I'll box your ears, the pair of you!' she bellowed threateningly, with excessive bleeding from her lip, and a ginormous throbbing vein across her forehead.

Mokwug violently threw the two drinks in Herrifurus' direction. As she stormed off, she spat out further degrading comments, this time aimed at Harlem. 'The skies, help us! That cheeky, ignorant runt from that human lot will be our downfall... *Saviour*... my backside!' she muttered.

Harlem stared at Herrifurus with a gobsmacked expression. Herrifurus raised his arms, waving Mokwug away, but she had already left.

'Look after... look after the Tinted Goggles of Profundity, take good care... good care of them!' Herrifurus instructed.

'Herrifurus, if it's all the same to you, I'd prefer to keep them here; they'll be safer, *I'm sure...*' replied Harlem.

Herrifurus agreed to place the goggles in a paranormal safe that would become invisible and reappear only when Harlem called for it. Only he would know the code, and only he could open the safe. Even if others had somehow managed to uncover it and had accessed the combination, it could never be opened by anyone other than Harlem. No matter where he was in Enduring Crave, Harlem could access his safe at any time. This would be the most effective way to keep the goggles protected.

The two friends positioned themselves outside the rock on Pressing Matters Lane. It was almost time for Harlem to bid farewell to Herrifurus.

'It was nearly curtains... *nearly*... curtains, Harlem. I had completely forgotten that I had instructed Monocle Sway to keep track of your folks. I am a clot of immense... of immense proportions. Disgraceful timekeeping... *disgraceful...* timekeeping, I'm afraid, but you should be on your way soon. Before you go, tell me who you are afraid of. Who is it that makes you want to run?' asked the well-meaning Herrifurus.

'Don't laugh, Herrifurus, but it's my old next-door neighbours. They're mean, selfish, and too absorbed in themselves. They don't give a hoot about anyone else. Always looking down and laughing at the poor and regularly mocking the less fortunate. Toeknee and Hellaine Maloney; that's who! They have lots of money and firmly believe they're superior to the common person as business owners. Rude, obnoxious, and all-around horrible. Fat cats, and that's putting it mildly. They eat and eat like a pair of pigs, only that would be an insult to a swine. Toeknee tried to ban kids from playing in the street; he didn't own the road but acted as if he did. He would drive at us kids and try to run us over with his custom black Range Rover, registration plate F1 MAL. In their eyes, they are above the law. He once knocked me off my bike, demanding I move out of his way as I held him up, despite him being fifteen feet from his driveway. He swerved at me, and I fell off my bike and broke my leg! Toeknee flung open the car door and charged, waving his broken golf club at me, shouting, "Do you know who I am?" That's his catchphrase!' explained Harlem.

'Tell me, Harlem, are you still terrified... terrified of these dreadful characters?' asked Herrifurus with care and compassion.

'Probably would be if I ever crossed paths with them again,' he answered honestly.

'Harlem, never be unsettled, no matter how much or how little someone throws their weight around, living with the assumption that others are subservient to them because they are worse off... worse off... in life. Money, fame, and power do not... do... not... decree they are worthier and more exceptional than any fellow human being. Only in their minds... in their... minds... Who is more affluent, the man with the money and few true friends but many lickspittles, or the poorer man with a friends list so long it enriches... enriches him more than currency ever could? Harlem, you have turned away from being jittery about these two vile people you speak of. Think... look deep... look... deep. When did you last meet them, within your own eyes... within... your own eyes?' asked Herrifurus.

'*Of course*, the pig clowns! It was Toeknee and Hellaine on the cobbles. He went to swing at me with his broken golf club. Toeknee always displays that golf club, brandishing it at people. Why doesn't he use his hands instead? "Do you know who I am?" How pathetic does that sound? How could I not have realised who it was when I first saw them?' enquired Harlem.

'Because, Harlem, this is how you see them up here... up here in your mind. A pair of pig clowns - you see them for what they truly are, treating money as if it is of no consequence and informing people that they have plenty of it. Eating way too much unnecessarily will get you... will get you... fat! These two are detestable characters. But remember this always: what does scare us can scar us! The difference... the difference being the letter E. Never be scared of anyone, for Everyone is Equal! We know that money does not make you truly rich, but love and genuine companionship do. Toeknee does not understand this feeling, as others are terrified of him. The true number of friends *is* the measure of a man. Toeknee sees money as not the root of all evil, but profit and greed! You cannot take it to the grave with you! A wise man once said, "All the money in the world won't get you into Heaven or allow you to buy your way out of Hell." Never a truer word spoken! *Money is the folly... the folly of man!*'

After a quick shake of hands and a firm pat on the back from Herrifurus, Harlem was racing purposefully back down the cobbles. He had to be home before Mum and Dad arrived. He re-emerged at the gravel track and dashed the rest of the way to the house. It was a massive relief, as his parents were not yet home.

They returned two minutes later, bringing a visitor with them; Grandma had come to stay for a week or two.

# CHAPTER TEN

## Meeting Jonathan North

The chains were becoming increasingly eroded; Harlem was finally unshackled, all thanks to Grandma. Ok, Harlem and his friends shouldn't have broken into the school. Big deal, just kids on an adventure; get over it, Mum!

The world goes on, and Grandma, forever a champion of Harlem, had pestered Mum daily and piece by piece. Through sheer persistence, Mum cracked and finally relented. Harlem was allowed out of the house if he stayed away from trouble.

It was Saturday morning; Harlem was up bright and early with a spring in his step. A critical mission awaited.

He washed, dressed, and departed the house in no time. Jumping on his bike, Harlem pedalled furiously toward his destination. On arrival there, and in little more than a whisper, he called out: 'Margo, wake up, it's Harlem!'

'Harlem, come away from the bungalow; if my dad sees you, he'll drop. He'll go spare, come away quickly!'

Harlem revolved to find Margo, Phillip Day, Steiney, and Tubbs McLard resting on their bikes. Margo insisted everyone move a safe distance from her home, but as they did, they heard yelling coming from the bungalow.

Harlem turned to see an elderly man dressed in a police uniform bawling at him.

'GET AWAY FROM HERE, WHAT DO YOU WANT? CLEAR OFF, I SAY!'

The five youngsters did indeed 'clear off.'

Harlem put his head in his hands. 'Margo, is that old man *really* your dad? He looks about a hundred. No, he can't be,' stated Harlem with exasperation.

'For your information, Harlem, he *is* my dad, that's Sergeant Nutmeg! He's not quite a hundred; he's still a couple of years away. You'd better make sure he misses you snooping around here again. Anyway, Harlem, what brings you here so early?' queried Margo.

'Margo, I need that key to get into school.'

'And *why* might that be?' asked Phillip Day.

'Look, I can't tell you. I'm not sure what I'm looking for,' replied Harlem evasively.

Margo stared and blinked at him, looking pensively, as though she was trying to figure out the real reason as to why Harlem wanted the key.

'I think he wants it to get into school,' added Steiney.

'Yes, I bloody want it to get into the school!' exclaimed Harlem, with a hint of annoyance. What else would he possibly use it for?

'Harlem, have you got any goodies on you? Any biscuits or chocolate? Maybe some crisps?' asked the ever-hungry Tubbs.

'No, Tubbs, *sorry*, but I'm not a corner shop this morning!'

Harlem was tetchy, even though he didn't want to come across that way.

'It's to do with the ghost boy, isn't it?' asked the inquisitive Margo.

'I don't think he's a ghost, but yes! Now, please, can I have the key?' asserted Harlem impatiently.

Margo and the others gaped at Harlem with a silent expression. If this boy wasn't a ghost, who or what was he? Margo reluctantly handed Harlem the key.

'*Here*, I think you're being reckless!' she added.

'Thanks, Margo! You lot, don't follow me, it might be dangerous! Don't ask questions either; I don't have any answers.'

'But, but, what…?'

'Not now, Margo!'

Harlem pointed sternly at each of his friends, one by one, gesturing that none of them were to shadow him.

'I need to find out for myself what I'm looking for. I promise I'll see you all later when I am done,' declared Harlem.

A few minutes later, Harlem was beside the school gate, lugging a weighty state of nerves: fear, panic, apprehension, suspicion, and adrenaline. He was a little daunted by Jonathan North; the school itself was unremorseful and intimidating.

Harlem entered the trees beside the school, abandoning his bike as he proceeded. He purposefully twisted the last three rails until each one was detached. He squeezed through the gap, jumping down onto the yard and placing the removed rails onto one of the felled trunks.

Harlem glared over the dismal schoolyard, which exuded an aura of stone-cold horror. The yard, utterly desolate, was devoid of warmth or pleasantness. The entire school compound seemed tainted with danger, as if gripped by horrendous atrocities from the past that refused to fade away into yesteryear, creating a palpable sense of suspense and anticipation.

Upon reaching the kitchen door, Harlem inserted the key; however, the door would not open, no matter which way he turned or jiggled the key. His first notion was that Mum had changed the locks after he and his friends broke in.

Harlem began skulking off, weighted by a feeling of disappointment. Whilst heading away, he gave ear to a tired creaking noise, which made him whip round to witness the door slowly drifting open. Harlem was not alarmed but filled with pure relief at the prospect of entering the school.

Inhaling a much-needed breath, he cautiously entered the kitchen, recalling the feeling of finding himself in an old Victorian workhouse.

If it could talk, the kitchen would surely narrate some torrid tales of events from an era long ago; it was so old-fashioned and outdated. Even the colossal fridge-freezer was a throwback to the '50s.

Harlem was curious as to what was inside the fridge compartment. He peeked in, finding a mouldy, outdated tub of margarine and ten packs of orange juice cartons. Upon closer inspection, it was evident that someone had consumed the orange juice and left the empty cartons in the fridge.

Beyond the kitchen stood the assembly hall, which doubled as the canteen. In the corner was a small theatre stage where the annual nativity play would be held. The curtain was up, so Harlem took the opportunity to walk out onto the stage. He stared at his invisible audience; what would they make of his story?

His search continued, and Harlem carefully explored the school gymnasium. Harlem frowned at hundreds of sooty handprints on the wall-mounted climbing frame and gym horse. Some appeared old and faded, while others were fresh as if they had only been made that morning.

Harlem next found himself standing in the lower hall, with two rooms to the left, both of which were classrooms. One of the two rooms on the right was the teacher's break room; the second had become a dumping ground for old storage. Some of the items were probably decades, if not centuries, old.

As Harlem speedily entered the first classroom, he opened the door to observe one of those mysterious shadow-beings with piercing blue eyes writing on the outdated, revolving, wall-mounted blackboard. The shadow-being wore a black cape and a mortarboard hat.

Six other shadows were positioned at old-fashioned, individual school inkwell desks. None were paying attention in class; three shadows were giving off faraway looks of boredom and exasperation. The fourth had been idly staring at the clock, the fifth was asleep, whilst the sixth doodled with his pen and notebook. Upon Harlem barging into the room, the seven shadow-beings were caught off guard and immediately absconded through the walls. Both Harlem and the shadows had had the fright of their lives.

The room next door was another outdated, long-forgotten classroom with an exceedingly high ceiling and windows that could only be opened with a hook and pole. This classroom also came complete with the old school inkwell desks. Both rooms contained old-fashioned, cast-iron radiators, presenting a musty, unused, unloved, derelict quality.

Harlem searched the teacher's break room. Suddenly, the radiators began clanging noisily. Harlem was unsure whether the clanging was due to Jonathan North's clanging or the old radiators.   Perhaps this was the kind of noise they occasionally made, worn down over the years, creaking and barely clinging to life.

'JONATHAN NORTH, WHERE ARE YOU? I KNOW YOU'RE HERE, STOP PLAYING GAMES!' Harlem yelled out angrily, but he received no response.

Harlem was eager to find evidence of Jonathan North, but could Harlem be wrong? Indeed, was there a ghost boy at school?

Harlem soon discovered the long, spiteful, silent and haunting corridor Mum marched him down the last time he was here. The corridor stretched from the main entrance to the lower hall, and Harlem strongly believed the long passage was designed to take everyone's spirits away when they entered the school.

'COME ON, JONATHAN NORTH, SHOW YOURSELF!' he shouted again.

Harlem was becoming increasingly agitated, having searched the entire school, including the toilets.

Jonathan North was not hiding in the boys or the girls' lavatories. There was just one last room to investigate. Opposite the toilets lived a dark and fearful set of stairs leading underground.

Harlem used his phone as a flashlight to slowly navigate the stairs. At the bottom, he found a heavy, bolted, oval black door that had rusted over the years and was now excessively covered in thick cobwebs and several layers of soot.

Harlem suspected Jonathan North could not be hiding on the opposite side. Despite this, Harlem attempted to turn the handle; it was soundly locked.

With the inside of the school complete, Harlem carried the agonising idea that he had made a massive blunder in assuming that Jonathan North was trapped in this school.

He exited the school interior, ensuring the kitchen door was firmly locked behind him.

Not wanting to be caught, Harlem hurriedly turned right at the kitchen door, then followed the building down the side and to the front. He stared at the bell tower and the gargoyles.

'Unused for years!' he muttered, referencing the bells.

Next, he approached the school gates, where Harlem had stared at the boy on his first visit to Wishwisely, but there was no sign of him here today.

Harlem continued covering the school perimeter, stumbling down the narrow alley to the left of the building. Back at the rear schoolyard, Harlem even checked in the coal shed, quickly closing it again when the coal began falling out.

Harlem had completed his exploration but failed to find Jonathan North, now perceiving this trip as a complete waste of time. But then, could it be that Jonathan North didn't desire to reveal himself today? Whatever the answer was, Harlem had no urge to return.

He trudged despairingly towards the gap in the rails, presenting a sunken, dismayed, and disheartened expression. Gripping the three rails, he stepped cautiously onto one of the two large, felled tree trunks and just as he was to exit the grounds, an invading, unapologetic shiver ran through his body.

*'I say, old boy, are you looking for me?'* drawled a voice behind him.

Harlem sprang sharply; the voice had made him jump like a jack-in-the-box. A shabby-looking boy stood facing Harlem, a boy of the same age as him, give or take a couple of months.

This stranger was dressed in an outdated, tattered school uniform, consisting of a grey V-neck sweater, a dirty, white short-sleeved shirt, short black trousers, grey socks pulled up as high as possible, and black slip-on school pumps. His hands, legs and face were icky and grubby, and his finely parted blonde hair had become grotesquely greasy and needed an urgent shampoo.

Harlem timidly stepped down from the tree trunk and carelessly tossed the rails on the floor. 'You're Jonathan North; I've been looking for you!' he exclaimed.

'Yes, I know, old boy!' replied Jonathan North.

'I was shouting your name, calling you out!'

'I know, Harlem, I was watching you; *however*, you *do not* want to call me out, trust my words!' remarked Jonathan, who then started laughing, thinking that the idea of revealing himself right at the end was both amusing and sinister.

'Why didn't you show yourself earlier?' asked Harlem, disgruntledly.

'Watch how you're talking to me there, Harlem! *I must say I don't like it!* Now, why would I show myself at the start? Where's the fun in that? Why ruin a good show, eh? At least I let you into the school.'

'How do you know who I am?' queried Harlem with genuine surprise in his voice.

'Really, Harlem Hodge? I see and understand all that there is to know. I must say, you do disappoint me… You aren't what I expected at all. You… *you*… are supposed to stop me from achieving my wish? I laugh at the very idea!'

'I see you're modest, Jonathan; arrogance will be your downfall,' warned Harlem.

'Harlem, I'm a genius, in case you missed it. I've forgotten more about Enduring Crave than you will ever learn. You don't know the foggiest about what you're supposed to be preventing, do you?' he sneered.

'*A genius…* do you say? Ok, a genius imprisoned here for the last sixty years. Very clever of you, some genius you are!' retorted Harlem.

Jonathan pulled the most villainous face and pointed threateningly at Harlem before quickly composing himself and placing his filthy hand back by his side. He then smiled and pulled two cartons of orange juice from his old-fashioned, short trouser pockets. He offered one out to Harlem.

'Care to wet your whistle, Harlem?' Jonathan asked calmly.

'If you don't mind,' replied Harlem.

As Harlem went to take hold of the carton, Jonathan North cruelly snatched it out of reach.

'I do mind, you can't have one, these are mine! As the day of my liberty beckons, my thirst and hunger grow strong... *These taste bloody good...* I've waited a long time to taste sweetness like this. For the record, I was betrayed... in a most sinister act. But fear not... for soon... I will have my revenge on Herrifurus and all who assist him. I assume he's still performing his bumblesome moronic routine?'

'Herrifurus is brilliant; watch what you're saying, Jonathan!' asserted Harlem.

'Be careful, Harlem, I won't tolerate one more outburst. Indeed, Herrifurus is brilliant... at being a prat! Did you know that his middle name is incompetence? You haven't seen through him yet, as I do. Lightning never strikes twice in the same place, but put Herrifurus in charge, and it would. He's so bumbling and very predictable. Very callous... or is it... *calace*? A name we both know... a name I adapted for.'

'Jonathan, what did you do to end up under lock and key at school?' inquired Harlem after a long pause.

'Herrifurus and his gang of decision-makers denied my wish! Who are *they* to call my outcome? What gives *them* the right? In my opinion, waiting here is necessary. Herrifurus has merely deployed a delaying tactic, yet he is the one who counts the clock of despair, for it is his secrets that shall be eradicated. I shall have the last laugh, for when my wish comes true, I will also bring down the end of Enduring Crave; all down to me... and me alone!'

'But that will mean the end of the world!' cried Harlem with alarm.

'Harlem, do you know what naivety is? Look it up in the dictionary. It's all part of his senile routine... *poppycock*... all of it! With Enduring Crave gone, I shall have the power over all the wishes of the past... for there will be no forthcoming ones, and the world will still go about its business!'

'That's all lovely stuff,' remarked Harlem, 'but you still haven't answered my question about how you ended up here.'

'I was betrayed at the dead of dawn. Having outsmarted Herrifurus and his band of miscreants, it was all going swimmingly, but out of the blue... deception came! The conspiracy brought about my fall. Herrifurus couldn't do it himself; he got another to do his dirty work, with my punishment to be incarcerated here for sixty years. Before, as a pupil here, I excelled and shone, which brought on resentment. For my crimes of the desire to learn, to take on the education given to me... to make better my knowledge, I would be forced into the coal shed by the brutes of the day... for brawn fears the brain. The door locked; isolation can be a wonderful thing. Solace: No better company than my own, for what could the bullies do to me once I was inside? They have no class... no culture. I was safe; I put my plan together... I had resorted to it; my eyes opened to me. I became attached to the coal shed; I still spend much time there.'

'That's why I saw soot prints in school!' replied the curious Harlem.

'Yes, Harlem, *how elementary of you to deduce that...* honestly! You see... I was sent here to wait out six decades to the day. To jolly well think about my actions, as such. Herrifurus didn't send me here in the present; I was sent to wait one day behind real-time. Whilst the world and his dog were living Wednesday... I was twenty-four hours ago in Tuesday... alone in my personal time prison. Herrifurus cannot be responsible for harming a human. That is why I've not aged; I've never seen my old days. Nor when I'm free will I rapidly age to catch up to where history intended. That's another sixty years from now. Herrifurus is so pathetic... he couldn't even get the punishment right. There was a twenty-four-hour time delay, but this fractured after only one year, and I returned to real-world time -'

'-Sounds like a despairing tale, Jonathan, how very tragic!' sniggered Harlem.

'Interrupt me a second time if you dare!' threatened Jonathan, whose eyes had turned stony-black. 'My ageing hadn't altered; I remained the same as the day I was incarcerated, with no need for food or drink... sixty years to see out... nearly twenty-two thousand days. My hunger was to be free, my thirst for revenge on Herrifurus. Glitches would occur, and my isolation would be displaced by moments of presence. I could sometimes be seen but never heard, as if my tongue had been removed. It dawned on me that I now had the power to spook the wretches of the school... *oh, how the tables had turned.* Despite being in true time, I could do the impossible... walk through walls... disappear... all sorts of antics. I created the legend of the ghost boy, leaving warnings everywhere adults couldn't see them, including on the blackboard when the master vacated the room. I would erase my threats before grown-ups could witness them. I created a lore, one in which adults were prohibited. Visualise the beggars' faces when chalk scrawls on the board all by itself, only to vanish moments later. I terror-struck the young sods not to blubber to the teacher, or the ghost boy would come after them. I would appear in class and then withdraw, leaving the learners in a frenzy while the master faced the board. At last, I had attention… they were talking about me. Over the years, the jackanapes would include their additions to my story; everyone has heard of me, even you… *which*… I find *very* peculiar indeed! This school hasn't had a new pupil in years… *so*… how did *you* hear about the ghost boy?'

'When do you get out?' asked Harlem, ignoring Jonathan's question.

'Freed from school? Soon enough, Harlem, soon enough! How, you'd like to know? Well, that cat won't be let out of the bag today. I will permit you to feel even more anguish before then. Ever since you stepped foot in Wishwisely, I've become stronger with the ability to sense your presence. One Sunday afternoon, I heard noises that were far clearer than ever since I became trapped here. Colours more beautiful than I remembered blossomed. Sensations, it was a pleasure to get pins and needles—such tingling, how I had set my heart on those feelings. I knew you were coming; you called out to me unknowingly when you passed the school. Now, I ache with the strength I gather. But I must say, I am vexed, no pupils… now you and your mum come to Wishwisely. A new Headmaster... *very interesting indeed*. But I will call and visit her at my house.'

'Your house, what do you mean, Jonathan?'

'Yes, Harlem, my house... the house that Godfrey North built. It belongs to me... It's my birthright!'

'We bought that house; it's ours now!' argued Harlem.

'You're right, it is your house now... *but soon*... well, soon it shan't be. I will take back what belongs to me!'

'Jonathan, sixty years of being confined to this loathsome school. What a pity!' declared Harlem.

'DO NOT PITY ME! I do not ask for or need it. *You* will soon require condolence, Harlem.'

'Sorry, Jonathan North, you misunderstand. I mean, it's a pity you weren't destined here for a thousand years!' laughed Harlem.

'A good game, you speak, Harlem, really you do. *Such bravado*... but come the day, you will bury your head in the sand or sit back in the armchair. Nothing you think otherwise shall alter my course to change destinies. Herrifurus cannot help you; he cannot stop what awaits. He isn't human, he cannot think like us... *Well*, certainly not like me. He puts all his eggs in one basket with you. I see cracks where there shouldn't be... You will rue the day you stood here belittling me. Fragility is so transparent... I can see it in your eyes. All I say is factual; disregard that giant imbecile's non-human nature. Herrifurus is the biggest hypocrite in the universe. Enduring Crave, *ha*, and all for the good of humankind. What of Herrifurus? What or who does he sacrifice? Not himself and not that wobble gob Mokwug!'

'Jonathan, Enduring Crave was created to give mankind hope,' reasoned Harlem.

'Yes, Harlem, mankind! But they didn't fulfil *my* hopes. Herrifurus chose not to do so. He could have done and should have done. I begged and pleaded; this wouldn't have been necessary had he listened. I didn't request this; it was put on me; life is cruel, so get used to it!'

'What did you wish for?' enquired Harlem, urgently wanting to find out.

'Not for your eyes or ears! Sixty years and for what? Time is almost up... look at me... *look... at me...* fourteen years old for six decades. Harlem, you cannot begin to comprehend the knowledge I have ascertained. The changes I have witnessed - technology, events, discoveries, and man's progression! I shall be the creator of it all; I will change my destiny and more!'

'Yeah, but you won't have your wish.'

'Au contraire, Harlem, I will have my wish and all wishes that never came true, for they painfully reside unanswered for eternity. They will all be mine!'

'Good grief, Jonathan, you're going to steal other people's wishes!'

'Yes, Harlem, a jolly good idea, don't you think? I await your challenge: shake my hand. It is what all great opponents should do. It is the art of respect before battle.'

Harlem had no desire to grant Jonathan's request. He turned and headed for the gap in the three vacant rail slots. Jonathan shook his head in disappointment at Harlem's refusal to shake hands, while staring deep into his adversary's back. Harlem immediately became statuesque, unable to move on his own free will.

Jonathan next glared at the three rails on the ground, then eyed the gap where they had been removed. Incredibly, the rails were now repositioning themselves without physical human intervention.

Whatever Jonathan's evil thought process, he had made it happen.

'Come back here, you rude so and so, and shake my hand. You aren't leaving until you do!'

Harlem, having lost control of his bodily functions and movements, was embarrassingly and forcibly made to step backwards towards Jonathan. Once Jonathan had released his holding spell, Harlem spiralled to face the cocky antagonist, who wore the smuggest of faces. Begrudgingly, Harlem shook hands with Jonathan, two hands accepting one another with a semi-tight, insincere grip.

To add insult to injury, Jonathan embraced Harlem with a lasting, crushing hug and a mighty pat on the back.

'Make sure you replace the rails yourself, this time, Harlem, that's a good chap.'

Harlem expressed disgust as he stepped off the trunk and onto the wall. Having replaced the rails, he collected his bike from the trees. As he footslogged, Harlem concluded Jonathan North was following him on the opposite side of the wall, making threatening gestures.

'TICK-TOCK, TICK-TOCK, TICK-TOCK. Mountains crumble, and seas boil. Man retreats to his final view - the ledge before the tumble—a vacuum of oblivion, such wasteful toil. TICK-TOCK, TICK-TOCK, TICK-TOCK.'

'What a bum!' declared Harlem, describing what he thought of Jonathan.

'Yes, Harlem, and you are the deuterostome! *Now*, I warn you to watch that potty mouth of yours. I *won't* tell you again!'

Harlem was beginning to understand what he witnessed at school on that first trip to Wishwisely. He'd observed evil rapidly rising; the whole school had been enveloped in this wickedness. As he approached the road, a hand grabbed him from behind.

'WHAT YA DOING?!' yelled the owner of the hand.

Thankfully, Margo found the startling sight of Harlem leaping in shock amusing. Margo wasn't alone - Phillip, Steiney and Tubbs were all puzzled as to why Harlem was so determined to visit the school this morning.

'*Well*, did you find him? Who is he?' asked Steiney, unable to hold himself back.

What would his pals make of it? Harlem couldn't be completely honest about why he had been searching. The five guided their bikes towards the front of the school, while the others continued to seek answers from Harlem. Harlem correctly sensed that Jonathan was nearby, now snooping on Harlem and his friends.

Harlem glanced back towards the gates; Jonathan was standing with his arms crossed. It was evident to Harlem that

Jonathan looked both baffled and shocked, as well as deep in concentration.

Jonathan placed one hand across his mouth, with the other slapping his forehead, before scurrying away.

'What are you looking at, Harlem? Is someone there?' asked Tubbs fearfully.

'No, there's no one here,' replied Harlem. 'I was trying to call out the ghost boy as the story intrigues me. I believe he was called Jonathan North, but I can't prove it; maybe he's the lad from that old crone's ridiculous tale!'

'North... *North*... Jonathan North, why does that name ring a bell? A few seconds ago, I would have put a face to a name.'

Margo was having a memory lapse. The others were beginning to experience the same lack of remembrance. The curious thing was that this forgetfulness had occurred rapidly.

Harlem was sure it was Jonathan North's doing, although he kept this idea to himself.

'Margo, I need you to go home and somehow access the police database. Search for Jonathan North, who disappeared from Wishwisely in 1965. Get all the information you can. Please do it now! Don't let your grandad see you. We'll wait nearby.'

'He's *not* my grandad; he's my *dad*. He never pays attention to me, so it shouldn't be a problem. I'll see what I can dig up on record.'

The five set off on the short trip to Margo's, who insisted that the four boys remain a safe distance and not get too close to the bungalow. The reservoir disseminated a calm, early Saturday morning spirit, where the world's worries were locked up for another time.

The Sun glistened across the water, and the presence of nosy, early morning animals who showed themselves briefly added to Harlem's positive feeling. He was sure Margo would uncover information on Jonathan North.

After what seemed like the longest fifteen minutes, Margo charged out of the house. As she approached, Harlem's positivity was suddenly overshadowed by an abrupt change in his feelings. Just staring at Margo's expression, he realised she was coming back empty-handed.

'I'm sorry, Harlem, diddly squats, I'm afraid. There's nothing about a Jonathan North of Wishwisely. I looked at the local and national databases. It seems like this boy never existed! I am sorry.'

'YOU BOY, WHAT ARE YOU DOING? HAVE YOU BEEN IN MY HOUSE? GET AWAY FROM HERE.'

It was Sergeant Nutmeg. He was fuming as he came marching out of his house at such a slow pace. He was dressed in a police uniform, with his hat proudly perched on his head.

'YOUNG HODGE, I WARNED YOU! GET AWAY FROM HERE NOW!'

Harlem pounced on his bike and began pedalling as if participating in the Olympic time trials. The four others struggled to keep up with him, but back on the village high street, Harlem stopped, both exasperated and annoyed.

'What's the old man's problem? Why does he always shout at me? Why not you lot, why only me?'

'Err, he doesn't take kindly to strangers,' replied Margo.

'He'll eventually come round in his own time… or ours,' added Steiney.

'The old boy's been at it for some years now; he doesn't take too kindly to townie folk. It's all a mystery to him. He's still trying to solve crimes that aren't crimes.'

'That's enough, Phillip, at least my daddy's still trying! Everyone else has forgotten, haven't they?'

'Sorry, Margo, but he does need to retire, doesn't he?' replied Phillip Day.

'I'm hungry; let's go to the shop,' suggested Tubbs McLard.

After Tubbs purchased half the goodies from the shop, they set off on their bikes. Harlem wasn't in the mood for merriment. He decided it was time to go home; dark clouds were purposely deploying overhead.

Inclement weather was on the way, bringing further troubles for Harlem. As he raced home, thunder clapped and roared aggressively above, and then the heavens opened ferociously. Although he was almost at the house, the rain fell so fast and hard that Harlem was quickly drenched from head to toe.

Later, he stared out his window; lightning lit up the sky. It was only three o'clock, but the devious dark atmosphere made it seem a much later time of day and a good few months beyond August. There was a new conundrum for Harlem: why was there no record of Jonathan North? Had his family not notified the police about his disappearance? And what about the house?

Who had owned this house since the North family uprooted? How had Mum and Dad only paid £3008.56 for the property?

After tea, Grandma spent time with Harlem, presenting him with pictures from her childhood photo album. Grandma was reminiscing about her life, and although her brother Donny had long passed away, the loss still affected her greatly. She took pleasure in telling Harlem about the events relating to the photos.

'That's Donny and me when I was six at the beach, and that's Donny, who was ten at the time, flying his kite,' she pointed out.

Photo after photo was accompanied by a tale. In fairness to Harlem, he wasn't particularly interested in seeing these pictures. First and foremost on his mind were Jonathan North and Enduring Crave. He half glanced at the grainy, old, black-and-white photos. He couldn't fully make them out, but he pretended he was paying attention for Grandma's sake.

'Grandma, are you dying?' he asked.

'Don't be silly, no, I'm not dying. Where did that come from?'

'It's like you're reliving your life and all that!'

'No, I'm just lonely now that you're here. My parents, Donny, Grandad, now you and your Mum, you've all left me,' she sighed.

Whether she was intentionally guilt-tripping, Harlem felt sorry for Grandma, so he showed more enthusiasm in her picture book show until the end.

# CHAPTER ELEVEN

## The Countdown

Harlem hadn't disturbed his mobile phone in days and couldn't recall when he last had it. Although Harlem wasn't stuck to his device, he wasn't comfortable not knowing its location.

'Where is it?' he asked himself in frustration.

Searching was a welcome distraction with so much else to contemplate, mainly Jonathan North and Enduring Crave. The weather was not helping in any way, shape, or form. The rain continued to tease and torment Harlem. Mum sternly refused to allow him out in the stormy, wet downpour.

As the day wore on, the weather mimicked Harlem's feelings. It was dreary, cold, and dank. Harlem was burdened with gloom; his mood was severely claggy, which worsened by the second.

The rain persisted well into the afternoon and evening. Several hours passed. Harlem believed each raindrop hitting his bedroom window was mocking him personally.

'*Right*, that's it!' declared Harlem, who had determined it was time to escape from the house. Enduring Crave would be his second destination; first, he would visit Jonathan North at the school for a showdown. It would be a lifetime of confinement in his quarters if Mum caught him sneaking out, but the risk was worth any potential punishment.

Amid the night, he made his way to the school, having nothing to fear except fear itself.

After detaching the rails from the wall, Harlem trudged over the murky, waterlogged, concrete schoolyard. He had forgotten the key in haste, but that didn't matter as the kitchen door was found to be unsecured. This was most strange.

Slowly navigating through the kitchen, fumbling and groping with all limbs as he went by, Harlem started to believe that tonight's trip had been a grim mistake. What had he been expecting to achieve?

The assembly hall was miserly dark, with Harlem having no idea of the whereabouts of the light switches. He remained motionless, rooted to his spot, regretting the abrupt decision to come here at this time of night.

However, while contemplating this, the darkness was intentionally dispersed by a spotlight shining directly on Harlem and a nearby chair; the remainder of the hall remained in silent blackness.

'Welcome, Harlem, be a good chap and take a seat… SIT DOWN!' boomed a loud, cocksure voice, amplified by a microphone.

Harlem fearfully sat immediately, and then the whole assembly hall stage dramatically lit up like a Christmas tree, with disco lights scattering a rainbow of coloured beams.

Harlem lay eyes upon three mysterious but increasingly visible shadow-beings on stage—one shadow positioned at a grand piano, another on drums, and the third holding an electric guitar. Jonathan North cheerfully sauntered onto the stage, holding his microphone.

He looked ridiculous, dressed as Wolfgang Amadeus Mozart, wearing an extravagant red coat with a ruffle, short red trousers with white tights, and black slip-on shoes; the powdered wig and makeup on his face overshadowed all this.

Jonathan looked pompous as he strutted across the stage, carrying his conductor's baton in the other hand. It was sartorial elegance at its finest, but none of this made sense to Harlem.

Disco lights and electric guitar? Mozart would never have seen these in his time. However, this was Harlem's private show, produced by Jonathan North, so Jonathan conducted as he desired. It didn't have to make sense.

'We have an incredibly special audience member with us tonight,' confirmed Jonathan. 'The only audience member! If anyone is unaware, Harlem and I have business to attend to. All will be concluded soon, Harlem, old boy; tonight, there are no hard feelings. This one is for *you* and *only you*.'

Jonathan bowed theatrically and waved his baton with a flourish towards the shadow on the piano. The piano playing commenced with a slow, repetitive, yet pleasant melody that lasted around thirty seconds before being joined by the guitar and then the drums. The beat and tempo increased, and the show's star began performing his song.

'Let's not throw it away, like so many before us
I wish we could make it; please say you agree
If not, there's no time to fake it

If it's not going to be, it's not going to be
I've been kidding myself, working a lie
Convincing my shadow, everything's fine
Been fooling a dream, we're back on the lies
Until I'm home and finally realise
Though you kept quiet, you made up your mind
That final look, the look of goodbye
And I know you're not coming back
This time, this time, this time...

Our days are over, truly gone by
The unquestionable answer, nobody knows why
So, I say farewell; your hand slips away
You take your path, and I'll take mine

Now I'm looking to the future to see what it brings
I can't help thinking that we'll meet again
Cos a voice in my head turned to me, and it said
Just believe, and you'll see in time when you meet
You'll still love her
Love will remain, feelings the same
Years it may take, but my heart cannot break
You'll always love her

The future is tomorrow, gone is yesterday
I can't help thinking, was there a better way
One thing I do know is that each day that passes by
Brings me closer to you
And when full circles are complete

I'll land back at your feet
And lonely days will be destroyed
Seen no more, gone for good
And you'll be back with me


So now I know our days are not over
Not completely gone by
The unquestionable answer shall be rendered in time
For now, I'll say farewell, your hand slips away
You take your path, and I'll take mine
You take your path, and I'll take mine
You take your path, and I'll take mine


The song was complete; it wasn't half bad. Jonathan had fully theatricalised on stage. In another life, he would have made a fantastic musician. The stage lights dimmed, and the assembly hall lights returned. The instruments and the shadows had mysteriously vacated the stage. It was just Jonathan North and Harlem left alone in the room.

'Show's over, it's time you left, Harlem!' warned Jonathan.

'Not yet, there are a few things I need to understand,' replied Harlem.

'Oh really! I said it's time for you to leave!'

Suddenly, the dreadful and uncomfortable atmosphere plunged into diabolical darkness.

Music that reminded Harlem of a circus performance, also known as Entry of the Gladiators, weirdly began blaring out over the Tannoy.

The circus theme lasted twenty seconds before the stage lit up with those dazzling, scattered rainbow colours.

Still dressed as Mozart, Toeknee and Hellaine Maloney now accompanied Jonathan, but as Harlem had imagined them on the cobbles.

With one hand, Toeknee was waving his beloved but broken golf club; with his other, he struggled to hold back two hungry and vicious-looking rottweilers.

The two canines appeared ready to pounce, snarling ferociously, with spittle dripping from their jaws. Both dogs were restrained by metal chains, tightly gripped by Toeknee.

'DO YOU KNOW WHO I AM, DO YOU?' yelled Toeknee.

Hellaine began oinking with Toeknee, following, until both pig clowns grunted in unison. Jonathan stared at the Maloneys with an exaggerated, confused expression before pointing to Harlem and then to the pig clowns. He repeated this action three times, keeping his silly expression.

'I say, Toeknee, old boy, I told Harlem to go. Why is he still here? Now persuade him to get gone!' ordered Jonathan, laughing sardonically.

'MICKLES, PETERSON… GO… ATTACK!'

Toeknee released his grip on the chains, which clattered to the floor. Both the evil canines bounded towards Harlem, following Toeknee's unpropitious command.

Harlem was already gone; he had dashed across the assembly hall and into and out of the kitchen, firmly slamming the door on his way out and locking it. Mysteriously.

Harlem now had the key, despite not having brought it earlier. That didn't matter if he made it away from those dogs.

He charged over the schoolyard, crossing it with giant strides, on the home straight now, almost at the gap in the railings. Harlem leapt onto the felled trunk to find that the rails he had carefully removed earlier had somehow been replaced unfairly; there was no way out.

Harlem dreaded turning around and facing the scene behind him; the barking was becoming louder and louder. He abruptly but fearfully glanced back to witness the two dogs rapidly approaching.

Dogs can't open doors, and locked ones at that. How on earth had they gotten through?

The canines, Mickles and Peterson, homed in on their target. Harlem was frozen in place as the beasts approached.

All he could do was close his eyes helplessly as the two chewed him to pieces. This was it…

Harlem sat up in bed, his heartbeat thundering. He swallowed hard, panting desperately whilst trying to restore his heart to its normal rhythm. He stumbled out of bed, but his heartbeat refused to slow down, and he walked lazily to the front bedroom.

Upon looking out the window, his eyes landed on Jonathan North sitting on the green bench opposite the house.

Jonathan waved cheerily at Harlem with a big, satisfied grin. He next entered the red telephone box; Harlem heard the shrill tones of the landline downstairs, ringing out into the night. He rushed to answer the call before the noise woke the rest of the house.

'Tick-tock, tick-tock, tick-tock,' the voice through the handset whispered threateningly.

Harlem sat up in bed, drenched in sweat, his heartbeat galloping. He did a triple-take before realising he was safe in his bedroom.

'Just a nightmare, a bad dream, that's all. A nightmare within a nightmare,' Harlem tried to tell himself, although he didn't feel quite so reassured.

What did this dream signify? It felt so real – Jonathan, the shadows, and the song. Why were the shadow-beings performing with Jonathan, and why was Toeknee, the pig clown Maloney, still chasing Harlem, albeit via his dogs? Harlem had no further time to ponder these questions - he stared with disbelief as Larry Cornelius materialised in the room directly before him.

'No, *nope*, not happening. I'm still dreaming. Larry, you're not really here!' exclaimed Harlem, rubbing the sleep out of his tired eyes.

'And a fine hello to you, too, Harlem! I can assure you I am here, and you're not dreaming. I came on an errand sent by Herrifurus. You conversed with that ghastly Jonathan North in that unpleasant and outmoded school. You must report to Enduring Crave today. No ifs and no buts! Herrifurus has things to chew over with you,' ordered Larry.

'Chew, what things, Larry?' asked Harlem.

'What do you think? About Jonathan North, of course! You need a clear and sound mind for this, Harlem.'

Larry bizarrely presented a bronze, antique pocket watch from his improbable pockets. He flicked open the front plate and focused intently on the time shown on the dial; the black Roman numeral clock face stood out against the all-white background, surrounded by two golden inner circles.

'Fifty-nine years, add to this a further fifty-one weeks… exactly… now! Seven days and counting… one whole week. For this time at four o'clock, one hundred and sixty-eight hours from now… he will be free! We have exactly one week before he orchestrates his revenge. Be at Enduring Crave today. It seems you have not shown your face there for some time!' scolded Larry.

'I'm not allowed out in the rain; my mother would go mental. That's the only reason I haven't been,' grumbled Harlem.

'Be that as it may, what will you do about it? You must report in later today. Here, use this, but only if it is required.'

Larry tossed a purple umbrella, pulled from his improbable pockets at Harlem. Improbable pockets are named as such because any object can be pulled out of these pockets despite the improbability.

'Hopefully, it won't need to be called upon,' remarked Larry as he faded into obscurity.

'I wish it would stop raining for the rest of the day!' exclaimed Harlem in annoyance.

Three hours later, Harlem was out of bed. Having given up on its relentless tirade over Wishwisely, the rain had retreated, along with the absconding clouds. The Sun proudly commanded the sky, removing all evidence of the rain's torment. Harlem stared at his desk; the umbrella Larry had given him had vanished. Downstairs, Harlem found Mum and Dad wide awake, which was rare, so early in the morning, during non-term time. Mum must have woken Dad up to complete whatever tasks she had planned for him.

'What will you do today, Mum?' asked Harlem.

'We're just going to stay here today. Dad will mow the lawn and clean the patio while the weather is nice. *Aren't you?*'

Dad replied, like any downtrodden husband does when they have been assigned tasks they do not desire.

'Yes, my dear.'

Mum allowed Harlem to go out as the weather had changed for the better. He was, however, warned to stay out of mischief. Unlike in his nightmare, Harlem had no intention of going to school. His destination was Enduring Crave.

A few minutes later, Harlem happily stepped along the Cobbles of Hankering. Gazing at the untold and unlimited number of wishes zooming ahead, Harlem muttered to himself, 'We are a needy lot!'

Harlem heard dogs barking ferociously from deep within the unknown recesses of the ominous, humming smog. As he turned his head, panicked, Harlem caught sight of Toeknee, the pig clown Maloney, stepping out of the smog and onto the cobbles. Tony motioned his golf club at Harlem, then charged towards him while holding onto Mickles and Peterson, somehow managing to wave his broken golf club around simultaneously.

Ahead, and coming towards Harlem, was Hellaine, who was oinking as she drove a child's pedal car designed to look like a Range Rover.

The license plate F1 MAL was familiar to Harlem, and the real version of this vehicle was the one that knocked him off his bike on his old street.

Toeknee was both oinking and panting, and he was now stepping slowly. His size was not suited to running.

Onwards drove Hellaine; her manoeuvring and steering of the far-too-small pedal car were impeded due to the quaking of the cobbles. Harlem stood still, allowing Hellaine to get close. As she approached, just inches away, Harlem dramatically leapt over the pedal car.

This caused Hellaine to crash violently into Toeknee, who, moments before, had been barely standing due to his shortness of breath. Toeknee gave way like a fallen tree and collapsed, hitting the ground with the almightiest clonk.

Hellaine fared no better; the crash sent the vehicle hurtling into the air before it whizzed back towards the cobbles at high speed. The Range Rover landed ten feet from Toeknee before flipping over five times, leaving Hellaine upside down.

Mickles and Peterson switched targets in the confusion and began attacking the Maloneys. The dogs brutally ripped off both pig clown faces, but to Harlem's shock, instead of the gory sight he had expected to see, it was Jonathan North's head that now appeared where their faces had been.

The dogs vanished, as did the remaining parts of the pig clowns. Now, only one Jonathan North lay on the cobbles. He picked himself up, patted himself down, and gave a thumbs-up to Harlem.

'What on earth?' Harlem asked himself.

Harlem's past dread had collided with his present one, all in a matter of seconds. A foreboding rite of passage. A somewhat strange and inexplicable ritual. An initiation of fear from old to new.

There was no question about it: now Jonathan North had to be overpowered. Harlem couldn't allow Jonathan to come out on top and be fearful of him forever.

Harlem quickened his pace and soon reached the end of Pressing Matters Lane.

After entering the unusual doorway within the rock, Harlem found himself surveying Herrifurus' office. Strangely, unlike on previous occasions when he had visited, it had a credible look of an office. The mess, untidiness, and all the grime and clutter that had been present were gone.

The desk was immaculate, polished several times and glistening as if brand new. All those scattered pieces of paper that had lain about, covered in dust, had been cleaned and filed neatly in a plastic tray on the desk. The papers contained tasks Herrifurus had never bothered to complete, but here they were, all organised and awaiting action.

The green desk chair that had once matched its partner's untidiness was gone; a brand-new chair had replaced it, featuring beautiful, soft, and shiny leather. This chair was fit for someone of Herrifurus' stature and importance.

The freshly polished coat rack stood proudly on the back wall, adorned with a single coat. The woodworm had all but disappeared. The bookshelf was devoid of all those crumpled pieces of paper, which had been thrown away for good. Vases of tulips had been placed on every shelf, creating a warmer and homier atmosphere in the room.

The tulips were still alive and continued to breathe, having allowed themselves to be picked, knowing they would be returned to the ground, as this was another fascinating marvel of this secret world; picked flowers could be replaced with no damage done—a short-term lease, to brighten up the place, only for a few days.

A new, thick, red, shaggy carpet replaced what was left of the previous one. A thin, transparent plastic sheet had been left over the carpet to prevent anyone from leaving muddy footprints. The old and often ignored doormat had been disposed of.

What had happened to all those stacks of books and the long-collapsed piles that had been ignored and left on the floor for who knows how long? Harlem stared in disbelief at the walls; the outdated, chipped wood paste was gone. New wallpaper now adorned the walls, like Harlem had once encountered in his world. He called it the 'library effect'.

Every wall was covered top to bottom in wallpaper featuring a picture pattern that displayed a row of books on a shelf running the length of the wall. Below, another row of books and a shelf, repeating over. Every inch of all four walls, from left to right, contained the same repeating pattern. The books appeared too genuine, not imitations like the style he had seen before. Harlem stared at the wall before raising his arms to caress the wallpaper. The walls were smooth; it *was* wallpaper he was staring at, but Harlem knew there was more mystery to it than met the eye.

Harlem reached for a book, placing his hands carefully around the image of an interesting-looking hardback. As he attempted to pull the book from its position on the wall, the unbelievable result was that Harlem had loosened the edition from its location. Trying a second volume, that book was also removed.

All four walls had the same outcome. The person who designed this deserved a commendation. What a way to keep the office free from all those piles of books that had previously lain on the ground!

After gazing at the model of the Solar System, which looked even more spectacular with the dirt and grime gone, it was time for Harlem to move on. Herrifurus was likely to be inside Operation Flog a Dead Horse.

'Take me to the mezzanine inside Operation Flog a Dead Horse!' Harlem commanded.

After exiting the office, Harlem found himself at the bottom of the one-hundred-foot ladder leading to the mezzanine's top. No longer fearful of heights, thanks to his experience at the Inverted Blue Pyramid, he quickly navigated his way upwards to find Monocle Sway, Larry Cornelius, Mokwug, and a tense and fidgety Herrifurus.

'Blast it, Larry Cornelius, I want it up! *Where is my clock?* Blast it... blast it... already! *Come on, man... the clock... the clock...*' ranted Herrifurus.

'What's the matter, Herrifurus? Do you think a few more seconds and the world will cease to exist?' replied Larry, rolling his eyes.

'*Do not quarrel with me, Larry!* The clock... the... clock. Hurry up, I say!'

Herrifurus appeared to be having yet another temper tantrum. Larry dipped into his pockets and pulled out a magnificent, standing digital clock of a superb size. The screen was blank; it wasn't working. Herrifurus looked ready to explode.

'*Don't push it...* don't... push... it, Larry! *Batteries, man... batteries.* Are you taking the micky... are you... are you?' raged Herrifurus.

Larry hastily pushed two enormous batteries into Mokwug's hand, who slid them into place and began fiddling with the clock display, which showed a line of zeros.

Mokwug pressed and prodded furiously until she and Herrifurus were happy with the outcome.

The clock face now read: six days, nineteen hours, fifty-eight minutes, and twenty seconds... nineteen seconds... eighteen seconds... It quickly occurred to Harlem that this clock had one purpose and one purpose only. It was a countdown: dwindling seconds, then minutes, followed by hours, and finally days. At the very moment when the time was up, Jonathan North would be free.

Harlem sensed the panicked tension emanating from those on the mezzanine floor. Herrifurus turned and seemed relieved to find Harlem standing close by, as though he hadn't noticed his presence until now.

'Ah, Harlem, my boy... my... boy. You made it. *Come, come, we have chatter that requires our attention.*'

Mokwug, however, appeared dismayed to see Harlem. As usual, she couldn't help but be obnoxious with her horrible, acidic mouth.

'Look what the cat's dragged in, or did you just let yourself in? No manners with any of them from that human lot!' she spat.

'Not now, Mokwug, not now... not... now... I suggest you complete... complete a course at Miss Manners' Finishing School for Rude Girls. I will not listen to one more... one more distasteful remark! *Do not question me!* Go and find something useful to do! I believe the windows need a wipe, now shoo... *shoo!*' ordered Herrifurus.

'Very well, you ungrateful tizz!' voiced Mokwug, shaking her head at Herrifurus before irately turning to Harlem. 'And as for you, Harlem, look at that clock! Time is decaying, and the rack and ruin will have all been for nothing. Are you going to rescue Motherhood? Herrifurus may believe in you, but I can't see it. *Look at you, you're lost!*' she snarled, affording Harlem one last sneer before storming down the ladder.

Mokwug could certainly be intolerable with that tongue when she wanted to be. Larry appeared embarrassed to have witnessed such a poor display of behaviour. He intended to give Harlem some words of encouragement.

'Don't pay any attention to her. Believe it or not, Mokwug was in a pleasant mood. We've all had a mouth-flogging this morning. It's all par for the course. It's the very fabric of her clamour that brightens Mokwug's day.'

Monocle Sway also offered some words of support:

'Something comes… *of what*… no one knows. It's a facade with Mokwug. She means no harm; she's just playing to the gallery. A front to mask her fears… only don't say it to her face. If you do, she'll paste us across this room! Mokwug translates to "burden," and she now views humanity as a burden. She's been here for over two millennia, and let's face it, man does not endear himself to his fellow beings, let alone those here who sweat and toil to keep their existence afloat. If I may say so myself, those behind the scenes who graft tirelessly are perhaps entitled to be a tad aggrieved about it all. But, Harlem, my chum, I know you shall assert yourself and win the day! Stiff upper lip and all that!'

'Indeed… indeed… he will, won't you, Harlem? Yes, you will… you… will!' Herrifurus sincerely believed so.

Monocle and Larry bid farewell and went about their business, leaving Harlem and Herrifurus on the mezzanine.

'Harlem, glance upon the TV screen. Planet Earth… each green light you see flashing across the globe represents a million souls… See how many make the world glow. What happens in the coming days will dictate whether man's torch endures. Your meeting with Jonathan North occurred right on time. You have been set an unenviable challenge. You must remain calm and level-headed above all else. Do not respond to provocation from our absent… our absent… nemesis… Sixty years ago, he asked for what could not be delivered. Despondent, he distanced himself from me… *from me*… and became disassociated from us. Of course, Jonathan would occasionally visit our world and participate in his activities. Only now, I know what he was doing - devising his sinister plan and scheme. Today, he has had sixty additional years to implement and put it into action. We discovered his intentions just in time. *But I still have no understanding… no understanding of how he did it… no understanding at all!'*

'Did what, Herrifurus? What did he do?' begged Harlem.

'I do not know how, but Jonathan somehow accessed the Lantern of Infinite Wishes… that was… that was his crime—impenetrable… impervious… and human-repellent. *Whatever method and means he used, he broke… he broke in.* Wishes were stolen from those belonging to others… As you are aware, the lantern holds untold wishes still beating in the hope… the hope that one day they will become fulfilled. Even though the wish maker has departed the mortal coil, the dreams they created live in eternity. Unlimited energy amasses in the lantern, which, in the wrong… the wrong scheming hands, would do serious and irreparable damage. *One or two wishes taken; not much harm done, but pilfer a handful or more, and Enduring Crave would begin to crack…* The boundaries of our… of our world would topple, and this dimension would implode. What followed in the world of humankind would not be a picnic, mark… mark my words! The theft of wishes initiated a chain of events not seen here before... *before...* or since. Darkened clouds consumed our skies... in an instant, the Sun was cancelled. The torrents crashed in... the thunder and lightning persisted without repentance. The tremors danced on, and with newfound confidence, the earthquake heinously raised its grotesque grin... Jonathan was caught not long after he had plundered those wishes from within the lantern. He had returned to my office to taunt and mock... and mock me, for he believed he would have his wish... his wish... which I had refused. Before he found out that all he had achieved would count... would count for nothing, he set about using the stolen wishes as his weapon. *This should be impossible, but I am embarrassed to say he made it real.* Somehow... *somehow...* Jonathan made it happen. He now obtained power over those pilfered wishes. I recall one wish he used: revenge on the bullies at school who had made his life unpleasant. Sure enough, those bullies got what was coming to them. The tables were turned, and a new breed of maliciousness... of maliciousness now attacked Jonathan's tormentors. All set in the past... I viewed it with my own eyes... *my...* own eyes... I realised Jonathan did indeed have control over those... those snatched dreams. I couldn't allow him to continue; he had to be immobilised there and then. Jonathan was banished to the school to wait out sixty years. I cannot maim or harm any human, so this... so this was the most fitting punishment. Just before he was imprisoned, he delivered these chilling words:

**"Time waits for no man, but I have solace in knowing I have been spared. Time tells me a monumental delay is in**

my favour. You cannot stop time… and I will not halt in my revenge… for my revenge is more unwavering than the passing ticking of the clocks. Until we meet again, mark my words… I am coming… I am returning. The one who closes his eyes is ignorant of all that goes on. In sixty years, we shall meet again. I will not be stopped… never deterred… Victory is unabating… to splendour in the glory of Motherhood fell!"'

Herrifurus ceased talking; his face carried a look of severe worry, panic, and anguish. He had turned a whiter shade of pale than previously recorded, and his nose twitched relentlessly.

After nervously pacing up and down several times and yanking his ponytail repeatedly, he continued telling his tale, albeit with a significant sense of uneasiness.

'After Jonathan was locked in the school grounds, we set about… we set about putting things right. The unused stolen wishes were returned… returned to the lantern, but establishing which wishes were taken and used was vital. Once this was achieved, we had to effectively kill those wishes. Grottlers were sent to smash… to smash them, and sure enough… sure enough they did. The lantern settled, and Motherhood took back the skies. The unsympathetic black darkness had been bludgeoned from its perch. The Sun quite rightly restored its purpose. The rains ceased… the tremors vanished, and order… and order was on the track to being restored. Seven days without a wish, Enduring Crave was on lockdown. I temporarily put a stop to wishes arriving here. I did not… I… did not want them to witness the chaos and disaster that had been. And besides, putting everything straight for the longer term was the logical solution. But man, with his absence of hope so quickly... so quickly resorted to his most heinous of ways... a throwback to that bygone era before Motherhood. In such a short time, global tensions escalated to extraordinary heights... A war was being... was... being... readied. *Keep your fingers off those red buttons, you madmen!* Thank the dawn, for hope was re-instilled in humanity, and the danger averted. What happens next? Will Jonathan North finally get his hands on his wish?'

'Herrifurus, surely, he won't return for the lantern; isn't that too obvious? He must know that you're expecting him to,' pondered Harlem.

*'We must open our eyes... our eyes, who knows how an evil genius thinks? Who, I ask who, do you know*?' raged the infuriated ambassador.

'Herrifurus, I guess you're right. What did he wish for? What was the wish you refused?'

'That I am afraid, I cannot say... *cannot say*... You must figure... must figure it out yourself! This is part of the prophecy - Motherhood's terms.'

Herrifurus blinked at the clock and reminded Harlem that he had to think big, be brave, and not waver from what was heading their way. If he could do this, he would flourish; Harlem would be the saviour of Enduring Crave and the rescuer of humankind. However, he would never be able to tell anyone what had happened. After descending the ladder, Herrifurus and Harlem stepped into the boiler room again. In doing so, they emerged back in Herrifurus' office.

'How come you've decided to tidy up the place, Herrifurus?' asked Harlem, still shocked at the organised sight before his eyes.

'*Not me*... not... me... dear old Mokwug. If Jonathan North were to come out on top — and the world were to end— she wanted to go out knowing this office was in immaculate condition. Bless... bless her... she has the best intentions, you know.'

After bidding farewell to Herrifurus, Harlem returned to his world. As soon as he re-emerged on the gravel track, he was greeted unwelcomingly by the unusual and obscene torrential August showers, which had deviously stopped by to announce a personal hello. It was time for Harlem to dash home. Time is such a common word... how much time did humankind have left?

# CHAPTER TWELVE

## The Landlord's Plight

The silence was so loud that it bordered on becoming deafening. The dreaded anticipation of the forthcoming tribulations was impeding the usual hustle and bustle of Operation Flog a Dead Horse. The billions of Wantwots operated with a far greater lethargic disposition, resulting in a pace that was way off and concentration levels so low that they were off the chart.

The atmosphere and franticness that had once filled the cavernous room had subsided, and an overwhelming, subdued feeling had taken over. An untold volume of wishes continued plummeting into the Calace, and all these wishes still needed to be regulated and decided upon.

Operation Flog a Dead Horse must go on! The problem was that all eyes were on the enormous clock, causing the flying active Wantwots to crash into one another distractedly, dropping paperwork. In the chaos and disorder, those papers became misfiled. The employees at their desks had their heads turned in distress, resulting in some wishes temporarily shooting into the wrong dreamducts.

Harlem thought it hadn't been the most fabulous idea ever to have installed the clock unless the intention was to drive panic into all who still had a job to perform. It wasn't the most excellent idea... far from it!

Harlem hoped it would all be okay, but deep down, he knew Jonathan North would have to access Enduring Crave, for if this was his target, he couldn't obliterate it from the human world.

Whatever his dastardly plan, it had to be piloted from within, and Jonathan must have a base camp to put his scheme into effect. Implement the plot, see the first signs of carnage, and then penetrate his escape back to Wishwisely.

Harlem believed his opponent was ignorant of the tale; the very idea that denying humans the right to wish would mean global loss of hope.

This abandonment of hope would mean returning to the dark ages; only this would be the darkest days, man's last salute.

The days passed, and Herrifurus held his daily frenzied conferences on top of the mezzanine. The attendees were Herrifurus, Harlem, Monocle Sway, the irate Mokwug, and, depending on whether he had been drinking or not, Larry Cornelius.

The clock was rapidly running down the remaining few hours. The stress was distinctly visible on everyone's faces inside the panicked room. This would be the last conference before Jonathan North was free.

The one obstacle was that Harlem could not be in Enduring Crave at the time of Jonathan's release, which would be four o'clock.

There was no possibility of sneaking out at such an early hour or persuading Mum to let him leave. Would it be too late by then? Would Jonathan North already have an advantage over Harlem before leaving the house? It was now time for Harlem to head home. Would the next time that he reunited with Herrifurus be amid conflict?

That night, due to exceedingly high levels of worry and anxiety, Harlem was on tenterhooks. He did not have one minute of shut eye; he just lay on his bed, glaring purposefully at the clock. They do say time flies when you're having fun, but there was no hint of enjoyment as Harlem scowled quietly. So why were the moments whizzing past? Time also flies when you're worried to death and want the minutes to grind to a halt.

So soon, the unforgiving hour arrived; it was four o'clock – judgement hour, but nothing happened immediately.

What was Harlem expecting? The village offered only the uncomfortable sound of deathly silence —an absence of noise that heightened Harlem's thought process and uncertainty.

This ended at five minutes past four, with the peace rudely interrupted by the ringing of church bells. Mum and Dad were up; the bell chiming had woken them. They dashed into Harlem's room, squinting in the darkness.

'Where on earth is that noise coming from? It isn't from over the road. Whatever's going on?' yawned Dad groggily.

'Dad, it's the bell tower at the school!'

Mum swiftly butted in as usual.

'Don't be silly, Harlem, that bell hasn't rung in years. Why would you say that?'

'Mum, if it isn't from the church over the road, *where else* can it come from? Jonathan North is free at last, and it is his way of letting me know!' Harlem blurted this out, forgetting that his parents would not know what he was talking about.

The bells rang for precisely six minutes; the village fell silent once again.

'Go back to sleep,' demanded Mum.

Mum and Dad returned to bed, paying no notice to what Harlem had just told them.

To make things worse, the rains returned to tease Harlem. The timing was just in poor taste.

The inclement weather persisted throughout the morning, and Mum took great delight in informing Harlem that he wasn't allowed out. The day dragged on without incident, and there were no telltale signs that Jonathan's revenge had commenced. It was a typically quiet, rainy day in Wishwisely, except for the bells ringing early that morning.

Another night fell, and like the one prior, it would be a sleepless night for Harlem. At ten o'clock in the morning, loud thumping noises were heard behind the front door. Harlem listened to Mum scolding whoever had been knocking in such a manner. He slyly sneaked downstairs to catch Mum being Mum; sometimes, she possessed no filter.

'Am I really to believe you're a police officer? Have you ever heard of the term retirement? Are you serious?' she scolded. After further chatter with the mysterious individual at the door, Mum ordered Harlem over.

'Harlem, a Sergeant Nutmeg is at the door; he wants to have a word with you!' she barked, with a face of angered thunder.

Harlem was petrified; what reason did this old codger have for turning up on the doorstep? But, standing at the threshold was indeed Sergeant Nutmeg himself.

'Young Hodge, you are to accompany me to the station for questioning,' said the old policeman gravely.

'WHATEVER FOR?' yelled a furious Mum.

'Because this young man's phone has been found in my house. Also, someone has accessed police data files. I believe it was this little person standing before me. I have already had to warn him off several times.'

'I lost my phone over a week ago,' squealed the nervous Harlem, 'I've never been inside your house... honestly! Mum, tell him, please!'

'I think you need to come with me; hurry along now!' instructed the Sergeant.

'Now wait one minute... You listen here! Harlem's already told you he's lost his phone!' fumed Mum.

'But he's been snooping around the police station, *haven't you*, boy?'

'Only with Margo, she lives there,' admitted Harlem.

'Get in the police car, boy!' demanded the Sergeant.

Mum was adamant that Harlem was not getting in the car with the nearly one-hundred-year-old policeman; Mum and Harlem would follow Sergeant Nutmeg in her car instead.

As she escorted Harlem on the not-too-distant journey, she informed him again that he was grounded. Harlem knew that in the face of a possible calamity on the doorstep of Enduring Crave, Jonathan North had to be behind all this.

Harlem answered all the questions put forward by Sergeant Nutmeg, but the quizzing repeated itself ceaselessly, question after question, as if on an endless loop. The interrogation seemed to last for hours. Perhaps the police officer was bored; it certainly seemed that way.

Harlem secretly believed Mr Nutmeg to be a fool, so long consumed with the lacklustre inactivity of policing that he wouldn't know an actual crime if one came and bit him on the backside. But how had Harlem's phone made its way into the bungalow? How had Jonathan snuck in unseen?

Only after Mum argued back and confirmed Harlem's story about losing the phone did the policeman relent. Mum also corroborated that Harlem had not been out of the house the previous day.

For the fifth time on the way home, Mum smugly reminded Harlem that he was grounded indefinitely. The car halted outside the house, and the two entered inside to find an ashen-looking Dad standing in the living room.

'I say, the most baffling thing happened after Harlem was arrested,' he muttered.

Mum sneered. 'Harlem wasn't arrested; he was asked to come in for questioning. It was all a big mistake. That old man is out of his mind! Harlem's home, and that's the end of it!'

'Let Dad speak, Mum!'

'Thank you, Harlem,' expressed Dad. 'As I was saying… after you two had gone to the station, and not five minutes later, I heard a tapping at the front door. A scruffy little beggar stood there… he was about your age, Harlem. A bath wouldn't do the blighter any harm. Anyway, he welcomed himself inside, ignoring my protests. I politely asked him to get out, and he just grinned. He told me he wasn't happy with the wallpaper and carpets. Said they would have to go! The cheeky rascal headed upstairs and dived onto your bed. I informed him I would ring the police. "Go ahead, the policeman's a trifle busy right now," was the lad's response. He did a right tour of the house before reading my newspaper and proclaiming, "Not much in the media these days; I shall have to change all that!" The boy claimed that he lived in this house sixty years ago and that, by rights, the house was his. He said he would be taking it back. He wanted to know why the lavatory was no longer located in the outside shed. I pleaded with him to stop being silly and go. He glared at me and pointed to the front door. The next thing I remember is flying across the garden before being unceremoniously thrown to the ground. He had inexplicably tossed me on the lawn! I composed myself and timidly crawled back inside; the young scallywag asked me what it would be like if I had never been born, and that I wouldn't have long to think about it. He called me Dougie; I said, '*No. It's Mr Hodge.*' "Ok, Dougie," he replied. On his way out, he ordered me to tell you who needs friends like yours. Who is he? Whoever he is… he's delusional!'

'Dad, he's Jonathan North,' replied Harlem.

'He's a deranged little sod, isn't he! All that nonsense about living here all those years ago,' grumbled Dad, who was still shaking.

Mum wasn't prepared to stay out of the conversation any longer.

'Oh, stop with this, Harlem; someone's trying to get you into trouble. Silly games, that's all.'

'Don't believe me then, Mum! It's Jonathan North, and now he's free. My friends are in danger. I must defeat him - *forget this, I'm going out!*'

'No, you are not! You're grounded, mister!' stated Mum firmly.

'For once, I'm standing up for myself. Just try and ground me for longer!' yelled Harlem.

Mum and Dad couldn't believe what they heard, but it was too late; Harlem had already left the house. At that moment, he couldn't care less what retrospective punishment would follow.

Considering it was the summer holidays, Harlem spent far too much time at school. He managed a wry smile at this notion.

The endless rain had bitterly soaked Harlem, and now he was bogged down by the rainwater and saturated clothes. Not bringing his coat made him look like a drowned rat as he arrived at school. Harlem managed to dislodge the three railings, but he couldn't climb the wall due to the limited movement caused by his wet clothes sticking to him.

Harlem had come all this way because he believed his friends were at the school and in danger. He fell short at the final hurdle when they needed him the most.

Unexpectedly, Harlem was suddenly levitated onto the wall by a unique invisible force. He turned to witness one of the mercurial shadow-beings with piercing blue eyes reveal himself before flying off towards the trees, glancing back at Harlem, and placing a finger across the lips.

Harlem had no time to digest what he had just experienced.

He made the mysterious door at the bottom of the stairwell his only target. The cobwebs and soot had been disturbed, and the door was barely ajar, with the handle fixed downward.

Harlem forced the door open and followed the narrow, leaking tunnel, hidden for many decades, slowly tiptoeing forward, clasping and groping the walls, step by step, and becoming increasingly consumed by cobwebs. Harlem climbed a second set of stairs and found himself in the bell tower.

Jonathan North had been here recently, practising his ceremonial campanology—the art of bell ringing. With a derisory beam of light shining into the bell tower through a crack in one of the stones, Harlem barely made out four red bell ropes. Attached to one of the ropes was a handwritten letter, rolled up and fastened with a scarlet ribbon; it was addressed to Harlem, who held it up to the inadequate level of light available:

*Harlem,*

*What does a man do with his freedom? Will he sink or swim? Does he follow his convictions or simply remain subservient to his fears? My conviction in seeing the end of Enduring Crave cannot diminish. The bells signify my purpose. I am here; life is a show, and where is my podium? For those who run with me, share my podium. But your chums, where do they perform right now?*

*J North*

Harlem was forced to gradually pace cautiously back down the stairs and through the increasingly waterlogged tunnel. He spent all that time attempting to decipher the meaning of the letter. Podium is another term for stage; Harlem immediately realised that his friends must be on the school stage.

After dusting off the cobwebs, Harlem raced up the steps and into the assembly hall.

The stage curtain was firmly down; Harlem tossed it aside and found Margo, Phillip, Steiney, and Tubbs all restrained to chairs, their mouths covered with tape, with no thought of courtesy. Upon seeing Harlem, all four commenced mumbling and scuffling with their bindings.

One by one, Harlem untied his friends and removed their gags. No one could recall being abducted or explain how they ended up at the school.

However, all four did speak of waking up on the stage, silenced, to be met by a boy who greeted them when they shook from their catnap.

Harlem was steadfast in saying that it was Jonathan North. Who else could it be?

Situated at the extremity of the stage, Harlem saw a portable trolley that housed an early 1980s television and VHS player.

Harlem had never seen such a hefty, monstrous-looking TV before, nor did he know what a video player was, as this technology was no longer available. The TV promptly switched on, and the tape inside the video player began running.

Jonathan North was on screen, pulling an exaggerated, gleeful face whilst waving elaborately with both hands. The arrogant, self-gratifying swine, large as life, was showing off and playing to his audience.

The brute launched into a sentence carrying a slow, wicked, and menacing undertaking.

'Honestly, Harlem, do I have your attention, old boy? This is all too easy... I must say! The measure of a boy can be seen in the number of his friends, but surely, quality is better than quantity. Look at these four... You really do choose morons and oafs as friends... that's just bad form! This *is* interesting... we have time consumers here, *don't we*? Bully for you, Margo. Bully for you, Phillip. Bully for you, James. Bully for you, Tubbs. This was a surprise to me, I must admit! Harlem, you waste your time with these wretches... *So*, the question must be: how far will you go to save the other lot of bumbling clots? I sense you will do your best. *Cheerio*... we shall meet real soon!'

The television screen faded to static snow before abruptly shutting down, almost as if displaying a hint of resentment and regret for having presented such a monstrous exhibit.

Margo, Phillip Day, Steiney, and Tubbs wanted to leave the school premises immediately.

All four were experiencing terrible headaches and now felt sick; the four friends were squinting with severe pain. Harlem assured them it was safe to leave and that he would put things right.

As this wasn't a dream and because he didn't have the key, the kitchen door would have to remain unlocked, as he had observed upon arrival. Harlem replaced the railings in position and set off on the nerve-racking journey home.

The rain had eased off slightly, although it would be days before he thoroughly dried out. The fiery tongue lashing from Mum may speed up the drying-out process.

Walking by the school gates, Harlem listened to someone calling his name. He turned to find Jonathan North casually approaching.

Jonathan was holding a large black umbrella that contained hundreds of laughing yellow emojis patterned on top.

'It's a beautiful day in the neighbourhood… I say, *old boy*, you appear to be a little wet. I know somewhere we can go to dry off and talk, too… I can show you more of my power. Do not fear, for no harm shall come to you tonight. You see, Harlem, I'm taking in the sights of Wishwisely, remembering what it was like to stroll without limits. Enduring Crave can wait… *all in good time.* Come along!'

'Where to?' pleaded Harlem.

'You know, Harlem, I've always wondered when I would have my first pint… what would it taste like? I've been on Earth for seventy-four years, and tonight, I shall discover that feeling. We're going to the public house… *no ifs… no buts…* we are!'

'We won't get served, Jonathan, not a chance!' replied Harlem in disbelief.

'Harlem, you will be surprised; I want to show you something. Come along… come… along!'

Jonathan sheltered himself with the umbrella. The brolly was big enough to cover him and Harlem, but Jonathan allowed Harlem to continue getting rained on. The two reached the pub, which was named the Nags Head. It was a typical cosy village pub, the only pub in the village.

The outer walls were painted white, and the window frames were black; the establishment had an elegant, thatched roof. An old, black-painted wagon wheel rested against the front wall.

The pub sign did not feature a horse's head. Instead, it portrayed the face of a moaning, grey-haired old woman brandishing a rolling pin.

If Harlem could pick any drinking partner, albeit an underage one, it certainly would not be Jonathan North. Harlem was nervous as they entered the pub, but Jonathan was as brash as possible. The locals turned in their barstools and gave him a long gape. No doubt, they all shared the same musings, and that was that there's no way you two would be getting served here!

A withered elderly gentleman sitting in the corner stared intently at Jonathan. Jonathan, in turn, waved at the old man, who twisted away, placing his head downwards.

A fireplace with a warm, roaring log fire was situated in the opposite corner. The pub landlord leaned forward on the bar with his arms crossed. He hadn't taken his eyes off his underage patrons since they had set foot through his door.

'GET OUT AND SOD OFF!' he barked.

Jonathan wasn't deterred, sidling right up to the landlord.

'I say, barkeep, my fine fellow, two pints of your finest bitter and two bags of nuts. As you can see, my company is soaked and feeling under the weather, so we shall gather by the fire. Be a good chap and bring our drinks and nuts to us!'

The customers laughed out loud, but the landlord failed to see the humour in it.

He yelled at Jonathan.

'WHO DO YOU THINK YOU ARE, COMING IN HERE AND TALKING TO ME LIKE THAT? GET OUT; IF YOU DON'T LEAVE, I'LL THROW YOU OUT!'

Jonathan shook his head; he appeared calm, but a shaking rage rapidly replaced that. Jonathan was outwardly incensed and began pointing violently at the landlord. The barkeep inexplicably poured himself a pint of bitter and instantly forced the drink down his throat. The entire pint was gone within three seconds. He poured another pint, followed by a third. After quaffing three pints quickly, the landlord was wheezing and coughing and began spluttering while trying to catch his breath.

The landlord seemed to have no self-control over his actions. As the scene played out, Jonathan wore a sinister grin. Harlem was horrified to be in his presence and at what he was witnessing.

'Please stop it, Jonathan!' he begged.

'Very well, but only because I am thirsty,' replied Jonathan.

Out of pure terror, the man behind the bar poured the ordered drinks and brought them, along with the nuts, to the table as instructed. The clientele was collectively shocked and somewhat afraid, which was completely understandable. Jonathan explained that there was no need for distress.

As the evening passed, more village residents arrived to see what was happening. News travels fast in a small community; the story of the landlord's plight had quickly escaped the confines of the watering hole. Not everyone could fit in the pub, so a little crowd vied for position at the entrance door.

Jonathan was drunk, revealing all sorts of tales and yarns, slurring as he spoke. Harlem sat beside him, but after tasting just one sticky, treacle-like, bitter sip, he sensibly moved on to cola.

A small piano on the sidewall caught Jonathan's attention. Having had one too many, he stumbled over to the instrument. The arrogant rascal demanded that the piano be turned around so that he could face the crowd. No one was going to refuse him after the events that had occurred earlier. Jonathan sat on the piano stool and composed himself as he began the slow, repetitive, but pleasant melody. He allowed himself a smile as he focused on the task at hand.

'Let's not throw it away, like so many before us
I wish we could make it; please say you agree
If not, there's no time to fake it
If it's not going to be, it's not going to be
I've been kidding myself, working a lie
Convincing my shadow, everything's fine
Been fooling a dream, we're back on the lies
Until I'm home and finally realise
Though you kept quiet, you made up your mind
That final look, the look of goodbye
And I know you're not coming back
This time, this time, this time...

Our days are over, truly gone by
The unquestionable answer, nobody knows why

So, I say farewell; your hand slips away
You take your path, and I'll take mine


Now, I'm looking to the future to see what it brings
I can't help thinking that we'll meet again
Cos a voice in my head turned to me, and it said
Just believe, and you'll see in time when you meet
You'll still love her
Love will remain, feelings the same
Years it may take, but my heart cannot break
You'll always love her


The future is tomorrow; gone is yesterday
I can't help thinking, was there a better way
One thing I do know is that each day that passes by
Brings me closer to you
And when full circles are complete
I'll land back at your feet
And lonely days will be destroyed
Seen no more, gone for good
And you'll be back with me


So now I know our days are not over
Not completely gone by
The unquestionable answer shall be rendered in time
For now, I'll say farewell, your hand slips away
You take your path, and I'll take mine
You take your path, and I'll take mine
You take your path, and I'll take mine

There was plenty of merry applause, glass raising, and cheering from the clientele, not just from the trepidation of what might follow if they didn't cheer. It was a good song, and despite being beyond tipsy, Jonathan sang superbly, and his piano playing was effortless. He took a well-earned bow.

'Attention… *attention*, please! I must be going now; some I will see again in time; others I will not!' he announced to his audience.

The elderly gent, who had been in the pub for the whole duration and who had given Jonathan the fiercest of stares, stood up.

'Jonathan, are you taking us back in time with you, my old friend?' he asked.

'Indeed, Henry, I am. Only this time, everything will be different… we bookworms will not be the target… for the last laugh will be ours. The bullies will have their time in the coal shed!'

The diminished old man spoke once more. 'God bless you, Jonathan North, say it is so. Jonathan, where have you been? For youth treats you with grace and kindness. The woods have finally given up their secret.'

The atmosphere was one of widespread shock and contagious disbelief. The elderly, who had not been spared by Father Time and had witnessed the events of sixty years ago, recalled the long-forgotten past.

A dear, sweet old lady stared Jonathan right in his ghostly eyes.

'Are *you* the Devil?' she asked.

'No, Doris, not quite... *well*... not yet!' laughed Jonathan.

One more customer entered the pub, aggressively pushing past the crowd at the door - it was Mum. Jonathan spotted her immediately.

'Here she is, Major General, Field Marshal Arkle Stalin. Everyone is to stand to attention and salute! The nag has arrived!'

Jonathan found himself amusing and began chuckling fearsomely. When no one joined in, he gave that familiar glare of evil, and then laughter penetrated from all around.

'Tell me, Harlem's mum, what will it be like never to be born?'

No one in the pub could take their eyes off the events transpiring that night; it was all very peculiar and somewhat engrossing.

'Shut up, you silly boy! I think it's time you left - and stay away from my son! A filthy little lowlife like you has no place near him!'

Jonathan glared into Mum's eyes and hastily lifted his head to the ceiling. Mum was floating horizontally with her back against the ceiling, facing down at Jonathan.

'Please put her down, Jonathan!' begged Harlem.

'*Oh*, if I must!'

Mum was back on the floor, her lip wobbling. Harlem was sure she wouldn't cry, for he believed she had no tear ducts.

He swiftly exited the pub and escorted Mum to the car. As he did, he overheard Jonathan talking to the crowd.

'No one shall remember this night, for when victory is mine, this will have never occurred!'

Jonathan then followed Harlem to the car, laughing as he staggered behind.

'Honestly, Harlem, if this is how you act now, what will you be like when Enduring Crave plummets? This is merely the start of the games, just the beginning. You should pray and soon!' Jonathan tutted scornfully before disappearing into the night.

'Now you see, Mum, he is real *and* powerful. You were just a victim of it. Only I can stop him; I'm not discussing it further with you.'

'Is that the boy Dad said was at the house earlier?' asked Mum, still presenting a wobbly lip.

'Yes, but I'm not discussing anything else with you. You must let me face him; if you don't, he's already won. I must beat him; *I know I can*,' stated Harlem bravely.

Mum was perplexed. She had witnessed firsthand the power Jonathan North possessed. Harlem was henceforth ungrounded; he believed Jonathan had committed his first mistake.

# CHAPTER THIRTEEN

## The Zoo

Within minutes of Harlem sending his mother home from the Nags Head, he entered the office of Herrifurus, only to be greeted by an anguished-looking friend. Herrifurus had been concentrating fixedly on the solar system model.

'Ah, Harlem, I was not expecting you. *It is a little late...* a... little... late... We need fresh air... fresh... air,' he mumbled.

The two strolled out to Motherhood, Herrifurus holding his arms out to embrace the colossal terracotta tree trunk.

'Oh, Motherhood, we will undergo many challenges in the coming days. I implore you to stand tall and be our guiding light. For without Motherhood... we are... we are without life!' Herrifurus wiped away a tear running down his cheek. '*Harlem, we need to hasten... to hasten to the Zoo!*' he announced urgently.

After returning inside the marquee, they immediately exited again, with Herrifurus stipulating the zoo as their station. Moments later, they arrived at their chosen destination.

'Here we are... *here...* we are,' confirmed Herrifurus joyously.

The two stood in a field of the most splendid multi-coloured grass imaginable, surrounded tightly by tall, rainbow-patterned fir trees.

The field contained several colossal silver boulders positioned throughout, and one frightful-looking, depressing, blackened, misty cave. These were accompanied by an empty kiosk pay stand and a fully loaded old-style popcorn vending machine.

'Herrifurus, either I'm going mad, or I just don't get the joke. You said we were going to the zoo - I don't see any chimps or elephants around here. Not one tiger or zebra, not even a little meerkat!'

'Another good one, Harlem, quite the comedian on the… on the side, aren't you? This is not that kind of zoo. *Harlem, look over there… over there… do you see it?*'

Harlem spun in the direction of Herrifurus' finger. On top of the boulder in the centre of the field, Harlem witnessed a young man around eighteen, idling on a sofa, drinking beer and shoving slice after slice of pizza into his mouth. Tossing the empty beer can onto the floor, he opened a second. After swigging the first mouthful, the man let off the loudest belch Harlem had ever heard.

The slob then opened a bag of tortilla chips and poured the contents into his mouth. Half of the chips landed on the man's midriff; he began picking at and eating the crumbs one by one.

Further back on a second boulder, Harlem gazed upon a man roughly the same age as the layabout on the sofa, except this second person was in a sports hall, running up and down.

The energetic athlete dived to the floor and began performing press-ups, counting as he did to one hundred. He took a football from a sports bag and struck the ball with such an impressive strike that the football flew into the top left corner of the goal. The man then restarted his sprinting exercises.

'It is ok, Harlem, to get up close and personal; they will not bite. Here, have some popcorn, I always… I always love a good popcorn snack whenever I visit the zoo.'

Harlem smiled and gripped a handful of popcorn while moving in for closer inspection.

He now witnessed a third man appear on top of a third boulder. This young man was sloping unsteadily at a nightclub bar. The man was throwing back many alcoholic shots; he was drunk, and next started a scuffle with another patron.

The man, who only moments earlier had been consoling himself with tiny, alcohol-filled glasses, was now flat out on the floor and abruptly hauled out of the establishment by two burly door attendants.

'These three young men are the same… the same age… Several years ago, and within proximity, each wished… each wished they would become professional football stars. As you know, each wish is judged by an individual's means. Until the decision is made, they cart hope. We witness a live screening of the activities in which these three are currently participating. You could say we are watching a live TV show of all three individuals. To become the best, perhaps you must… you must train harder than all the others… Would it hurt to put in the hours of practice… *would it*… would it? It is late evening, and this active chap is in the gym doing what is required. One and three show no desire… no desire. Number two possesses all the qualities necessary to be accomplished. Soon, his wish will come

true. We shall facilitate his dream by boosting his skill levels...
I will increase his speed, strength, ball control and stamina. He
embodies someone who never gives up and consistently pushes
himself to exceed expectations. As for the other two, it has been
so long... *so...* long... since they last had the ambition to give
it a go. *Who knows when they last kicked a ball... do they
know?* The only application they have shown me is for
slovenliness and vulgarity. *Three-two-one; wishes denied for
the two oafs!* They shall be none the wiser and will continue
in their ways. They will make new wishes... wishes to instil
them with longing hope. Other wishes remain active from them.
These wishes have been waiting in the Fully Fledged Enclosure.'

The live screenings of the three men vanished, and a new
vision blurred into focus on the smallest boulder in the field;
only this boulder contained protective padding.

'Ah, Harlem, this is a wish that is young... is young of age,
one still in the bracket of Zoo Nursery.'

The personalised show followed a lady arriving home; her
children's babysitter greeted the woman, who apologised for
being late, climbed the stairs and entered her son's bedroom.

It was evident to Harlem that the child was poorly.

'What's happening, Herrifurus?' he asked both worriedly and
concerningly.

'My dear boy, this lady works four jobs... four jobs... just to
survive and care for her two children. She has nothing for
herself; just her babies... *just...* her babies. This lady is of
meagre means. Her boy weakens with a rare illness, and the
treatment required is not available... not... available in her

country. £70,000 is needed to send the boy for therapy. She does not have the wealth. While working one job this afternoon, we came upon her first wish in years. This wish has been granted; she will receive a knock at the door tomorrow. A briefcase containing £300,000 will be found on the doorstep. *No questions are to be asked...* The sterling is to be used... is... to be used... to send the boy away to get better... and for the woman's accommodation as she waits. In return, the boy will pull through and the lady will pay off her mortgage, giving up three jobs... I am placing extra concessions on this wish as she is indicative of someone who places others first.'

The image of the lady and her child instantaneously evaporated.

'Harlem, the nursery contains... contains wishes born from the last twenty-four hours. But permit me to ask you this: how many... how many wishes would you say are currently in the Fully Fledged Enclosure? *Take a guess...* a guess! *Take a guess, I say!*' stated Herrifurus jovially.

Harlem didn't have a clue; the field was vacant. He pondered to himself: was it a million, was it ten million? He had no idea.

'Herrifurus, *is it* five hundred million?'

'Harlem, I see you have guessed low. The exact amount is nine billion, six hundred thousand, and twenty-four, er, make that twenty-five. *No, it's now twenty-six.* You see, Harlem, in just that split second, the number has risen and continues to do so. One individual can carry many active hopes within them. Others have a wish list as long as their arm. Humanity is nearing eight billion; are they content with just one wish? Absolutely not… absolutely… not… Now you see the magnitude of our work here. *Look, study… study the contents of this field.*'

Harlem raised his eyebrows with curiosity. The field was empty, but seconds later, an image settled on the grass, then another.

Within a short time, the entire field was covered in impressions of wishes and the people under surveillance by Herrifurus and the Wantwots.

Still, the visions continued to appear; thousands became millions, overlapping with new images. The speed at which they materialised was simply phenomenal.

'Harlem, this is… this is just a tiny percentage of active wishes. A handful of sand… a… handful… of… sand… in a desert of wants. You must still observe what cannot be! Recognise when a wish must not be permitted. Lines… lines must be drawn. *Come with me to the Hogsty, and you will see better… will see better…* Look and understand… and understand more clearly!'

They entered the cave, a place of deep, unsettling darkness, where they were greeted by a peculiar sight: a soggy, malodorous patch of festering, decaying brown grass, bizarrely adorned with twelve dancing porcelain lavatories, their incessant opening and closing of both seat and lid a disturbing accompaniment.

Each time the lid and seat were lifted, the toilets would make disparaging comments such as "ta-ta, whiff face", "I think not, smelly", "Oh, boy, do you stink!" and "You're so full of crap!". These lavatories communicated with those wish makers, talking out of their egotistical backsides.

The wooden sign in this unpleasant and dismal cave read *"Hogsty"*. A new live reel appeared on the Hogsty rotting grass, and like anything in a Hogsty, it carried with it the hideous stench of excrement.

This real-time action footage displayed a man rushing down the street, attempting to catch up to a young lady. The man grabbed the lady by the left arm as he approached her from behind. She was crying and yelling at him. Somehow, she freed her arm, screaming for help as she escaped. The man no longer chased and returned to his car.

'This excuse of a man, this bully, who is abusive not only... not only with his tongue but with his fists, has laid his hands on that beautiful angel for the last time! *Who is he to think that any other Sapien is his personal property*? An object no longer, she is free of him forever! He can curse her no more. *The audacity of him to wish*... to... wish...that she would return to him and stay with him for good. *It boils my blood*... She will not... will not... be returning to this brutal imbecile. *The Hogsty is where a wish will not be entertained - no acceptance at any time... any time of day*! His wish bypassed the Nursery and found itself here, and rightly so... rightly... so. *Wish denied*! This is one wish I take pride in declining, but he will wish again. Remember... being a judge, jury and executioner to a particular wish cannot affect my thought process on what is yet to be... Harlem, there is one more scene you must witness. Observe, as it defines... defines the reason for Enduring Crave. A wish... a... wish... back at the Nursery!'

Outside, a new presentation magically appeared on the padded boulder, depicting a young lady grieving in church. She was sobbing uncontrollably whilst kneeling and staring at a photo of her mother. She smiled at the picture, but then the tears poured with meaning as powerful as twenty waterfalls.

'Harlem, I am not of this Earth, but I can feel the heartache of the hefty loss of a loved one. Unfortunately, one thing you can be sure of in life is that, at some point, we wave goodbye when our dear ones depart. Though we walk a long journey down that road... that road... with others who entered our lives by our side... we all have our last passage. It is the natural order... the... natural... order... when those whose final destination is untimely and their station is not ours, we continue ahead, dwindled in number... and carrying heavier hearts. Those who grace us on our first day of life are not all present with us at the end. Time may turn... may turn the page, but how we hunger for our missing, emotionally and physically. We lose something we never... *never*... get back. This dear lady suffers from just that. Her mother's loss is heart-wrenching. An unbreakable bond splintered... splintered in death! These last nights have been agonising for her, and it seems never-ending. What can she do? Where does she turn? All she can do is wish, as to wish is to hope... is... to... hope. To dream of seeing her mother again is to ask for a miracle... a... miracle, so I can never rebuff this. A mother's love can never be equalled. She has not wished for her mother to rise from the grave; had she done so, I could not allow it, of course. Although impossible, the wish to see her mum again for one last time will not be ignored. I will keep this wish alive; she will always live with that inner hope – a reason to believe, a purpose to follow, a bestowment of hope in her heart! This will impel her forward on her journey. The fire in the wish will never be extinguished even when her light flares no more...'

Herrifurus had tears running down his tired cheeks. Harlem, too, felt emotional.

'...To cancel hope; to deprive humans is to watch the world return to turmoil,' continued Herrifurus. 'We would find ourselves in a time... in a time before the Eight Curators bestowed upon humankind the gift of wishing. But there is hope, and this begins with the individual. Watch it multiply once, twice, and a million times repeatedly. Hope is contagious; the more abundant it is, the greater the good for humankind... If we lose, the world will be a barren, dusty desert of rock and wind. There will be nothing to recall humanity's unfulfilled dreams. The waste will be unforgivable and criminal. *Unforgivable and criminal, I say.*'

It had been a powerful, sincere, yet erratic speech by Herrifurus and a chilling reminder of humanity's indebtedness to the Eight Curators.

Harlem had now visited the zoo; it certainly wasn't what he had expected.

'Seldom do I take... do I take expeditions to the zoo with company; it is rather thought collecting. It is better to see humans in the flesh, well, not quite... *not quite*. The zoo makes it more realistic and offers a broader basis for decision-making. Visiting the zoo occasionally reveals clarity and unshackles the chains… the chains of complexity that go hand in hand with my residency here. Every wish vies for attention among the colossal numbers. Each one cries out… cries… out… for attention. "Don't forget me!" *Oh, the chaos and the ruckus.* "Accept me," or "I've been here the longest!" and "Why did that one get granted before me?" These wishes scream out… scream out for solace; it is a powder keg. Each wish turns on its fellow in line. It is not a first-come, first-served operation. *Consultation is not an option*… is not… an option. They will never… never listen… We must be on our way now. It is time to call on Backeyedjection. Let us make our next destination the ballroom.'

'How long will it take to get to the Calace?' asked Harlem curiously.

'Not long… *not long*… lucky this kiosk is here. Come, we can use the door to get to the ballroom.'

'Yes, Herrifurus, very lucky!' replied Harlem.

'*To my office right away.* At once… at… once,' ordered Herrifurus, using his ability to travel through doors in Enduring Crave.

As soon as the two arrived at the office, they swiftly departed, making the ballroom their next destination. On arriving in the ballroom, Herrifurus immediately consulted with Backeyedjection.

'Backeyedjection, what of the human world? Is there any unusual behaviour to report… I mean more unusual than is usual… than… is… usual. *Is panic increasing? Have significant doings occurred*?' he worried.

'Calm your panicky exterior, Herrifurus! Hold your horses; there is nothing out of the ordinary to report yet.'

Herrifurus and Harlem next discovered Larry at the bar.

'I hope… I… hope… you are not drinking at this time of day, Larry! *We are not*… we…are… not… a hotel!' he admonished.

'Just a fleeting drink, Herrifurus; I had to leave the operations room. It does nothing for my health.'

'Very well then, Mr Cornelius, you can… you can escort us to the mezzanine. It is time… time… for a conference! *Follow me*… follow… me!' ordered Herrifurus.

On top of the ridiculously lofty mezzanine floor, the three were greeted warmly by Monocle Sway but grumpily by Mokwug. In recent hours, tensions had been slowly escalating. The leadership team were beginning to step on one another's toes; it was not far from bubbling point. It didn't help that Mokwug was acting even more overbearing than usual.

'Herrifurus, you waste time believing in the boy from that human lot. I make no bones about my feelings!' she spat rudely.

'Excuse me; I am in the room. I also have feelings!' interjected Harlem, hurt by the unnecessary comments.

Mokwug pointed at the clock. 'You, *boy*, forty-eight hours creeps up since that rascal was free. Nearly two days… you are utterly useless and inept! An absolute shambolic doing! Is this your phoney war, is it?'

Herrifurus was not prepared to stand for this verbal onslaught.

'Mokwug, Jonathan North is still in his world. We have watchers and CCTV cameras throughout Pressing Matters Lane. If he tries to infiltrate here, we shall know... we... shall... know. We can do nothing until he makes the first move.'

Larry urgently attempted to calm the situation before Mokwug could get in another word.

'Ease off, Mokwug, calm down!' he implored hopelessly and nervously.

'Don't, Larry, how dare you tell me to calm down! If you do so again, I'll wallop you so hard that you'll wake up on Neptune! You are, need I remind you, simply a guest here and nothing more.'

That was a stunning piece of diplomacy from Mokwug. Larry was understandably hurt and angered by her unnecessary comments.

'You can find me at the bar; I'll wear a do-not-disturb sign. So do not disturb me!' he huffed.

Herrifurus blew a fuse, having heard enough vile remarks from Mokwug.

'MOKWUG, GET OUT... GET... OUT... AND DO NOT SHOW YOUR FACE... YOUR FACE... UNTIL YOU APOLOGISE TO LARRY AND HARLEM! I think that will take a considerable amount of time from now. You are a real piece of work! *Go away... get lost... shoo, shoo!* Monocle, take the reins until my return. Harlem and I are taking a trip to the human world. Come, Harlem, let's be off! We shall take in... take in... the sights of Wishwisely!'

A few moments later, the two headed down the Cobbles of Hankering. They chuckled jovially in a moment of tranquillity regarding Mokwug's comments to Larry.

As they stepped forward, hundreds of thousands of new wishes whizzed by, making their rapid way to the Calace of Judgement.

'Harlem, you understand… understand how imperative it is that we, that you, come good in all this. Jonathan North must be defeated!'

The unscheduled purpose of their journey was to visit the human world at the last minute and temporarily leave their woes behind. The two strolled around Wishwisely. The chat was light and pleasant.

The rains had ventured elsewhere; the cursed weather and its torment had said farewell for now.

Herrifurus loved the sights and sounds; he rarely left the confines of Enduring Crave. The locals were polite to their faces, but that didn't stop the two from receiving funny looks: Herrifurus for his appearance and Harlem for the earlier antics that had taken place at the pub.

After a hearty stroll on the high street, it was time to head back. The unhurried atmosphere was abruptly interrupted by the beeping of Herrifurus' mobile phone.

As he yanked it out from under his poncho, it was revealed to be an early prototype from the late 1980s. Monocle Sway was on the opposite end of the line. He was in a panic and in distress, speaking incoherently.

'Ease up, Monocle, tell me... tell... me... what has happened. What has Mokwug done this time? *I will box her ears*... so I will... so... I... will!'

'No, *it's not* Mokwug this time, though I wish it were. The wishes dropping into the Calace have stopped... they've dried up. We haven't encountered one for ten minutes. Something is wrong on the cobbles... a disaster awaits you! Hurry now, hurry back now!'

'We are... we are on... on our way, and how!'

As Harlem and Herrifurus appeared in the Meadow of Purple Purpose, Harlem sensed a menacing presence. At least one more entity was lurking in the meadow.

A fearsome and troubled storm was brewing; threatening dark clouds were merging overhead.

The increasingly forceful wind tossed the hovering sign disrespectfully until it could take no more. It fell, buried by the deep purple grass.

'Quickly, Harlem, to the gate... to... the gate...'

As they hurried, a gloomy pressure was gathering above. A lightning discharge suddenly set the sky alight; thunder duly followed. The gate was unfastened, beaten, and blowing back and forth in the gale. Herrifurus forcibly locked the gate as they moved beyond, but for no detectable reason, the gate toppled over.

'*Help me*... help... me, Harlem. *We must*... we...must... raise this gate!' shouted Herrifurus into the wind.

Harlem did his best, but it was useless; the gate was too heavy to lift. Harlem then glimpsed a horrendous sight ahead of him.

'Oh, my days. Herrifurus, look at the cobbles!' he shouted.

As the two faced the horrifying sight that befell them, they were both at a loss for words. A devastating situation had taken place on the cobbles. It was obvious to Harlem that even without a word being uttered from Herrifurus' mouth, he carried a heavy heart.

# CHAPTER FOURTEEN

## The Troubles with the Cobbles

There was outright devastation and destruction visible as far as the eye could see. Whoever or whatever wanted to demolish the Cobbles of Hankering had indeed succeeded in their mission. The once-perfect cobbles transporting wishes to the Calace of Judgement were no more. They had been uprooted, tossed, smashed, and cracked; some were split in two. It was a scene of unimaginable decimation and carnage.

'Look there, Herrifurus!'

Harlem nodded towards a wish that looked as though it was barely clinging to life. Yesterday, it would have fizzed along. But now it was stuck, slowly struggling to pull itself over to the next cobble, which, due to the displacement, was now a good foot away.

Please remember that wishes had always contacted every cobble on the once splendid blue and orange criss-cross pattern whilst on their journey for judgement. The cobbles were now smashed and disordered, so the wishes could not move forward.

The wish Harlem had first seen upon arrival had given up and said farewell; it was deceased. The first two cobbles had not been spared a different fate from the others; these, too, had been utterly obliterated. This meant that new wishes were unable to reach the cobbles. Herrifurus turned to see millions of wishes forming lines in the Meadow of Purple Purpose.

Each wish was becoming fidgety and unruly and plunging and jostling onward. New arrivals at the back were now impatiently stomping forward; it was becoming a horrid watch.

'Harlem, do not... do... not... step backwards! *Turn your head...* your head... see... see here!' ordered Herrifurus.

Harlem stared back in disbelief. So many wishes were rowdily cramped in the field that the tall purple grass had now taken on a flat, pulped appearance. A few minutes earlier, Herrifurus and Harlem had been stepping on wishes, unaware they were stuck in the field. Still, when the two had been consoling themselves at the sorry sight of the cobbles, millions more wishes had been made. Those wishes were stuck, swarming the field, trampling the grass.

'They will die soon enough! They are suffocating. It usually takes three seconds to reach the Calace. Now they are trapped, glued with no destination in mind, imprisoned in the purple meadow!'

'Do something, Herrifurus, you must!' demanded Harlem.

'Dear boy, what... what... can I do... *what can I do*?' he implored desperately.

If the wishes couldn't make it to the Calace of Judgement, their time would soon be up. One by one, the wishes fell silent.

'Herrifurus, is this what you expected?' asked Harlem.

'I didn't... I... didn't... know... what would come. This is far worse... far worse... than I imagined. We must get to Enduring Crave and quickly... and... quickly!'

Carefully negotiating their way over the broken and uprooted cobbles, Harlem and Herrifurus came upon an unknown number of wishes lying lifeless on the ground. Despite the pitiful and dreaded walk, they eventually arrived back at Herrifurus' office.

*'Another... another mess!* The humanity of it... of it all!'

Herrifurus was, regrettably, referring to the recent cleanup of his office; he much preferred a chaotic and jumbled workplace. The two did not idle as it was time to move on speedily. Operation Flog a Dead Horse was forced into silence due to the severe shock and stupefaction of the recent, tragic destruction. It was so overbearingly unbelievable. For the first time in sixty years and for only the second time in history, Enduring Crave had no new wishes to nurture.

As Harlem and Herrifurus dashed to the mezzanine floor, all heads turned towards Herrifurus. Every Wantwot stared at him, each seeking needed guidance and leadership.

A mighty, attentive level head was needed - could Herrifurus hold it together and be durable and unruffled, or would his ponderous side rise to the top?

Monocle Sway was inconsolable and heartbroken as he flapped around in distress. Larry Cornelius sat on the floor, shaking his head in incredulity. Mokwug was undeniably angrier and more irritated than ever.

She was seething as she carried a rolling pin in her right hand, whilst smacking it into her left palm. She glared at the two with her frightful eyes.

'Left your post, did you? Abandoning and absolving responsibility, are we? You and he from that human lot are as bad as one another!'

'Mokwug, I foresee... I... foresee a bleak ending for that rolling pin. Do not tempt... do... not... tempt me... *Mark my words*... I will stick that rolling pin where the bravest of the brave dare not go!' warned Herrifurus.

Mokwug snarled, giving Herrifurus the impression that she wanted to slog him with the rolling pin.

'*Mokwug, do not stare at me... at me in that fashion. It is becoming boring and predictable... and predictable!* When you are quite settled, show me the CCTV, and order in... order in the watchers,' instructed Herrifurus.

Herrifurus and the personnel chosen around him inspected the CCTV footage of the cobbles' demise in detail, now displayed on the enormous TV screen. This meant every single Wantwot was able to turn and watch in disbelief.

The cameras captured the destruction; however, nothing and no one could be seen creating or indeed causing the decimation. The watchers, a selected bunch of Wantwots stationed on Pressing Matter Lane, had also delivered their grim and appalling accounts.

The watchers had been caught off guard, for no presence had been detected. The cause of destruction was now being speculated and theorised. Witness statements and CCTV footage showed that the obliteration had lasted for a full minute.

In a mere sixty seconds, the cobbles had been annihilated. There would be no more hankering.

In the operations room, the panic was widespread. No beings had been spotted before, during, or after the event. So, the question was, "Was the attack orchestrated from within the human world?" No one knew if Enduring Crave would be next. How, when and if?

'Everyone... everyone... *I need your attention*... your... attention... A tragedy has occurred. We must all focus. Resolve, and resilience must be... *must*... be... exhibited... Be on the lookout for anything that seems out the ordinary. Watch out for any ambush that may be stalking around the corner. To humankind, it will be as if the right to wish... to wish... has been removed... Today, that hope is no more... is... no more... This is only the beginning, the first step on man's stairway to self-destruction.'

Following Herrifurus' rally call, Mokwug crassly intervened, whinging and whining and displaying her never-ending annoyance at Herrifurus, prodding him several times in the chest with those powerful fingers. Mokwug let it be known that she believed Herrifurus must accept some responsibility for the cobbles' destruction, as he had left his post to go galivanting around Wishwisely. It took a good few minutes before Harlem dared get a word in edgeways.

'Herrifurus, did Jonathan North ever have mind control powers?' he wondered.

Mokwug quickly chimed in. 'Mind control! What do you think this is, *sorcery*? I have a good mind to take hold of you by the scruff of your neck, young man!'

Harlem, on this occasion, paid no attention to the ever-disgruntled Mokwug.

'Herrifurus, he has a strange power over the mind. I saw him influence the landlord. He did it to my dad when he visited our house. He *even* commanded my mum; no one's ever done that... *and* Jonathan dominated me at school!'

'Quite the storyteller, aren't you? An overactive imagination from an underactive imbecile. *Honestly*, that human lot!' sneered Mokwug.

'Put a sock in it, Mokwug!' replied Harlem in an increasingly confident manner; he wasn't finished talking. 'Herrifurus, I believe Jonathan North has somehow come by or gained mind control. Did Jonathan ever wish for superpowers or brainwashing abilities? Could he have wished for it whilst trapped in school?' asked Harlem.

*'Harlem, what have we learned... what... what?* Even if Jonathan had indeed... *had*... indeed... wished for, as you say, superpowers, it would not be entertained. An immediate... an immediate rejection. That wretch lost the... the right to wish six decades ago!'

'Well, he's somehow attained control and the power to dictate what others do. I'm telling you!' insisted Harlem.

This hit a nerve with Mokwug. 'Oh, you're telling us, *are you*, Harlem? Herrifurus, this boy is a crackpot; he's a younger, smaller version of you. Even skimmed milk masquerades as cream.'

In tandem, both Harlem and the increasingly frustrated Herrifurus turned to Mokwug and yelled:

'SHUT UP AND GET OUT... GET... OUT... NOW!'

Herrifurus and Harlem next agreed that a visit to the cobbles was in order, if only to depart from Mokwug's presence for a while. As they toured the devastated path, trying to comprehend just how this tragedy had occurred was staggering. Was the Phantom of the Cobbles genuine or not? Could the destruction be the result of a natural disaster, such as a tremor? Had this tremor been restricted to the cobbles only?

The answer had to be 'no' as Jonathan North was on the loose, and it would be way too much of a coincidence. Jonathan was somehow behind this. Harlem and Herrifurus examined the length of the cobbles, but it had been a pointless task to root out the cause of destruction.

A chilling wind came rushing by, ushering in guilt and remorse. Harlem had felt this sensation; Herrifurus had been ignorant; he was still woeful.

During the unceremonious walk back to Enduring Crave, Harlem frowned at the pitiful scenes ahead. His attention had been removed from what was immediately in front of his feet. Due to the displacement, two broken cobbles ended up on top of one another, and without realising it, Harlem stepped on the double-stacked cobbles, causing both to separate violently. Losing balance, he inadvertently stepped backwards. Instantaneously, Harlem found himself standing on the gravel track.

Harlem didn't know what to do. Should he go home or try to get back to his secret world? As he peered into the churchyard, a notion of soon-to-be peril fluttered around him. The rain clouds above let loose their load, and the rain soon attacked its intended target. The decision was made for him, and Harlem sprinted home. As he made his way indoors, flashes of lightning lit up the bleak house.

Mum had, unbelievably, forgotten the events in the pub, and to add insult to injury, Dad couldn't recall what he had related to Harlem about being tossed into the garden. Both his parents had complete amnesia. That meant that Mum couldn't remember meeting Jonathan at all. It was back to square one; Harlem would not be allowed out in the rain.

Harlem was livid but not surprised, as nothing now made him wide-eyed. The mystifying thing was: how had they forgotten so soon? However, the bonus was that they couldn't remember Harlem running off and disobeying them. Even more puzzling was that Mum had not scolded him for returning home so late. It had just struck midnight.

Harlem wasn't going to sleep anytime soon. He had missed that evening's episode of Dirk Hader and His Excess Baggage; he would have to watch it on catch-up. In his failure to concentrate on the task, he accidentally clicked on a previous week's episode, in which Dirk made supercharged rocket jetpacks for the dead to use in the spirit world. Harlem watched uninterestedly before realising halfway through that he had already watched this episode.

Harlem switched off Dirk Hader, having had the urge to check the news stations. There was a breaking story on BSNews:

In the most northerly town of Canada, the residents of Alert, in the Qikiqtaaluk region of Nunavut, had begun an uprising.

The town of Alert is the northernmost inhabited place in the world.

No one knew why this uprising had begun, and no explanation was offered. The people of Alert had become incoherent and irate. Harlem listened to the bulletin with considerable interest.

'Maurice Pinprick here… for BSNews Canada. I am here in the most northerly town of Alert, where the residents all seem to have taken leave of their senses. Approximately two hours ago, state officials received a call for help. The people of Alert have gone mad, attacking one another and everything in sight. The reason and cause are not determined, but I have Mike here. Mike is a resident, and we hope to get Mike's version of events. Mike, can you tell us what's happening?'

Mike grabbed the microphone and glared gravely into the camera. 'Hope is gone… it's gone, I tell you. We are all doomed… doomed!'

Mike wrenched the camera away from the cameraman and tossed it to the floor. Harlem could see only an image of the snow-covered ground. The camera had been picked up within seconds, and the news crew attempted to continue the broadcast.

'This is Maurice Pinprick, here at Alert; I can tell you I have lost hope. I have lost hope… it is gone… GONE!'

The live broadcast was quickly removed from the air. Harlem flicked through every news station available to him. There were no further reports from other news channels about the events in Alert, nor were there any similar incidents anywhere across the globe.

Harlem wondered whether the Alert chaos was related to the cobbles. He wasn't sure; if this were the case, it would affect the whole world.

Where was Jonathan North? He had disappeared, but where would he be hiding? His dastardly scheme was underway and being implemented as planned. What was his next move? These were the questions that Harlem put to himself.

Providence had been placed on Harlem – save Enduring Crave and humankind. But right now, Lady Luck was abandoning him.

Harlem woke up feeling extraordinarily disoriented. After eventually coming around and fully opening his eyes, which had been covered with sticky sleep residue, he unhurriedly worked out the time. Holy Moley: it was half past two on Saturday afternoon.

Harlem couldn't recall the last time he had slept this long. He hurtled downstairs and straight into the living room. The curtains were closed, and upon peeping out of the windows, Harlem gazed at his parents' cars. His parents must still be in bed.

Harlem would leave them there, as it would make his life easier in the moment.

In his frantic rush downstairs, he hadn't initially noticed the newspapers on the front doormat. It was odd, as there should have only been one newspaper, but there were two.

Harlem registered that these were two different editions of the *Daily Grind*. On closer inspection, one was Saturday's edition, and the other was Monday's.

This wasn't possible, as it was Saturday today. How did a newspaper from two days from now get delivered by the paperboy? It couldn't be a newspaper from the future; the rational explanation was that today was Monday.

Harlem had fallen asleep around half past one on Saturday morning and had awoken at half past two Monday afternoon, giving Harlem a marathon nap of over sixty hours.

Dad never had a paper delivered on Sunday; that was his day to stroll out and purchase one from the shop, if only to get away from Mum for five minutes.

It immediately crossed Harlem's mind that he had been inactive for two days.

Harlem snatched Saturday's newspaper and read that the frenzy in Alert had unremorsefully spread through Canada like a crazed and unrelenting wildfire. The sudden, ferocious popular uprising was so severe and unforeseen that the commotion and out-of-control mayhem caught the government off guard. Thus, those in charge had mobilised the troops to suppress the mob and quell the disorder happening across the nation.

The mania and uprisings were contagious and spreading rapidly.

Harlem now concluded that the chaos had to be linked to the destruction of the cobbles. Perhaps humans had begun to realise that they no longer carried wish-making capabilities.

Even if the words 'I wish' could still be uttered, maybe people sensed that it fell on deaf ears.

The protests and uprisings were massive in number and over such a widespread area, and despite the mammoth, maddening crowds, had resulted in surprisingly few casualties.

The people demanded that their voices be heard, but the powers that be would not listen.

Harlem then studied the published edition from today. It quickly became apparent that the situation had worsened significantly.

The uproar had advanced across the border and into the fifty states. Anarchy prevailed, and it only grew nastier.

Those who still held on to hope were the targets of those who had lost all hope. Those without were singling out those with.

Gangs of wayfaring lost causers had begun yanking active hopers limb from limb and forcefully rapping heads in a desperate attempt to uncover hope; these scenes mimicked a zombie disaster B-movie.

Official state buildings were ablaze. Blocked freeways were cluttered with deserted and neglected cars and trucks, many of which were now raging in flames as their owners had abandoned them, desperate to escape the reckless, charging frenzy. Clashes with the police and other forces had become excessively feral and savage. The curfews that had been implemented were naturally being resisted. Looting and careless attacks were out of control.

This movement wasn't restricted only to North America. It continued to spread southwards until every South American country was breached by spiralling, out-of-hand violence: anger, frustration, bedlam, and lost hope were all part of the recipe. What had begun as a minuscule disturbance in Alert had grown and developed into a full-blown pandemic. Two continents and their people were amid an altercation that didn't look like it would end soon.

Madness was consuming the world. Harlem had read enough; he tossed the papers into the air and sprinted to the Childhood Tree.

The tension only increased when Harlem looked down at the decaying wishes in the Meadow of Purple Purpose. No matter how much hope he carried that the cobbles would be miraculously rebuilt when he arrived, they weren't.

It seemed to Harlem as if the destruction had occurred a long time ago; the ruins looked dated, as if they were centuries old.

As Harlem walked with extra diligence, he came upon more wishes rotting on the ground. Herrifurus was waiting outside the rock, looking outraged.

'*Where in dawns blazes...* dawns blazes... have you... *have you been*?' he asked frustratedly.

'Please don't yell, Herrifurus,' replied Harlem. 'I've been asleep. I think Jonathan North might have drugged my parents and me.'

'I see, but for dawn's sake, do not... do... not... repeat that to Mokwug. She will hit the roof... the... roof... then me and lastly you!'

The atmosphere in the operations room was uninspiring. The once hectic hustle and bustle was now all but a distant memory; it was all very mundane. The Stream of Mean Dreams Returned to Human Beings was without the usual hideous content, as no new selfish excrement and stool dripped in.

Herrifurus had ordered that the channel of the stream be washed and cleaned. Thousands of Wantwots were busying themselves with tiny mops - all to rinse away the repulsive stench that still lingered. Thousands more were cleaning the conveyor belt and the dreamducts; others were painting the walls.

On top of the mezzanine, Harlem was informed that Mokwug, assisted by a troupe of Wantwots, had hastily but successfully installed CCTV in various parts of Enduring Crave on Saturday.

The relaying images were now openly visible on the humongous TV and being closely scrutinised.

Backeyedjection had been relocated to the mezzanine, along with his desk and portable monitors. He was immersed in his work, his eyes spinning faster than ever. Every news station and media platform covered only the out-of-control chaos and the accompanying troubles that came with it. The hysteria was now worldwide.

If Harlem had continued to read the newspaper or switch on the TV, he would have realised this sooner. Now, the sheer magnitude gripped him.

'*We need time*... we... need...time... There is still hope out there, in the form of wishes that have already been granted. More hopes lay in the wishes... the wishes still to be determined; those of the Fully Fledged Enclosure. However, we have three to four days at best... at... best... we need a solution. *Think, Harlem, think*... think!'

'Herrifurus, what happens in three to four days?' asked the fearful Harlem.

'Harlem, humankind will begin to bubble and boil... bubble... and... boil... Self-destruction stage number two: what you see now is only the first step. As those with hope are attacked without prejudice, their hope also dwindles. We must find Jonathan North. If we do, we may see this out.'

Operation Flog a Dead Horse was, without warning, plunged into chaotic darkness as a thunderous 'BOOM' shook the entire Calace of Judgement. A moment later, the lights returned but quickly went out again.

A second striking boom was heard, followed by a third. Each time the noise blasted, the lights briefly extinguished after the tumultuous shaking.

'*The Grottlers!*' cried Herrifurus. 'Access all cameras... all cameras from the Whitewash Woodland. Monocle Sway, do it... do... it... now!'

With a speedy tapping of keys, the TV screen contained only the nine images from the nine cameras positioned in the woodland on Saturday.

The booms, shakes and loss of light were becoming so frequent that Mokwug had to bring in candles to make the room glow. There was no emergency lighting, so it was good old-fashioned candles to the rescue.

Herrifurus and his team witnessed, with horror, Grottlers disappearing from the woodland on their way to the human world to destroy wishes. They were targeting already granted wishes, but these were not wishes that had been granted in error, nor were they used as an act of evil.

Each time a Grottler marched off on his one-way journey, the uncompromising boom echoed, followed by the dreadful tremors. The extinguishing of the lights represented a Grottler leaving this world.

'Monocle, turn on… turn… on… the map of the… of the world!' demanded Herrifurus.

The map of the world indicated the Grottlers' arrival to obliterate specific granted wishes. Each time a Grottler woke and went to war, a white dot appeared on the screen, signifying the location of the Grottler. The Grottlers were targeting the entire world. So many were now on the march that thousands of candles were required to alleviate the darkness.

'Harlem, Mokwug, come with… come… with… me! We must go to the Whitewash Woodland. *Make haste with me… with… me!*' ordered Herrifurus.

In the Whitewash Woodland, the three stood in utter disbelief as they watched the little statues come to life and stretch. The Grottlers gave a final salute to Enduring Crave before disappearing.

The animals in the forest were terrified and ran to Herrifurus for protection; he advised them all to hide out in the garden.

In parts of the woodland, the whiteness had begun to recede; not too much, but it was noticeable. A red, sticky liquid replaced the purity that was disappearing more quickly by the minute.

'The woodland is beginning… is beginning to corrode. The Grottlers are a part of the fabric… the fabric of the forest. Remove too many too soon, and the woods begin to feel the loss. It shall not sustain itself for too long!'

Mokwug immediately grabbed the phone to ring Monocle Sway. 'I need a count of how many Grottlers have gone to battle. I want an answer now!'

'Hold your horses, Mokwug,' replied Monocle. 'Give me a few seconds... these things take time. Ah, here we are... *crikey... that's not good...* not good at all... So far, just under a million have given themselves up in the name of Enduring Crave.'

Mokwug hung up without so much as a 'thank you' to Monocle Sway. Herrifurus caught a glimpse of a Grottler waking up just a few feet away. The little fellow yawned and stretched.

Herrifurus seized it, plucking it from the ground and holding it to his face.

'What are you doing? *Tell me...* tell... me!' demanded Herrifurus.

'My order is to defend Enduring Crave,' replied the Grottler. 'For this, I would gladly lay down my life. I have been tasked to terminate all the wishes of one individual. I must be leaving for duty calls... Ulaanbaatar, Mongolia, is my destination.'

'Yes... *yes...* but... who ordered you?' asked a choked-up Herrifurus.

'Herrifurus, it has been an honour. If I do not return, I tried in vain to defend my kingdom.'

Just like that, the Grottler was gone. Herrifurus was now more distraught. Not only that, but he still had no idea who could have authorised the orders. Who was sending these tiny bleeders on their plight? It was niggling away at Mokwug as well.

'Herrifurus, only you can decide, not I nor the Wantwots. What's happening?' she asked, aghast.

Harlem had begun to think logically. Who else could it be but Jonathan North? He had to be the one who was instigating all of this by cunningly and deviously overriding the system.

'Herrifurus, it's Jonathan North. This is his work. First, the cobbles — eradicating the route for new wishes to arrive at the Calace. His second move is to begin destroying granted wishes. His third and ultimate aim is to get his hands on the Lantern of Infinite Wishes. That's his end goal; he craves whatever wish you refused. That wish is the reason for all this… and the wish is still in the lantern. Jonathan won't stop until he has it, except… it isn't *his* wish.'

'HARLEM, MY BOY!' yelled Herrifurus. 'You could be… you… could be right!'

'He could equally be wrong,' added Mokwug. 'Conjectures and suppositions. Venture this path, and it may lead to a dead end.'

'Mokwug, Harlem is on… is on to something. *In Harlem, we trust… we trust; Harlem means vanquisher!*'

Harlem grinned as that last part of the sentence was familiar, whilst Mokwug objected.

'May I ask a question? What does Jonathan gain if the world is destroyed? Why would he see off humankind? It would all be pointless.'

'Mokwug, he isn't aware of the repercussions,' replied Harlem. 'Jonathan didn't believe what Herrifurus had said when we spoke in school. Jonathan believes humankind will still go about its business when all this is over. All this cobbles nonsense and Grottler stuff is just Jonathan showing us how monstrous he is. He is a self-declared evil genius. Jonathan North must be somewhere in Enduring Crave.'

'Harlem, an impossibility of the highest... *the highest order*. This cannot be... cannot... be.'

'Come on, Herrifurus, get with the times! Sixty years ago, Jonathan was last seen heading into the woods. He has another access point, kept secret and unknown to you. He must be here in this realm... that's why he doesn't know what's happening in my world.'

On returning to the top of the mezzanine, Monocle Sway hastily met the three and swiftly informed them that Larry Cornelius was once again drunk, this time at the bar.

It was a long climb up to the summit of the spiral staircase. Inside the ballroom, Larry was found lying face down on the bar. He was babbling and making no sense at all.

'Tchoo monkeyed, wee tyred, woohoo!' he slurred.

Larry rolled over, falling from the bar and landing flat on his face.

Herrifurus was out of breath, having climbed the spiral staircase, so it was left to Mokwug to carry Larry off to bed via a secret, revolving, hidden door next to the bar.

'Harlem, on reflection, how can you even think... even... think... of Jonathan placing his grubby mittens on the lantern? It is now under lock and key, safeguarded in the Calace. Even... even... you, Harlem, do not know where it is hidden. *Need I...* need... I... remind you that to find the Calace of Judgement, you must wear... wear the Tinted Goggles of Profundity or dictate where you intend to head from my office, and even then, you would need permission. Jonathan North has neither… has neither of those.'

'Herrifurus, please do not be blind to what you cannot see. Look at how far he's come; he's shut down the cobbles. What about the Grottlers? He's capable of all that, and his final move will be for the Lantern. Jonathan will already know where the Calace of Judgement is, having spoken of the Calace to me… so he knows its existence. Herrifurus, something's niggling at me; I must go. I'll return as soon as I can.'

As the two friends stood outside the rock on Pressing Matters Lane, Monocle Sway informed them over the phone that the number of Grottlers sent off on the journey of no return had hit five million.

'Trust me, Herrifurus,' exclaimed Harlem. 'It may be tomorrow before I return.'

Once back in Wishwisely, Harlem rushed to the school. His destination was the classroom where he had interrupted the shadow-beings.

He leered at the hieroglyphics on the blackboard.

His concentration was suddenly cut short by the chief shadow-being appearing from within the blackboard, still wearing his mortarboard hat and cape.

'How does one exist on a dead planet?' asked the shadow in a quiet, guilt-ridden, and trembling voice. 'A planet that is long unremembered and forgotten. Planet Permeatus, detected at the border of this universe and the second universe, *is* that very planet. A planet of waste, rot, and cavities, deprived of attention and extensively overlooked. It is with great hardship, defiance, and difficulty! One must persevere by dropping in under the cover of light onto foreign spheres. By infiltrating the penumbra of beings on those orbs, we generate enough energy to live a further one hundred years of human time on Earth… *But…* please forgive me; I digress without introducing myself… I am Symptom-Hazard, General of the Shadow Squatters! We do not harm those whose shadows we intrude, and all energy for life-giving we do not keep. We ourselves are penetrated by my fellow species on return to Permeatus. We collect the energy and nourish our dying with life. If I take one hundred years and feed nine of my species back home, it is ten more years of living for each. The disadvantage is the endless missions of gate-crashing inhabited planets. Our actions may be illegal in our system, but we mean no harm and cause no harm. Permeatus, so distant from any living planet, allows us to hide in the shadows. We go unnoticed; this is the reality of our tenebrosity…'

Symptom-Hazard abruptly ceased talking and nervously glanced around the room, acting paranoid as if dangerous forces were spying on him. Symptom-Hazard urged Harlem to come closer. He began speaking, but his tone had now become more panicked and distressed.

'But we were unmasked… *found out…* by the hideous and villainous Demon of Daric. We were ordered to go to Planet Earth and be enlisted of a boy. The demon directed us to follow the boy's sinful schemes and plots to bring about the downfall of a secret world. If we refused, *we* would be destroyed! The most nefarious and detested characters in Hell would not want to ingratiate themselves into this boy's service. We have, I regret to say, obeyed his every command up to now. But we are free of his shackles at last. Our mission has been fulfilled.'

With a final scowl around the room, Symptom-Hazard retreated to within the confines of the blackboard.

# CHAPTER FIFTEEN

## The Grottlers Rise in A World Gone Mad

The birds had initiated their daily singing ritual a little too early this morning. The time was ten to four, and the incessant sounds of the birds suggested to be amplified twenty times to Harlem, who wanted nothing more than complete silence to ruminate on the despicable actions of Jonathan North. Was that too much to ask?

It had been yet another sleepless night with every question he gripped at yearning to be set free with answers.

What was Symptom-Hazard's task? Why had he confided in Harlem? And whatever happened to Vincent Garrison? Where *had* Father Time vanished to?

Harlem continued to study the current play of affairs throughout the world.

Chaos had taken control of the planet, augmenting each time a Grottler destroyed a wish. Parts of cities all over the globe were ablaze. Safe zones and exclusion zones had been readied; however, nowhere was impregnable to the ever-consuming madness. There was still a chance if only civilians were clashing, protesting, looting, and setting fires out of lost hope. It would be a whole new scenario if the pandemonium spilt over to government and military officials.

People who owned a wish in the Fully Fledged Enclosure still held on to hope. Smash that hope and wish, and then those people would join the raving, zombified loons. Ever increasingly populated, the furious mob became the driving force behind the steamroller of devastation.

Across the globe, attempts to evacuate cities had failed. The warped and out-of-control minds would not allow any idealists to escape. It was a plague of desperate zombies purposefully drifting in all directions.

Harlem was sure that Jonathan North was unaware of the dire situation the world had found itself in. Earth could be destroyed in the next few days, and it simply made no sense; Jonathan would never get his hands on the wish he so badly desired.

On stepping out of the house, Harlem purposefully visited the church over the road. He recalled Jonathan advising Harlem to pray soon. It seemed an odd thing to say, and Jonathan couldn't possibly be in church; he would have burst into flames as soon as he opened the door; the Devil is not permitted to enter a sacred space.

As he set foot in the churchyard, Harlem remained unsure of what he was searching for. Was he looking for a sign, a vision, or a voice – or did he need to meet someone? If so, then who? Could it all be part of Jonathan North's games? Did Jonathan expect Harlem to pray?

Inside, Harlem was startled to see that the congregation filled the pews. All worshippers were praying sincerely, for the world's end seemed imminent. Without warning, a man with a fearful and suspicious expression swiftly stood up before hastily leaving. Harlem followed, making sure he wasn't spotted.

A bright white light suddenly appeared in the churchyard, followed by a minute rumble.

This terror-stricken man was frozen with dread as a solitary Grottler stood before him. The Grottler was as large and brash as life; it was no longer the gnome-like statue it once was, as it now stood six feet tall. It gazed directly into the man's tearful eyes.

The Grottler placed its left hand on the man's forehead before exploding into a cloud of white dust. The man immediately became increasingly agitated and irate, shouting and cursing the state of his life.

It was clear to Harlem that he had lost all hope. He would soon be one more adding to the tidal wave of anger as he ran off, yelling and cursing.

Several minutes later, Harlem headed for the Childhood tree in the centre of Wishwisely, but as he exited the churchyard, he bumped into his four friends.

'Harlem, have you come to help us? Is that why you're here?' asked Phillip Day whilst tasting a fingertip full of earwax.

'What do you mean?' replied Harlem.

'He means Jonathan North!' exclaimed Margo. 'Are you here to stop him from hurting us? That boy dances with the Devil!'

Margo held her hands to her head, suggesting she suffered from another headache. Her eyes were tightly closed as she grimaced in pain.

'I'm going to try and save the world. There isn't much time, but I have a plan.'

'What are you on about, Harlem?' asked Steiney. *'What do you mean, save the world?* We want you to help us escape that servant of Hell!'

'Harlem, you're the only one who can see us. Nobody else has noticed us for decades, except for Mrs Wormpick. No one remembers us. You must be here to rescue us now that Wormpick's retired. Please... *please...* say you're going to free us!' pleaded Tubbs.

Harlem was bereft of understanding. Save them from Jonathan North, but in what context? Margo and the gang had no inkling as to what was happening across the planet. What were they implying? Free them from what?

'Yes, I'm here to help all of you!' reassured Harlem. 'I'll be back soon, trust me. But now, *I must go*, keep your chins up and stay away from that school!'

'Don't go... *don't go*,' begged Steiney, but it was too late.

Harlem mimicked Herrifurus as he hugged the Childhood tree in Wishwisely. He had never really taken the time to gaze upon its beauty before. Right now, he imagined what it would have been like all those years ago when Godfrey North wandered into the field and planted seeds. Instantaneously, those seeds interweaved with Motherhood, and this very tree grew. Godfrey was a good and kind individual, as were his descendants, who had been allowed access over the years.

What went wrong with Jonathan? How had he sneaked under the radar, and why had he been accepted?

The Meadow of Purple Purpose had miraculously recovered as the grass towered tall and proud, releasing the irritable itchiness; the unknown number of wish fatalities no longer weighing it down.

The wishes had all decomposed, and no telltale signs remained - nothing was left of those once active hopes.

The out-of-this-world setting, with a permanent, premature sunset and dozens of aimlessly drifting puce asteroids unhurriedly passing by, was a welcome sight. The peculiar floating sign was repositioned in its rightful place, and the gate was restored to its former glory.

Harlem was overjoyed to see this, but the happiness was only fleeting. As he closed the gate behind him, Harlem faced the deteriorating cobbles.

Every day that passed made the cobbles look more antiquated by five hundred years. In a week or two, there would be no evidence remaining and nothing to suggest that this once wondrous marvel had existed.

Upon arriving in Enduring Crave, Harlem headed straight for Operation Flog a Dead Horse. The entire room glistened and gleamed. The Wantwots had cleaned the room, providing a glimmer of sparkle in an overcast environment. The Wantwots, now that their task was complete, idled with no purpose to serve.

On top of the mezzanine, Harlem was gloomily informed by Monocle Sway that two billion Grottlers had now entered the human world. Mokwug stomped over, looking to stir up a clash.

'*You*, from that human lot, are you still adamant that the Devil's hiding out in Enduring Crave? Under our very noses?'

Larry Cornelius, now nursing a major hangover, dared to mock Mokwug.

'Well, Mokwug, let's face it. Anyone could be hiding out in that moustache of yours!'

Well, that was it! Mokwug threw a punch, and it didn't miss. Poor Larry was airborne; he flew a fantastic thirty feet before crashing to the floor. It was hardly a fair and even brawl. The little jester was only teasing, but Mokwug didn't have a funny bone or a sense of humour. Herrifurus became incensed at Mokwug's uncalled-for violence.

'Mokwug… Mokwug… *what on earth…* on earth… did you do that for? You big… you big bully, you! This is unacceptable and unforgivable! I will not… will… not… tolerate fighting. It is always… always you, Mokwug! *There shall be no more… no more of this nonsensical behaviour!* Morale shall not be dented more than morale is already… is already dented! This is exactly what Jonathan North wants. Go and stand in the corner and think about… think about your actions!'

Whilst Larry lay comatose, Backeyedjection began frantically gesturing that events had taken a decided turn for the worse. War was looming all too rapidly. To calm the raving, trouble-causing masses and to put an end to the maddening drifting crowds, leaders worldwide blamed other nations for the disorders and troubles.

Strengths of power placed on show, with some nations displaying the might of their military. Some states had mobilised troops to the borders. A few smaller countries, who already had strained relationships with each other for years, had started firing potshots: a missile here and one in response there.

Nations were forging alliances, and three opposing factions were emerging. Meanwhile, the furious mob had infiltrated Downing Street, the White House, and the Kremlin.

Reasoning was like cloud dust; it couldn't be found, no matter where one searched. The politicians and the armed forces chiefs, all those wielding some authority, were also beginning to suffer the effects of being unable to wish, some having lost all hope.

None had ever been placed under such pressure before, so naturally, they acted out what humankind does best: preparing for self-destruction through war.

Enacting all the bravado nonsense, not one was prepared to back down; to be seen as weak, it would soon be Sapiens' curtain call.

'Herrifurus, why don't you grant all the wishes that you can from the Fully Fledged Enclosure? Wouldn't this help alleviate the shortage of hope in my world? Let's try it before the Grottlers get to destroy them!'

'Absolutely, Harlem, absolutely!' replied a perkier Herrifurus. 'Why didn't... why... didn't... I think of that? This instant, what a splendid... a splendid notion. Of course... *of...* course... this will help fill the void of hope. *Stupendous... stupendous idea.*'

It was a stupendous idea; the only problem was that Jonathan North had foreseen this and had somehow overridden the system, blocking the granting of wishes. No matter how many times Herrifurus attempted to grant a wish, and no matter what the wish was for, it was 'access denied'.

Each time a wish was granted, a cartoon image of Jonathan North tutting and raising his eyebrows appeared on the monitor.

*'When I get my hands...* my... hands... on that blighter, I will give him... give him what for! The impudent rascal. You just... you just wait... you wait, Jonathan North. *I will send... will send you southwards!'*

Herrifurus was seething to the point where steam appeared to be escaping erratically from his ears. He was crimson with rage; he desperately wanted to give Jonathan North what he deserved.

'The Fully Fledged systems are down!' shrieked Monocle Sway. 'The Grottlers are coming! Those poor defenceless wishes may as well paint a target on their backs.'

Herrifurus was now letting off more steam than ten saunas combined.

'Herrifurus, I have to go,' asserted Harlem. 'You're going to have to forgive me, but I think I may know who destroyed the Cobbles of Hankering... It's only a hunch, but it might just hold water.'

'Ok, Harlem, but before... before you go, please help me... help me put Larry Cornelius to bed.'

Seeing the two clumsily and haphazardly carrying Larry down the mezzanine ladder and then up the spiral staircase was a sight. Herrifurus was so befuddled by Jonathan North that the quicker, rational route of exiting the boiler room again escaped him. Even though Larry was small, it was hard to move him as he was a dead weight, fast asleep.

Harlem and Herrifurus each grabbed a leg and pulled and yanked Larry up the spiral staircase. It was an almighty endeavour to get to the top, and Herrifurus appeared ready to collapse from exhaustion.

Once in the ballroom, Herrifurus lay himself down on the freezing floor and attempted to suck in all the oxygen on site.

Harlem giggled, although he knew it wasn't appropriate. It was a sight to see; both Larry and Herrifurus lay down, side by side. One was unconscious, the other unfit.

After fifteen minutes, Larry was, without deference, dragged up the stairwell behind the secret hidden door next to the bar. The cold, echoing stone stairwell led up to the magnificent, red sapphire dome on top of the Calace.

Larry's bedroom was situated underneath the dome. Harlem and Herrifurus gently lay the jester down on his bed.

'Harlem, please wait… wait a few minutes while I make Larry a mug of Wake Up as Right as Rain Tonic. I will be back in an instant!'

This tonic consisted of two crushed teeth from the Sabre-Tooth Tiger, one tablespoon of human tears, one egg yolk from the egg of the dodo, a pinch of Mokwug's rage, one whole withered orange peel, a dash of salt and a tablespoon of cane syrup. Oh, and 50mls of brandy. All mixed in with two nostril hairs from a Woolly Mammoth.

Harlem stared at Larry; what a plucky and courageous, yet stupid, comment to make to Mokwug that had been. Harlem was now more than aware of what could come his way if he, too, were impertinent again towards Mokwug.

The booms and tremors pressed onwards and upwards towards the top of the Calace. Larry's bedroom light fared no differently. The Grottlers remained restless.

Herrifurus eventually returned and poured the Wake Up as Right as Rain Tonic down Larry's throat. Larry woke up right as rain but immediately began venting his anger about the absent Mokwug before declaring 'goodnight'. Larry rolled over in a huff and fell asleep immediately.

'Herrifurus, do we only have a day or so left?' implored Harlem.

'At best... at... best... if we are lucky; who knows? *Man's situation worsens by the second; go and follow... and follow your suspicions.'*

A brief time later, Harlem again made the school his primary focus.

Harlem was determined to establish communication with Symptom-Hazard, but would the shadow be willing to reveal himself once more? Only time would provide the answer.

The following morning, Harlem, now dressed in camouflage, had crawled no more than thirty feet into Mucky Waters. He rested flat on his stomach, disguised and spying on the surrounding areas with his binoculars.

Remembering an old pair of green and black combat trousers and a T-shirt in his wardrobe had brought about this not-so-bright idea.

Dressed in combat gear, he covered himself in face paint — green, brown, and black — added a few twigs and leaves, and he was ready to drop in behind enemy lines. He would be in stealth mode and would go undetected!

Lying motionless, Harlem believed his combat attire had the opposite effect. Harlem felt ludicrous, carrying the notion that he stood out like a clown juggling next to a vicar while the clergyman gave his speech at a funeral.

It was hardly inconspicuous.

However, no one could distinguish Harlem; he hadn't invaded far enough into this unforgiving territory.

Harlem must not let himself be identified by the BinBags; they would surely give his game away if they spotted him.

It had been a poor decision to come here alone. Harlem couldn't exactly travel beyond the swamps and bogs. What if something happened to him? Should he fall into a swamp, he would sink, and no one would be any the wiser.

Harlem retreated, inching and wriggling himself to the very edge of Mucky Waters. He hid in the overgrown field on the outskirts of this horrible, reeking, long-forgotten wilderness. His covert mission was to uncover whatever it was that he was searching for.

What was hiding in there that held so much of Harlem's attention? Why was this place so vehemently occupying his mind, especially when the world was so close to the final war? Something didn't sit right in Mucky Waters.

Time continued to ebb away, and back in the other world, it was becoming increasingly credible that the end was nigh. Diplomacy was still sought, but couldn't be found amidst all the anger, resentment, anarchy, madness, and hatred. With no solution, then, the outcome would be blood, death, fire and then nothing – the end.

Harlem remembered his experience within the Inverted Blue Pyramid. When we are at our lowest point – rock bottom – we rise, for it cannot get worse. What could be more disagreeable than the destruction of all life on Planet Earth? This was the most sunken Harlem would ever feel - his very own rock bottom. There wasn't much time, but perhaps enough to come out on top. Harlem still carried hope as he returned to the Calace of Judgement.

Harlem no longer cared about his appearance as he accessed Operation Flog a Dead Horse, despite the giggles and pointing fingers aimed his way. The Wantwots tittered, reasoning that Harlem looked absurd dressed in his disguise. Somehow, he had managed to create a little light relief. Now it was time to go to work; it was time to earn his real stripes.

Backeyedjection, Monocle Sway and Herrifurus were present on top of the mezzanine. Mokwug was sulking and seething elsewhere, and as for Larry Cornelius, he was in bed with a concussion—the Wake Up as Right as Rain Tonic hadn't worked perfectly.

Monocle Sway buzzed on over to Harlem.

'*I say*, young chap, can this really be the moment to play toy soldiers? If you wait a day, you can participate in the real act… though it will be over frightfully lively.'

'Monocle, I'm not playing games… certainly not war games. Herrifurus, you need to come with me now! *No arguing*, let's be off!'

'Harlem, you will hear no protests from me… *from*… me… but where are we… are we going?' enquired Herrifurus.

'You'll see,' replied Harlem.

Shortly afterwards, Herrifurus and Harlem were crouched in the overgrown field at the border of Mucky Waters. Harlem had been here himself not too long ago. Herrifurus confusedly stood up.

'Kneel, will you, Herrifurus!' demanded Harlem.

Unsure why they had come here, Herrifurus probed in his unique way.

'When I see more than one person… one person… sticking out a hand to catch the same bus… it doesn't make sense. *Is it a game*… a… game? Five folks at the bus stop… do they all feel the need… the need… to throw out their hand? Are they cheated without participation? Strange activity… for it takes one… takes one… to catch the driver's attention. *It makes no sense at all*. Harlem, I don't understand why we are here. *This, too, doesn't make any sense…*'

Harlem stared in confusion at Herrifurus. The only one that did not make sense was Herrifurus.

'Herrifurus, *listen to me!* Jonathan North is in Mucky Waters. The one area of Enduring Crave that nobody ever visits. He's at liberty to come and go unnoticed. This is where his portal to this world is located; you would never know it was there. Over sixty years ago, he made a wish, but you held back and refused to grant it. After months of distancing himself, he had concocted his plan with those Wantwots who no longer had a purpose. Jonathan North had a route into Enduring Crave…

and not just through Pressing Matters Lane. No one knew of his schemes, for he never once gave any indication of his evil machinations… Don't blame yourself, Herrifurus, but he came here repeatedly to conspire. I'm afraid to say that Jonathan gave these Wantwots a determination and a revenge… in the darkest and most disconsolate area of Mucky Waters.'

'To the centre… *make haste…* make… haste with me! *Right now, and straightway.* Follow me…follow me' declared Herrifurus.

'No need to walk, Herrifurus. I'll spare your legs, look at this.'

Harlem gleefully pointed at a yellow amphibious vehicle, a miniature hovercraft concealed by the wild grass. A white wooden door and frame were hanging out of the back seats of the hovercraft. A second door and frame were lying on the grass.

'*Where the blazes…* the… blazes… did you get this? Do you care to… care to… explain… Harlem?'

'Not yet, Herrifurus, come on… let's be off!'

The two hopped into the hovercraft, and Harlem put his foot down hard on the accelerator. The amphibious vehicle charged off ahead, gliding over the swamps and bogs, through the trees and knocking over several BinBags in its path. The hovercraft and its two occupants had quickly become coated in filth and mud.

'*Blast it…* blast… it… I hadn't planned a bath until… *until Christmas of next year!*' grumbled Herrifurus.

Upon reaching the centre of Mucky Waters, the engine ceased, and the hovercraft came to rest at the edge of a small bog adjacent to the path.

'Where did all the Wantwots sneak off to? We haven't come across any of the turncoats, have we? Wait until… until I get my hands… *my hands on them!*'

'*In there*, Herrifurus!'

Harlem gestured and nodded to the largest swamp in Mucky Waters. The swamp resided on the opposite side of the tangled path.

On Harlem's first visit through Mucky Waters, something didn't appear quite right, but he hadn't considered it much until now.

'It isn't a real swamp; it's a fake! It's a sunken building, with the roof designed to fit in with the surroundings. It looks like a swamp, but it isn't. It's a plain old roof with mud, slime, and duckweed on top!'

Harlem did the unbelievable; he exited the hovercraft and charged down the path before leaping straight onto the swamp. Inconceivably, he didn't sink; it was a solid roof, precisely as he had suspected. Herrifurus followed, completely mystified at Harlem's discovery.

Tangled and tucked away between reeds and water lilies, Harlem stumbled upon a roof hatch. After forcibly twisting the handle, he heaved the hatch open. Harlem and Herrifurus instantly peered inside to see what lay in the unknown depths below.

What was unearthed resembled Operation Flog a Dead Horse, but on a considerably smaller scale. The room was devoid of life, but it was evident that recent activity had taken place here in this bunker. Every smart screen continued showing live events concerning the Grottlers' actions.

Whilst Herrifurus attempted to comprehend the technology he was staring at, he held the unnerving feeling that it was applied science he wasn't aware of; all present-day mechanics, technology, and gadgets – all far superior to the outdated machinery in the Calace.

'Herrifurus, this is where the orders are directed to the Grottlers. It's from here that Jonathan and his allies operate. They've created a new technology which deliberately wrecks wishes, overriding and destabilising the command at the Calace. This is sixty years in the making... Herrifurus, who came up with the idea to build the Calace?'

'It was Monocle Sway. He was most persistent... *most*... persistent... Stating that we must upgrade to new engineering. *Why... why do you ask?*'

'Just wondering,' answered Harlem.

'The Wantwots were to leave no trace... no trace of the old '60s hardware behind. As we moved into the Calace, the obsolete gadgets were fired... were fired into the Sun. Alas, our so-called modern engineering is but decades old. We simply do not have a big enough budget to keep up with today's smarts,' groaned Herrifurus.

'Herrifurus, I think for the most part, the old equipment was sent to the Sun. But what if the Wantwots from Mucky Waters snuck in and stole enough apparatus to make this bunker their operational base, all instigated by Jonathan North and his confidante, who built the bunker in the ensuing years? Reverse engineering your instruments and bolstering new devices and advanced technology as time passed, so his plan was ready to commence when he was free. A dastardly scheme to destroy the cobbles, smash granted hope, and override you to permit wishes in the Fully Fledged Enclosure. It was all ordered from within this hidden den, but what irks me is that the Calace was built after that swine was sent to the school... so how does he know about the Calace? How did he adapt?'

'Harlem,' replied an emotional Herrifurus, 'are you saying there is a traitor... *a traitor*... in Enduring Crave? *Are you, are you?*'

'Exactly! Jonathan couldn't do this alone with just the Wantwots from Mucky Waters. There's a traitor in this world! A traitor who was pivotal to the plot!'

Herrifurus dropped to his knees, placing his head in his hands before bursting into tears.

Harlem tried his best to comfort him, but it was no use. The soft and tender approach wasn't working, so Harlem sensed that he needed to be sterner.

'Get up, man! What's wrong with you? Planet Earth could be destroyed real soon, and you're on the floor, sobbing like a baby. Let me get you your warm bottle of milk! Stand up, man, and be counted. You're supposed to put humankind first. We can deal with the traitor when we win - we must win. Now, stand up and do your job! Show your true bottle!'

Herrifurus ploddingly stood upright, urgently wiping the tears from both eyes.

'Thank you, Harlem, for those… for those much-needed words. *You are quite right*… quite… right… *I will box the traitor's ears when I find out who it is*… who… it…is…'

The two peered down into the bunker once more.

'Hold on, Herrifurus, *wait one minute*. Let's play toy soldiers for real!'

To Herrifurus' utter bewilderment, Harlem now inexplicably held a grenade in his right hand – where on earth had that come from? Grinning at his companion's dumbstruck expression, Harlem deftly pulled out the pin and dropped the grenade through the roof hatch. Harlem and Herrifurus hurriedly dived out of the way as an ear-splitting explosion ripped apart the inside of the recently discovered bunker.

'Another one for good measure!' remarked Harlem.

Harlem tossed a second grenade into the operations room while Herrifurus could only look on, aghast. This follow-up detonation finally ended the unsolicited mischief as the entire interior of the base was blown to fragments.

'Herrifurus, get hold of Monocle Sway right now! Find out the position of the Grottlers!'

Babbling over the phone, Monocle jovially informed the two that the Grottlers had laid down arms. Travels to the human world had all but ceased. The Whitewash Woodland was noticeably quiet at last. Harlem could overhear the Wantwots celebrating in the background, but an individual standing behind them immediately interrupted the short-lived moment of joy in Mucky Waters.

'BRAVO, BRAVO, BUT THE SHOW DOES GO ON!'

The roar had alarmed Harlem and Herrifurus, who pivoted to find Jonathan North slowly clapping his hands.

'Now don't be smug, *my less than fine fellows*,' Jonathan's voice was urgent. 'My secret bunker had done all it needed to do. *Goodness gracious*, Herrifurus, you look... *how do I put this*... you look... terrible! Have I been on your mind? For you have been foremost in my thoughts. The days have not been kind to you... *yet*... I invariably remain the same. Do not be swallowed by self-satisfaction; this is just a minor hindrance, for my plan is almost complete. Four billion Grottlers have been terminated, as have the smashed cobbles. No new wishes are being attended to... well, boo-hoo! Do you think humanity is upset with me?'

'Jonathan, two worlds will be destroyed by this,' reasoned Harlem. 'This one and ours.'

'Don't you see, Harlem?' replied Jonathan, 'once I hold what I want, then none of this will ever have happened. But in the improbable event that I fail... *then so be it!* The world can say goodnight if I don't get what I want. Please excuse me and forgive my short stay. I must be off; I have an appointment at the Calace of Judgement. I wouldn't bother chasing me... not that you are capable, Herrifurus, toodle-oo.'

Jonathan scampered away laughing, but before Harlem could give chase, a swarm of sickly-looking Wantwots dived-bombed the two. It was an assault that lasted around five minutes.

The Wantwots were incapable of causing harm, but there were so many that Herrifurus and Harlem could not escape the swarm.

Then, as quickly as the attack had begun, it was over. Jonathan had disappeared, using the confusion to escape. Harlem and Herrifurus returned to the hovercraft dejectedly.

'Take us to the Calace... the Calace... at once—this *instant and right away*. We must arrive before he does; Jonathan has the jump... the jump on us. Let's be off, I say!'

'Herrifurus, Jonathan North isn't heading to the Calace now. He wants us to panic and give chase. He'll arrive in his own time and in all his glory. Let's go and gaze at the horizon.'

The hovercraft speedily raced away from Mucky Waters, leaving it safely behind in the distance. Upon arriving at the Path of the Life, the horizon had developed large, thunderous, ear-splitting cracks and had severely weakened, becoming increasingly faded. Conspiring black clouds were circling overhead.

'The actions of either world will impact the other. The boundaries of Enduring Crave are preparing for the worst. Inclement tides are shifting into... into this world. If Jonathan wins, we will be no more. If war is the answer, then we shall say goodnight as the planet erupts... *as the planet erupts*... If we win, and win we must, then the boundaries will... will rebuild.'

If Jonathan were to get his hands on the lantern, then yes, it could be the end of Enduring Crave. He had penetrated it once, and now he had more help than he did over twenty-one thousand nine hundred days ago.

'Harlem, this mind control you speak of; it unsettles me. Where did... *where*... *did*... Jonathan obtain this deviousness?'

'Herrifurus, I wouldn't worry about that for now... let's focus on the lantern and the cobbles. Come on, we need to make our way to the Calace.'

Before heading to the Calace of Judgement, it was essential that Harlem first return to the marquee. Harlem desired to stash the hovercraft out of sight; it would be their secret for now.

# CHAPTER SIXTEEN

## Fighting Wrongs

Harlem and Herrifurus headed straight for the ballroom within the Calace of Judgement. Despite the room being gigantic, cold, and unwelcoming, the ballroom walls still glistened majestically. The four scarlet-marbled, diamond-encrusted walls radiated wondrous displays of beaming ruby light.

'The lantern is secured... is secured and hidden in this wall. If that rotter removes it, a chain reaction shall commence. The Calace will rumble, the foundations will plunge to their knees... *Maybe not right away, but soon!* The cracks will not... will... not... end here... They will separate and head in all... in all directions of Enduring Crave. Increasingly, this world will fracture and ultimately disintegrate. Whether Jonathan succeeds in stealing a wish or not, removing the lantern shall be the... the deciding factor!'

'*Why*, what's changed?' asked an astonished Harlem. 'What if he just takes the lantern but can't access it? Why would Enduring Crave end? It doesn't make sense.'

'The Eight Curators have watched and asked themselves... and... asked themselves... how much time and help does humankind need? Twenty thousand years, and we are still spoon-feeding them. There comes a time... a time... when even the most persistent patience runs dry. Don't blame a clown for acting like a clown - stop going to the circus! Man's actions over the last few days have led them to conclude. However, if we defeat this royal pain from the rear, the Curators may think... *may*... think twice!'

Herrifurus cautiously glanced around the ballroom, ensuring no one was eavesdropping.

He motioned to the lantern's approximate location within the wall.

'Harlem, the lantern is impossible to identify; embedded within the diamonds of the wall. The powerful ruby radiation overpowers the golden rays illuminating the lantern. *Impossible*... impossible... for him to place his dirty mitts on the Lantern of Infinite Wishes!'

Beyond the Doors of Red Envy, an immense sense of relief was felt due to the Grottlers having been halted from their mischievous doings. A small victory: one battle won, but the war wasn't over.

On top of the mezzanine, Harlem and Herrifurus were ambushed once more by Mokwug.

'Took you long enough! Four billion of those darlings were destroyed, and for what? Very belated it is, so do not make merry in your achievement!'

'*Buzz off*, Mokwug!' insisted Monocle Sway. '*Buzz off*, why don't you?'

'YOU BUZZ OFF, MONOCLE!' snarled Mokwug.

Monocle decided it was wise to widen the gap between himself and Mokwug, becoming a shrinking violet. Herrifurus placed his face in his hands and shook his head despairingly before turning to Backeyedjection.

'*Backeyedjection, I demand an urgent update.* What goes on... goes on in the human world?' he enquired.

'Four billion lost Grottlers has taken its toll,' stipulated Backeyedjection. 'Man's endurance diminishes as we speak. With the inability to wish added to the dilemma, time is fast running out.'

The fools locked within their underground bunkers were getting itchy fingers. The red buttons could soon be pressed. With a shortage of hope, there was no reason to continue. These fools would take the whole world into that last goodnight. But with a glimmer of hope, it would be so different.

The rhetoric spewing from the mouths of world leaders signalled that the end was fast approaching. The three opposing factions had ordered a one-hour deadline. In sixty minutes, the red buttons would be operational. The world and its population were in a frenzy. Pre-Armageddon was such an abominable time.

This was not the moment to surrender, nor the time to raise the white flag.

Harlem was thinking firmly, but what was he overlooking? And then the realisation arrived... 'Harlem means vanquisher!'

'What... what... was that... *what was that*?' replied Herrifurus.

'Herrifurus, the message I received – do you daydream of living in a fantasy of a village? You sent them, didn't you? You know which one I mean. It wasn't Father Time; it was your doings, where is Vincent Gassison?!'

'Guilty... guilty as charged. The messages, visual or otherwise, were only... were only paintings in your mind. My dear friend Vincent Garrison is missing; he has been taken and *time-napped* for fifty-nine years, but when and where? He is in danger; I just wanted to gaze at him one last time, so I included him in my communication with you, allowing me to tune in and contact you via your snow globe outside my office, eight globes... for the eight children of Human. Only one is broken... that of Jonathan North. Very seldom do we take this action. It has only been afforded to the descendants of Godfrey North, and now you; it isn't for anyone and everyone; that would... would be unwise!'

When Harlem enquired if Herrifurus had sent the images of the witches to Harlem, Herrifurus was stumped and shocked. He had no answer, for it was the first he knew of Harlem's sightings of the witches, or as Harlem now knew them - the BinBags.

Was it possible that they had gotten inside Harlem's head? Perhaps when Enduring Crave opened up to Harlem, the BinBags took advantage of this opening to make their grim announcement.

Harlem now inexplicably held a megaphone to his mouth. Of course, it wasn't the first time that day that Herrifurus had seen him holding objects that seemingly came from nowhere, but the Ambassador was too distracted by the urgent situation to comment.

'Attention, Wantwots: listen up!' demanded Harlem. 'Take note, we need calm heads both in this room and in the human world. Start sending paintings to your people —every man, every woman, and every child aged twelve and above. Tell them: go home and make a wish, for dreams and wishes are just minutes away. *Do it now*, go home to wish, you will be heard!'

The Wantwots began carrying out Harlem's instructions as fast and chaotically as a whirlwind. Every monitor was switched back on. The Wantwots, stationed at their desks, pulled out snow globes, tiny pieces of paper, and pens from the drawer. The message that Harlem had dictated was feverishly noted down.

The paper was astonishingly inserted and then shredded inside the globe, and when the Wantwots began shaking the globes, the snow fell. Communication had been sent to half of the world's population.

Because the whole world was awake, the Wantwots immediately swapped places at the desks so their colleagues could send messages to those who should have been asleep.

The process was repeated until everyone who still carried the right to wish received their mind art. Would this work? Could this make the humans see sense?

Four minutes later, Backeyedjection began hopping up and down with great glee.

The crowds in the street were dispersing; the citizens were heading home. It was a glimmer of hope, as those on the move included politicians and military leaders.

Herrifurus and Harlem were aware that they had only bought time. The pressing of red buttons would only be delayed. Harlem once more held the megaphone to his mouth.

'Wantwots: please listen. We have bought some time, but this is merely a temporary measure, for it will soon become apparent to humans that their wishes are not forthcoming. Folks may be able to say, "I wish", but it won't be long before the realisation again hits that there is still no hope. *Unless that is…* the cobbles are restored. Monocle, Mokwug, remain here - tune into the CCTV along the Cobbles of Hankering!'

Harlem and Herrifurus immediately descended the ladder and aimed for the boiler room. It was essential for Harlem to take one more look at the Childhood tree in the centre of Wishwisely.

It was a sorry sight as they hastily headed down the ruined cobbled path.

Upon entering Harlem's world at the gravel track, Herrifurus requested a short rest to catch his breath, which Harlem refused; both immediately twisted and headed towards the tree. Harlem experienced an almighty shiver running through his body. This was the signal; it was time to return to Enduring Crave.

Their extremely brief trip was complete.

The return walk to the whopping rock should have been much quicker, but Herrifurus slowed proceedings down.

When they finally arrived, it was time for Harlem to give the order.

'THE COBBLES OF HANKERING, GET HANKERING!'

As soon as Harlem uttered those words, the most insane, unbelievably mind-blowing chain reaction began. The cobbles started to repair themselves. It was as if Harlem and Herrifurus were watching the destruction in reverse. The cracks receded, and the uprooted cobbles returned to their original positions. Smashed cobbles became whole once again. Cobbles flew back to their position within the path.

The two were standing and watching the carnage, which was being played back at twice the speed of real-time. Within sixty seconds, the Cobbles of Hankering had been restored to the perfect formation they had lain in for over twenty thousand years. It was a phenomenal piece of engineering.

Herrifurus stared at the young boy before him; how could he have known how to communicate with the cobbles in such a way?

Ten seconds later, Herrifurus was distracted as a wish flashed down the cobbles, immediately followed by a second.

After two minutes, over seventy million wishes whizzed along the cobbles and onto the Calace of Judgement.

After five minutes, the total number of wishes exceeded two billion. Due to the events of the last few days, it was understandable for humankind to dream so desperately. The cobbles were quaking fiercely, with no intention of slowing.

'The cobbles will handle... will... handle the aggression... They celebrate... celebrate... alongside humankind. *The cobbles are in joyous mode*. Harlem, I do not... do not know how you did it. *Jolly good*... jolly... good... but dare I ask how?'

'*Sorry*,' responded Harlem, reluctantly. 'You'll need to wait a little longer. Come on, let's head to your office.'

'*I could run*... could run... a mile in celebration... *in celebration!*' bragged Herrifurus.

'*No*, you couldn't, Herrifurus, you liar!' laughed Harlem.

'I suppose... I... suppose... *I couldn't*... I couldn't!' chuckled Herrifurus.

The two were again ambushed by Mokwug, who was waiting to pounce in Herrifurus' office. Her mood had not improved. 'You, *boy*, from that human lot, how did you fix the cobbles?'

'I didn't,' responded Harlem. 'But I know who did; say hello to Symptom-Hazard.'

The shadow emerged from within Harlem, giving Mokwug the fright of her life. She began jabbing at Symptom-Hazard, but, made of shadows as he was, her fists passed straight through him. Two minutes later, she was still shadowboxing. Eventually, she wore herself out and dropped dejectedly into the chair.

Symptom-Hazard looked exhausted just from watching her.

'*I say*, is the old girl always like that?' he asked aghast.

'*I'm afraid that is the case*... that... is the case. *She knows no better*... no... better!' replied an embarrassed Herrifurus.

'Herrifurus, this is Symptom-Hazard, General of the Shadow Squatters. The ones who restored the cobbles. Symptom-Hazard -please allow your squad to reveal themselves.'

A second shadow-being emerged, this time from within the General. A third appeared from inside the second shadow.

Each time a shadow appeared, a new shadow emerged from the one before, like strange Russian nesting dolls, until ninety-nine shadows and Symptom-Hazard filled the room.

*'My limitless tidings to you all...* to you... all. *Thank you...* thank... you!'

'No, Herrifurus, our endless apologies to you!' expressed Symptom-Hazard. 'Jonathan North forced our hand. He despatched the Demon of Daric to snatch us, for we are the only lifeform who could destroy the cobbles in such a fashion. They ransacked the first two universes, prowling for ones who could perform such impairment. Once the cobbles were destroyed, our purpose was served. The wait for destruction was complete once you two departed for your walk around Wishwisely - a trip I mind-bent and coerced you both to take... After the ruination, we were abandoned and trapped in the portal. Jonathan no longer had a purpose for us, but we escaped inside you, Harlem. We have no idea what other misdeeds he might be slyly concocting. Jonathan demanded access to our power, arguing that once we capture a shadow, we can read its mind or even mind-bend it. Jonathan used us for his own ends, be it controlling the landlord from the pub, taking the memories from your friends, or keeping you and your parents asleep. We defied his order; we awoke you in time. Every peculiar activity was ordered by Jonathan but effectuated by a squatter. Great power comes to those willing to listen to the whispers of their spirit instead of shouting to the world... Notwithstanding reading and hearing Jonathan's commands, his mind is an unwritten page, as if the ability to pry into his thoughts or, indeed, mind-bend him had been cut off and sealed away in an impenetrable vault... Herrifurus, beware: a being travels to school to rendezvous with Jonathan. An underling under the darkest clouds... that even the Shadow Squatters are rendered blind, we were still ordered to disperse whenever the subordinate was enroute. I believed it was the demon, but it is indeed your traitor.'

'When I discover this backstabber... this... backstabber... the culprit... the culprit will beg... will beg for my forgiveness,' shrieked Herrifurus. 'I will show them the road to what for! But Harlem, I must... I must enquire, I must... I must! How did you know about General Hazard and the Shadow Squatters?'

'Even before I moved to Wishwisely, I saw shadows in my room manoeuvring on the ceiling. As the days passed, I caught a glimpse of them several times; these shadows are gifted at staying out of sight, so were they intentionally revealing themselves? A nightmare I had presented me with a new puzzle. In my dream, I was searching for Jonathan in school... and he and several shadows were on stage playing in a band. When I woke up, I knew they were working together, but I had no idea why. I figured out what was happening only after Symptom-Hazard came forward at the school. When I returned, I asked the General if he could restore the cobbles and reverse the destruction his team had caused. He told me they could; they had already secured the Meadow of Purple Purpose gate as a show of remorse. Shadows are a peculiar phenomenon; they can appear in front of or behind us. We rarely see what shadows are doing from behind. Shadows can be withdrawn or up close and personal, very definitive, or not. It all depends on the light; these shadows had seen the light. They regrouped and waited in Wishwisely. I had to be one hundred percent certain before taking action. After we destroyed the bunker, I knew I had heard the truth. Symptom-Hazard approached me when he could have remained hidden. On my orders, the Shadow Squatters reversed their actions on the Cobbles of Hankering. For those sixty seconds, they made amends. The shadows were working from behind. It's incredible what they can do from behind!'

'Jonathan and that incessant song!' added General Hazard. 'Harlem, Jonathan would sing to us on the hour, *every hour*. You must work out what it means!'

Harlem insisted that the Shadow Squatters be allowed to leave; he would escort them back to Wishwisely.

Clasping onto the back of Symptom-Hazard, Harlem flew with the shadows over the topsy-turvy, shaking cobbles until they had passed beyond.

Back at the Childhood tree, the General advised Harlem that for their crimes of betraying Jonathan and the demon, Planet Permeatus would likely be destroyed.

The shadows apologetically bid farewell and departed, but not before stating they would cross paths again.

There was no chance that Harlem would be able to stroll his way back to Enduring Crave. Humans were making endless wishes that meant the energetic shaking and quaking of the cobbles were not safe or practical for walking on at this time.

That didn't matter, as Harlem now had a jetpack that enabled a speedy and safe flight back to the office. He discarded the jetpack outside the rock, and as Harlem entered the office, Mokwug struck.

'*Well*, boy? You, from that human lot! How long have you known about the Shadow Squatters? Tell me, I do not trust you! Herrifurus, Harlem is dishonest and holds back secrets. Just another Jonathan North in the making, a carbon copy!'

'*Want to be angry… to be angry, do we?* After all this boy has done, still you cannot say 'well done' or 'thank you'… *You horrible, craggy grunter*! I will give you a reason to be mad… a real reason… a… real… reason. WATCH THIS!'

Herrifurus gazed into Mokwug's eyes.

'Are you watching, Mokwug? Do your eyes… do your eyes follow? *Do they follow me, do they, do they, I say?*'

Herrifurus grabbed the neat and orderly papers from his desk and hurled them at Mokwug. Next, he yanked out several books from the wallpaper and tossed them around the room before tearing and ripping away large sections of wallpaper.

'Do you see what I am doing? I am acting ungrateful for all the hard work that you did for me; I show… I show no gratitude. Disrespecting and expressing no understanding… no… understanding of your emotions. Take these flowers and return them to the tulip fields. Do it… do… it… at once… AT ONCE!'

Mokwug, head down, gathered the flowers from the bookshelf and departed the office. Herrifurus had made his point. He calmly composed himself as he pulled down and straightened his poncho.

'What a pain in the backside... the... backside... *How that woman cannot say thanks is beyond me*! Is it not obvious that not all of humanity is like Jonathan North? In her eyes, you all have the potential to be.'

Enduring Crave was not home and dry just yet. Jonathan North remained in this realm and would not stop at any cost until he had the Lantern of Infinite Wishes within his grasp.

'Harlem, we have had a great victory today; be it not all for nothing. It would be futile to have saved... have saved humankind in the short term if we cannot... cannot rescue Motherhood. Save Sapiens from themselves whilst we go down in flames; mankind will abruptly follow. Have we just... just delayed the inevitable?'

'No!' replied Harlem. 'We still have time... how much time, I don't know. Let's prepare for one last showdown with him, who has been stuck in time. Come on, back to the Calace!'

As the two descended the spiral staircase, it was business as usual in Operation Flog a Deadhorse, with wish after wish plummeting onto the conveyor belt, which was functioning on overdrive.

Harlem peered into the channel at the start of the Stream of Mean Dreams Returned to Human Beings. Already, and so soon, drip after drip of unending human stool and excrement had filled the now almost overflowing stream.

Typical humans, despite the near wipe-out, many wishes that arrived and continued to do so contained selfishness. People's priorities were misguided, failing to prioritise the collective good of humankind. Just looking at the drops of vile backside egotism, it was evident to Harlem that some folks would never change.

There had been a brief celebration when the wishes returned to the cobbles. The Wantwots had joyously set off party streamers and tossed confetti around the gigantic room. That merrymaking had long finished as the Wantwots were now back working resolutely.

Mokwug had returned and couldn't leave things be, not even for one minute. She was upset about the mess, annoyed that the room had been cleaned thoroughly just recently.

'IF YOU THINK I'M TIDYING THIS MESS UP, YOU'RE VERY MUCH MISTAKEN!' she yelled, but no one was listening.

'Herrifurus, we wait for Jonathan North,' declared Harlem. 'We could move the Calace, but he would find us in no time. Revenge guides him; he wants his wish… and that's it!'

A few minutes later, a hungover and still slightly confused and concussed Larry Cornelius haphazardly stumbled over the mezzanine floor.

'What's going on? How have the Wantwots returned to their stations? The last thing I recall was a pervasive sense of doom and gloom, and it felt utterly hopeless. The Cobbles had been destroyed,' he mumbled, blinking confusedly.

'It was… it… was, Larry, *but not anymore…* not… anymore. How bad… how bad is your head?' chuckled Herrifurus.

Larry was in complete shock. Before he was walloped, everyone had been highly pessimistic. But now there was hope across the world, hope in both worlds; yet still, time passed, and the wishes of humankind continued to drop in. It would all have been for nothing if Jonathan North had the last laugh.

# CHAPTER SEVENTEEN

## The Storming of the Calace

Those unfortunate enough to be amid the lengthy, dejecting interlude on the mezzanine floor, were somehow able to withstand Mokwug's insufferable antics, who tutted relentlessly and unnecessarily flung her arms about in dramatic fashion.

Mokwug seemed intent on making this the 'Mokwug show'.

Herrifurus frowned indignantly; his loyal assistant was becoming an overbearing nuisance; she had become a monster-sized burden.

Perhaps the translation of Mokwug carried a new meaning; mankind was no longer a burden from afar. Now, it was her presenting a further weight to carry, one that she imposed on her colleagues.

The wait for Jonathan's arrival made Harlem think deeply about recent developments. What did Philip Day mean when asked if Harlem had come to save them? Margo then added the narrative of Jonathan hurting them and that Jonathan dances with the Devil; what did that stand for? Why did his friends ache with migraines when mentioning Jonathan? Another puzzle was Symptom-Hazard's reference to Jonathan's song. Harlem pressed, stirred, and prodded the depths of his mind for telltale clues and answers.

'Herrifurus,' began Harlem, 'the wish Jonathan stole from the lantern sixty years ago…'

'Which wish... *which wish, I say?*' mumbled Herrifurus.

'The one he used as revenge on the bullies at school. The one where a new breed of mean now roughed up Jonathan's bullies. You said it was all set in the past!'

'Alas, why do you... do you... speak of this... of this... wish now?' replied an increasingly ill-tempered Herrifurus, whose cheeks were now glowing.

'You never destroyed it, *did you?* You haven't been able to find it,' expressed Harlem.

'*Must I say...* I... say alas... once more? Harlem, you are correct... the wish still eludes me. We have explored all frontiers, but alas... alas... the wish does evade.'

'Jonathan doesn't own it,' replied Harlem. 'Until recently, he assumed the Grottlers had smashed it. He was completely stumped when he saw Margo and the gang outside school.'

'Casualties of war... of... war! Harlem, those four chums of yours were indeed... were... indeed... Jonathan's bullies, but his lust for revenge overstepped the mark... Your friends are to be captive hereafter, for eternity... *for...* eternity... with no escape, eternal damnation with pain, misery and endless suffering from the very name and thought of Jonathan North. Until the wish reveals the hidden location from where it is concealed, they remain ill-fated, unremembered, and tossed aside by all but one of humankind. *Oh, I have meddled as far as one can... can possibly meddle...* We keep an eye out; old Wormpick looks in on them, but a wish remains unbroken. I cannot... cannot... interfere with concessions as there is an absent wish to *concess* with! Education and endless innocent games help to alleviate their pain ever... ever... so slightly. Mercifully, that imp Jonathan was himself trapped in time, which limited the nightmarish reality of your friends and allowed Jonathan to be ignorant of them in school. But the one who pilfered the wish remains hidden... remains hidden... in the call of time!'

'Herrifurus, it's been said that Jonathan dances with the Devil,' expressed Harlem. 'It's possible the Devil has it. Not the actual Devil, but an entity that could be misidentified as such - I mean the Demon of Daric!' After a long pause, Harlem added to his collection of questions. 'Herrifurus, *who* is Wormpick?'

'WHAT'S THIS NOW?' yelled Mokwug with an overbearing urge to meddle in the discussion.

'*Shoo, Mokwug, go away*... go... away... this topic of conversation excludes you and shall continue... shall continue to exclude you!'

Herrifurus signalled in the direction he expected Mokwug to trot. He was simply in no mood to entertain this burden right now.

'*Would you believe*... would... you... believe... Wormpick is the alter ego of Mokwug. A long time ago, all the loving, caring, polite and respectful parts that had forever been trapped deep within Mokwug escaped in a new form. Wormpick was created; she resides in Wishwisely, and you have met her. Wormpick is the keeper... the keeper of the Windmills!'

The conversation was tactlessly interrupted by a growl from Mokwug.

'Herrifurus, I thought you'd slipped up when I first arrived in Enduring Crave. I am the eighth child of Human to have accessed this world, but you said what had only been told six times before. I hastily but incorrectly challenged this. The sixth and seventh arrived here together,' declared Harlem.

A further distraction arose, causing Harlem to fail to complete his point, and once more, Mokwug was the culprit.

'Well, *come on*, you from that human lot, how will Jonathan North access the Calace?' questioned the irate Mokwug, who deliberately bit down ferociously on her lip, causing gushes of blood to drip on the floor.

'I don't think it will be by land,' hypothesised Harlem. 'A storming of the Calace awaits; it's a shame we haven't got an army to defend us!'

Harlem thought it was slightly absurd that the only army Enduring Crave had was in the form of the Grottlers. However, there was no further time for waiting; a thunderous clunking commotion initiated at the Doors of Red Envy.

BANG-THUD-BANG-THUD
-BANG-BANG-BANG-
BANG-BANG-BANG
THUD-THUD-THUD

The doors yielded, and in soared the billions of pasty-looking Wantwots from Mucky Waters, some of whom were returning to the Calace of Judgement, others visiting for the first time. The attack was a well-organised aerial bombardment. The invading Wantwots dived and plunged in on their kin who were hard at work, whether at the stations or on running duties.

A warning siren blasted out across Operation Flog a Dead Horse. It had been triggered far too late, as the raid, so intelligently swift in coming, had caught everyone unaware. How *had* the invaders infiltrated the Calace?

Those positioned on top of the mezzanine were not ignored. The Wantwots from Mucky Waters swooped on the senior staff, but Herrifurus and Mokwug received the most attention. The Wantwots were so small and squishy that, as had happened earlier at the bunker, they didn't hurt when they nosedived in, headbutting relentlessly, but merely served as a distraction.

Herrifurus noted Harlem clutching a tennis racket; Harlem was whacking the unwelcome ones with the racket. It was a fantastic Wantwot repellent. Who knows where he had discovered it right in his time of need?

'Harlem, *over here*... over... here!'

Harlem tossed the tennis racket to Herrifurus, who began swatting the little pests.

'Take that... and that, you tiny blighters... *You tiny blighters, you!*'

The Ambassador of Enduring Crave was swatting away; what a great backhand he demonstrated, followed by a brilliant lob. The Wantwots were hitting the floor hard.

'Game set... game... set... *and match*... and match!'

'*Not yet*, Herrifurus!' shouted Harlem, who was indeed correct; thousands of Wantwots were still charging and attacking the hierarchy. Mokwug attempted wild swipes, but it was most difficult as she aimed blind. Poor Monocle Sway and Backeyedjection fought valiantly, but neither was built for brawling. Larry curled up and cowered as the raiders went about their assault. Herrifurus continued to whack the opposition.

'*New balls*... new... balls... please!' he ordered, as though he was participating in a tennis match.

Operation Flog a Dead Horse was entrenched in battle, but Harlem sensed that Jonathan North would not bother getting his hands dirty by participating in this fight. Jonathan would be heading for the lantern. Harlem escaped and descended the ladder, urgently needing to get to the ballroom. As he aimed for the spiral staircase, there was a great deal of cover to allow him to charge unnoticed; he disguised himself under the clouds and swarms of battling Wantwots.

As Harlem drew near the spiral stairs, he observed Jonathan North standing approximately halfway up the steps.

Jonathan appeared to be laughing diabolically, as a stereotypical villain, while attempting to take over the world. Harlem began speeding up the staircase, but Jonathan sensed this. Realising a pursuit was underway, Jonathan hastily scurried back to the ballroom. When Harlem entered, he found his nemesis groping at the walls, searching for the Lantern of Infinite Wishes.

There were four walls in the ballroom; the alarming concern to Harlem was that Jonathan appeared to be searching within the correct wall; not only this, but he was exceedingly close to his prize. Jonathan's hands were rooting deep inside, displacing and pushing around the diamonds within the walls.

'Give it up!' demanded Harlem. 'Jonathan, you don't realise what you're doing?'

'Do you know the definition of madness?' scoffed Jonathan. 'It's offering the same thing repeatedly but expecting different results. I'm the only one who evolves; I'm always adapting and creating new plans. It is Herrifurus who does not change; he constantly bangs his knee. I'm too close for you to stop me now!'

'Bangs his knee, what do you mean?' asked a puzzled Harlem.

Jonathan sighed. 'If I sit at the table, I get up and bang my knee. The next time I sit at the table, I get up and bang my knee again. If I keep doing this, I must be doing something wrong, so there comes a time when I pull my chair out a little further. *Guess what*? I don't bang my knee when I get up!'

Now it was Harlem's turn to groan.

'Jonathan, if it's your wish you seek, *you're too late.* It won't be within the lantern.'

'I am very much aware of that, old boy. Do you have anything of value to say? *Even you*, Harlem, know I lost the privilege of wishing long ago. My wish, the one you speak of, was never in the lantern to begin with,' stated a cocky Jonathan.

'I know what wish you had refused,' confirmed Harlem. 'You're attempting to steal someone else's wish – another with the same hope. Bad form, naughty boy… thou shalt not steal!'

'Thou shalt not care!' replied Jonathan arrogantly. 'I had my wish denied; who cares if I take what does not belong to me? For the maker no longer needs it.'

'Jonathan, if you find and remove the lantern, it will be destroyed along with the Calace... taking Enduring Crave with it. Is that what you want?'

Jonathan was becoming increasingly frustrated with all the questioning aimed at him. His mannerisms appeared feverish.

'I will be out of here before the walls crumble,' chortled the troublemaker. 'The Eight Curators will say goodbye to this world... but not mine! They may have lost patience with us... but it shall not matter... they will never know!'

'I never mentioned the Eight Curators!' responded Harlem.

Jonathan aimed his standard evil stare at Harlem, but unbeknownst to him, creeping up behind was Mokwug and Herrifurus. They had fled the insurgency in the operations room.

Harlem was astutely aware that he had to distract his combatant long enough for him to be grabbed.

'Jonathan, I've been to church. I know, and I know it couldn't have been easy for you. But this insanity isn't the answer. Let it go!'

Jonathan was becoming increasingly shaky; his voice carried a tone of increased anger, resentment and hatred.

'*Let it go...* never! Harlem, you know not what it feels like... do not preach to me that you know. Who told you?'

Mokwug was right up close behind. She grabbed the young imp, wrapping her meaty hands around Jonathan. Mokwug squeezed so tight that Harlem believed Jonathan would snap in two.

'*Got you*, you little sod; you haven't changed, have you! And I'm not referring to your clothes, you shabby scoundrel!'

Mokwug was incensed. Harlem instructed her to escort Jonathan to the office, wait, and hold him until both he and Herrifurus returned. For once, she didn't argue or object. Jonathan was hauled off, kicking and screaming.

All the while, the battle of the Wantwots continued, but the unemployed Wantwots were weaker. The fight was never going to go their way. It was all a diversion set up by Jonathan. The loyal workers in the operations room were coming out on top. The solution for those on the back foot was to retreat. The blobs that Harlem and Herrifurus had swatted slowly began to come to life. Dazed and bruised, they led the exodus.

Harlem and Herrifurus had remained in the ballroom. Without warning, the absconders flew in and aimed straight for the secret door leading to Larry's bedroom. Harlem and Herrifurus followed up the stairwell.

When the two entered the bedroom, they witnessed the last of the first batch of retreating Wantwots departing through an open window high up in the glass dome.

'Herrifurus, that's how they accessed the Calace, carrying in Jonathan North with them,' Harlem pointed out.

'But... but... but how on dawn's sweetest day did they know... did... they... know... where the Calace was?'

'Come on, Herrifurus, let's go back to the office. Let's make sure we collect Larry and Monocle on the way.'

Operation Flog a Dead Horse was bursting with an overwhelming sense of relief. On top of the mezzanine,

Backeyedjection was trying to reposition his trusted TV monitors, but the majority were smashed, innocent victims of the attack. There remained a few hundred sickly brown Wantwots lying unconscious nearby. Larry and Monocle were intensely flapping and kicking at them, respectively. As they woke up, the remaining infiltrators staggered off; it looked like they were flying drunk.

Many more followed from all over the humongous operation room. In total, around fifty thousand stragglers left the room. As the very last one exited, a thunderous cheer erupted.

Harlem, Herrifurus, Monocle, and Larry Cornelius headed to the boiler room. This would be the first time the latter two would discover the secret method of travelling to and from the office. It had never been identified before, as everyone was so preoccupied with their work, with Larry often being intoxicated.

On entering Herrifurus' office, they discovered Mokwug clinging to Jonathan as if her life depended on it.

'Put him down, Mokwug,' assured Harlem. 'He can't run anywhere.'

Herrifurus was blocking the exit, but Mokwug was taking no chances. She reluctantly dropped Jonathan before joining Herrifurus, standing in front of the only way out.

'OW, THAT HURT, YOU BIG BULLY!' cried Jonathan.

'*It's over*, Jonathan!' declared Harlem. 'The Grottlers are asleep, and the cobbles restored. Even you couldn't have failed to see new wishes dropping into the Calace.'

The problem was that Jonathan hadn't spotted the wishes tumbling in. He was oblivious to it, as he had exclusively concentrated on the chaotic scenes with the fighting Wantwots while celebrating his arrival at the Calace.

It was all his doing, his victory invasion. Jonathan hadn't seen the woods for the trees.

On hearing all this, Jonathan became enraged, pointing his finger towards Harlem sinisterly as he threatened whatever fiendish punishment he had in store for his adversary.

'Behave yourself, Jonathan. We know all about Symptom-Hazard and the Shadow Squatters.'

Jonathan tried his best to belittle Harlem, but his attempt was poor. 'Lies, Harlem, all lies. You are such a fibber, codswallop, all of it!'

'Mokwug, please restrain this rotter from interrupting me if you would be so kind,' asserted Harlem.

Mokwug once again grabbed Jonathan and placed her considerable right hand across his mouth. His mumbles were no louder than a mouse's squeak. There was a subdued silence in the office as no one knew how to proceed to the next appropriate course of action.

'Let him go, please, Mokwug,' insisted Harlem. 'Will you give all this up now, Jonathan?'

'NEVER!' was the response from this peskiest of all pests. Jonathan hadn't finished yet; more cockiness was to follow.

'What are you going to do with me? *Send me back to school... put me in another time prison*? I shall wait even longer the next time. You see, Harlem, however, I pay for my crimes... I will not age. Herrifurus cannot allow that; he has already stolen sixty years of my life. Isn't that true... you

ponderous imbecile... you massive clot!' Jonathan stared
malevolently at Herrifurus.

'Yes, I am afraid... am afraid to say that is true... that... is...
true,' confirmed Herrifurus. 'Only when he stops going about
his nonsense... his... nonsense... can he regain a normal life.
Sorry, I have to say that I do not believe it will be anytime soon!
But what to do... what to do... with this... with this scoundrel?
Put him back in school, and at this rate, he heads... he heads for
eternal life! The very purpose of school is to learn lessons. What
lessons have you learned, you impudent swine, tell me... tell...
me? *No, I will inform you of what you have learned - the
square root of nothing... of nothing!*'

Steam was once again escaping from Herrifurus' ears. His
cheeks were now crimson with irritation. However, the
conundrum was about establishing a new penalty for Jonathan
to pay for his most recent heinous deeds.

As the ideas for the most suitable punishment were put
forward, Harlem sensed a new presence approaching the office.

'Herrifurus, as I was saying earlier before Mokwug put her
oar in, the sixth and seventh humans to arrive in this world came
together, didn't they? That is why you informed me about what
had only been expressed six times in the past.' Harlem turned
back towards Jonathan - 'You expected me to go to church and
pray, but when I saw a Grottler destroy a wish out in the
churchyard, I laid eyes on something else. It was a gravestone –
Stanley and Mary North: Died December 11th, 1964. I
understand your pain, Jonathan, or can I call you Donny?'

Jonathan, who had solemnly stared at the floor in his realisation that his plot had failed, immediately lifted his head when he heard the name 'Donny'. Grandma entered the office.

'Hello, Donny, isn't it time you changed your clothes?' joked Grandma, with a nervous laugh.

Jonathan was speechless; for a self-confessed evil genius, he had no idea that Harlem was his great-nephew, and he had undoubtedly never reasoned on his sister turning up at this juncture; he wasn't sure if she was still alive. Jonathan was so preoccupied with Harlem on that first encounter at the school gates that he hadn't noticed the elderly lady with him.

'Florence, it's truly wonderful to see you, but before the day is through, we will be a family again, me, you, *and* Mother and Father. Your showing up will not stop or deter me. I shall have the wish. The lantern will be mine!'

Mokwug once again silenced the wretch as Grandma approached Harlem.

'As a young girl, I couldn't pronounce Jonathan; it came out as Donny, which stuck as the years passed. We discovered Pressing Matters Lane and visited it on numerous occasions over the course of a year. After the deaths of our parents, Donny increasingly became isolated; he had changed, having become unlikable and nasty. One wet evening, he returned home, distraught and angry. Herrifurus had refused his wish and had cancelled it there and then. Donny vowed revenge, and nothing would stop him. I assumed it was temporary, but it didn't seem to pass as the weeks and months went by. He was heartbroken and believed his wish was a way to reunite us with our parents. The hope was to go back in time to prevent their deaths. Donny understood that wishes of time travel or bringing back the dead could not come true, but he wouldn't be reasoned with. Rage and revenge filled his days, and he became the target of the school pupils. Donny would sneak off at night. Only now do I understand where he was going - to his secret portal to this world. One morning, after months of hurt, he informed me he was heading for the lantern, believing he would finally receive his wish; his desire was too great. I had to inform Herrifurus, but I was too late; the Lantern of Infinite Wishes had been opened, and wishes had been removed. Of course, it wasn't his wish within the lantern; if Donny could find one like his own, he could use that wish. One that had been kept alive for another: someone else's hope!'

Grandma repeatedly shook her head at Jonathan.

Mokwug growled mulishly. All this growling and snarling caused spittle and saliva to drip heavily onto Jonathan's head.

'Donny had been caught in the act,' continued Grandma, 'resulting in damage and destruction - the dark clouds and tremors, the earthquakes, and floods. Thankfully, he had not handled his ultimate wish. He would have to be punished; his quest wouldn't halt if he weren't. He couldn't be allowed to destroy both worlds. I was only twelve, so I wished he would be confined to school for sixty years, for his well-being. If he were trapped in school, he could not cause harm. Even back then, I must have known why I deemed it sixty years. Shortly after,

Herrifurus informed me of Motherhood's new prophecy for the future: My Grandson would face Jonathan North in sixty years… Harlem, you know the rules; I could never have told you such a tale!'

Harlem smiled and hugged Grandma, but it was a sad and sorry story and still painful for Grandma to talk about and relive.

'I know, Grandma, that's why you came to Wishwisely with me. It was time to return; you hadn't set foot in that house for sixty years. You were enchanted; it brought all those memories flooding back to you. You were very quick to pass by the school, and it was time to inform me of Donny in the churchyard, which was a very appropriate place to do so. Such a coincidence that the crone told us the story of the North boy and the abandoned house; that was a great trick, but who was she?'

'Why?!' asked a jocular Herrifurus, '*She is Wormpick, our eyes and ears in the camp…* in the camp… of Wishwisely.'

'Harlem, how did you know Donny is Jonathan?' asked a curious Grandma.

'That song, that incessant song as Symptom-Hazard described it! Jonathan was singing about a girl; it couldn't be a long-lost love of a girlfriend; it had to be his sister. The Shadow Squatters had placed the song in my head, but then Jonathan sang it when we were at the Nags Head. He misses you, too, Grandma; the song was about the hope of him one day reuniting with you. One more thing, though, you sold the house to Mum and Dad, didn't you? £3008.56; that is how much the house would have cost back in 1965; you sold it for what it was worth when you last lived there.'

'*Indeed*... indeed!' replied Herrifurus. 'All set in conjunction... in... conjunction with Motherhood's prophecy. *Start with your mother, grant her wish for promotion, bring her here, and you would follow.* Your Dad always does as... as instructed, so there would be no opposition from him. The moment you wished... you... wished... for adventure was the cue... the cue... and this confirmed the prophecy. *Perfect planning... perfect planning!*'

'Excuse me... excuse me!' demanded Jonathan. 'You chatter amongst yourselves as if you are victorious. The day lives, and I will triumph before it no longer breathes. The lantern will henceforth be in my possession. Harlem, you understand we cannot end the story here!'

Harlem acknowledged that Jonathan was correct; the two would have to face off in a final showdown.

# CHAPTER EIGHTEEN

## The Final Showdown

Harlem didn't know how he and Jonathan would ever settle the situation. Whatever the final showdown, it had to be one of Harlem's suggestions, but what could it be? There could be no weapons as such; it had to be a battle of the minds. Harlem stared around the office before gazing at the one coat on the coat rack.

The coat belonged to him; Harlem had left it there that Sunday when he and Herrifurus had arrived late at night to start the tour of Enduring Crave.

Although it seemed like a long time ago, Harlem remembered what was in the pockets, having placed something in them earlier that week, something to show and wow his friends.

'Before the next move, I just need to go to the little boy's room; please excuse me a moment!' announced Harlem.

Harlem exited the office and returned a brief time later. He once more eyed his coat.

'Jonathan, you have already been outsmarted and will be again. It's time to call this whole thing off! You are neither an evil genius nor just a genius. You are a dim-witted so-and-so who has overstayed his time and some!'

Jonathan was seething. 'Outsmarted me? Hardly! I was careless in my actions. You happened to discover my base, and as for the cobbles, you required help from those who betrayed me. I *am* a genius, and you will *not* outsmart me! Look how far I have come. The day shall be mine! I rely not on technology but on what is in my head.'

Harlem was aggravating his nemesis and continued to berate Jonathan.

'Jonathan, I'm not talking about stealing my phone... and using it against me or kidnapping my friends with the help of the Shadow Squatters. If I outwit you and fool you, will you lay down arms?'

Jonathan could not resist the challenge.

'Game on, for you cannot outsmart me; these are simply more ill suggestions and notions!'

'Very well,' responded Harlem. 'A no-holds-barred winner-takes-all challenge. If I win, you stop this madness. If you win, you get to take the lantern. Is that fair? Do you agree?'

'Positively, honestly,' replied Jonathan. 'You can trust me; I wouldn't tell you untruths; that wouldn't be cricket. But fear not, for lies do not come your way. It is you, Harlem, who will be stewing in your juices. You cannot pull the wool over my eyes!'

Herrifurus frowned at Harlem, shaking his head in displeasure. His body language and tone signalled he didn't have the same assurance as Harlem.

'Do not be silly now, Harlem. *This is not the time...* the time... for uncertainties!'

'It's ok, Herrifurus, we have nothing to worry about. Jonathan won't win, and he's promised to call it a day after all. He will have to eat those words, believe me!'

Mokwug tutted and grunted noisily; she possessed no belief in Harlem, who instructed Grandma to remain in the office. Everyone else was to head to the ballroom.

'Jonathan, the ballroom is cold. Will you object if I wear my coat?'

'Not at all,' confirmed Jonathan. 'It will not save you!'

In the ballroom, the four attendees watched anxiously as Harlem and Jonathan stood face-to-face, trying to figure out what the other was thinking.

'Jonathan, are you ready?' enquired Harlem.

'Of Course! Let battle commence!' he replied boldly.

Harlem took two steps back. 'Jonathan, do you see this silk handkerchief? I shall now make it disappear... If you can tell me where it is, once it's vanished, *you win*. To prove there is no trickery, I will take off my coat. Guess correctly... and the lantern is yours.'

'That's it, that's your gamble?' replied Jonathan. 'You can't make things vanish; I say you can't... *I can*... and very soon I will make you *all* disappear... now get on with it and stop wasting my time!'

Harlem waved the handkerchief in his right hand before pressing it into his clenched left fist. He pulled both hands away, and the handkerchief was nowhere to be seen. It was all very theatrical and entertaining. Jonathan was rattled, instructing Harlem to make it vanish again. Harlem duly obliged; he redid the trick five times. Each occasion baffled Jonathan, who, as Harlem knew he would, was searching so hard for the handkerchief that he never once noticed the fake thumb now placed over Harlem's real thumb.

A simple and basic magic trick had fooled Jonathan North, yet the troublemaker did not admit defeat. Instead, he accused Harlem of skulduggery and sorcery.

This was not the perceptive Jonathan that Harlem had encountered previously. Harlem then dutifully pulled out a deck of playing cards and adroitly shuffled the pack.

'Jonathan, pick a card, any card… don't show me your card, but I'll tell you which card you picked!'

'*No, you will not!*'

Jonathan grabbed the full deck out of Harlem's hand before throwing the cards straight at Harlem's face. Jonathan bolted over to where the lantern was, as near as dammit hidden.

Harlem was stunned momentarily; when he raised his head, Jonathan had his hands inside the wall, frisking and probing for the Lantern of Infinite Wishes.

'Harlem, it is I who fooled you. You need to know one thing about me: I am a compulsive liar!'

Furious fondling and fiddling followed until Jonathan placed his grubby hands on the lantern. Harlem shouted for him to stop; if Jonathan removed the lantern from the walls, the Calace would start to crack. This was the Eight Curator's last straw. But Jonathan would not listen to reason.

The walls began rumbling whilst the floor fluctuated diffidently before becoming more brazen. The chandeliers swung violently above with an undeserved confidence.

As all this was happening, Jonathan only paid attention to the lantern. He procured a miniature golden key from his pocket and inserted it into the tiny lantern keyhole.

Jonathan turned it steadily, and at once, the lantern was open.

The most wonderful, golden haze drifted outwards and surrounded itself around and over Jonathan North. He now owned the lantern's power and over all the wishes inside. Herrifurus looked heartbroken.

'The key… the… key… was destroyed by me… I fired it into the Sun. It is a key that no human being could ever… could ever make or recreate. *The lantern*… the… lantern… should be human repellent. A tragedy has unfolded, for the lantern is breached. *Everybody needs a dream world, and now that dream world is gone…*'

Mokwug violently snatched hold of Harlem. She was visibly horrified at what had just happened.

'I told you, Herrifurus! Him from that human lot has betrayed us. Harlem allowed this to happen; he was too overconfident. He's no more than a conniving, little, scheming, underhanded giblet. I ought to box his ears! Herrifurus, you have been both ignorant and blind. That Human lot, indeed!'

Herrifurus plucked Harlem away from Mokwug, and a verbal wrangle commenced between the two.

'MOKWUG, SO HELP ME... SO HELP ME! I may do... may do... something... something... I come to regret!' threatened Herrifurus.

'What's that, Herrifurus?' replied Mokwug in a wicked tone. 'You do not have the energy or the brain capacity to do anything imaginative. *Good God...* you couldn't even feel the wool as Harlem pulled it over your eyes, good grief!'

Herrifurus started dancing his feet back and forth whilst raising his fists, motioning that he was willing to land one on Mokwug.

'*Come on, Mokwug, put them up...* put them... up... *Come on, girl*, fight someone your own... your own size!' he threatened.

Perhaps this spat would have lasted longer had it not been for Jonathan North shouting and triumphantly waving the lantern around to win over everyone's attention.

'I say, old beans, such a ruckus! Is my last memory of this place going to be the sight of in-house fighting? Herrifurus and the meathead spatting like this. *Deary me!* As for you, Harlem, it was a no-contest; you never did land a punch on my nose... I must be going now. At last... I hold the wish I yearn for; I wish to go back to December 10th, 1964!'

As soon as Jonathan muttered those words, the pace of destruction within the ballroom intensified. The walls bulged, and the ceiling appeared ready to collapse.

The chandeliers crashed to the floor, cracking thunderously and splitting unapologetically into large sections. The ballroom was crumbling as large shards of glass heavily rained down on it.

Harlem instructed everyone to head for the Doors of Red Envy and make the office their destination. Mokwug took hold of Larry and Monocle Sway.

Jonathan was terrified. He was very much mistaken if he believed his wish would be instantaneous. Jonathan wept as Harlem sprinted and grabbed him. Harlem reassured Jonathan that they could make it to the doors. As the two dashed as fast as they could, they narrowly avoided being crushed by falling debris and exploding walls.

Herrifurus waited despairingly at the doors. Jonathan tripped and fell; Herrifurus stepped out and grabbed the very rascal who had caused all the crumbling chaos. He seized Harlem, pulling them through the doors as the ballroom finally collapsed.

The Calace had crumbled, but why hadn't the rest of Enduring Crave been annihilated? Herrifurus had let it be known that ruptures would appear throughout the realm.

Mokwug gripped Jonathan, who was still sobbing. Monocle Sway was slapping him with his little question mark wings. Larry was most distraught that the bar had been destroyed; he let it be known that he needed a drink. Grandma stared angrily at Jonathan -

'Donny, what have you done?' she asked furiously.

The rascal failed to answer as the reality of the situation had finally dawned on him.

'Calm heads... calm... heads... *if you please*... if... you... please!' begged Herrifurus.

'I would ask you all to refrain from worrying,' added Harlem. 'The Calace of Judgement is in fine working order... the Wantwots are buzzing away as we speak... Operation Flog a Dead Horse goes on! No cracks are headed this way. Enduring Crave... endures... come and see for yourself. Back to the ballroom, we go!'

Harlem led the way out of the office. Sure enough, the ballroom was standing unharmed: Upright, splendid, proud, and imposing as it always had.

Herrifurus and his team were baffled and mystified, silently gaping open-mouthed.

Jonathan glared in disbelief as it was confirmed that he had once more failed in his wicked endeavours. Larry peered over at the bar; overjoyed, he made his favourite place his immediate destination.

The others followed as Jonathan was roughly manhandled by the forever irritable Mokwug.

'A jolly good show, Harlem,' stated Monocle. 'The ballroom began to break up; we ran for our lives. That guttersnipe undid the lantern; I saw it with my own eyes. Are you suggesting we imagined it; is that what you put forward?'

'Monocle, that's exactly what I put forward!' responded Harlem. 'Symptom-Hazard informed me he believed there is a traitor here in Enduring Crave. A traitor who worked in league with Jonathan North. This is a fact I had already worked out. The only concern was that the Shadow Squatters couldn't tell me who the backstabber was. A body under the darkest of cloaks.'

Harlem looked fixedly at everyone in the ballroom. He paused before slowly continuing:

'Who is the turncoat? Whoever it is, they are in this very room! We have Mokwug, who is unashamedly anti-human and unafraid to hide her feelings. A craggy, relentless belittler, putting me down at every opportunity and mocking Herrifurus and me at every turn. Dear old Mokwug has become so tired that I can't blame her. She sees no change in humankind; is it worth continuing for her? Did she finally snap and say enough is enough?'

Mokwug growled and raised Jonathan over her head, displaying her strength. Herrifurus sighed and shook his head in disapproval.

'What about Monocle Sway?' continued Harlem. 'Leader of the Wantwots. The Calace was his idea... maybe he was in on it with Jonathan from day one. Someone informed Jonathan about the Calace... and yet... the Calace of Judgement was constructed sometime after Jonathan's imprisonment. Perhaps another motive... does he resent that his Wantwots are discarded and tossed aside once their purpose is up? Surplus to requirements - is this the reason?'

Monocle almost crashed to the ground in complete shock. 'How very dare you?!' he huffed.

Harlem persisted. 'And then there is Larry Cornelius, an overstaying guest of Enduring Crave, if I may say so. What rationale does he have for still being here, apart from living a life free of responsibility? Herrifurus' friends and allies left long ago after Herrifurus was exonerated. You don't work here; have you stayed to conspire with Jonathan? Are you envious of humankind and the help they get in the form of wishes? Leave or remain - you chose to remain! Although the invading Wantwots came in through an open window in the dome above Larry's bedroom, anyone could have opened it at any time. Larry had a concussion and a hangover; Mokwug was off being Mokwug - no one knows what she was doing. Could it be her who opened the window? What about Monocle? You could have slipped away from the operations room; with all the distractions, no one would notice!'

Harlem had offered a reason for the three to be the traitor.

Herrifurus was understandably heavy-hearted; one of his three closest confidantes was a defector. The anguish, hurt and pain were unmistakably visible on his face.

'I don't know what to say... to... say... I am dumbfounded. Say it isn't... it isn't true!'

'I'm afraid it is true,' avowed Harlem.

Harlem took hold of Mokwug's right arm as she forcibly gripped Jonathan with the left. Harlem guided Mokwug to the bar before steadfastly curling her arm around Larry Cornelius.

'Grab him tight, Mokwug, he's the traitor!' announced Harlem.

Larry struggled, but it was useless; Mokwug now had two culprits in her custody. Harlem then informed those present of his conclusion.

'Why did he never go home? There is no logical reason for him to still be here. Herrifurus' naivety, if I may say so, played a part in all of this. Larry was unwatched and able to come and go to the school as often as he pleased, all the time conspiring with Jonathan. Larry would exit this world through Jonathan's secret gateway. Larry left the window open; it was his pretence of being concussed and sleeping that he believed would be his alibi. Fooling us into thinking the wake-up tonic hadn't worked correctly. *But that could never be...* because Jonathan invaded the Calace from the air. That meant he must have encountered a pair of Tinted Goggles of Profundity, but from where? Herrifurus and Mokwug have a pair; mine are locked in my paranormal safe. Larry must have handed Jonathan a pair pulled from his improbable pockets. Larry has assisted in engineering the new technology and trickery that sent off the Grottlers. Those pockets are a gift from the demon, allowing them to obtain whatever they need. Larry was already here sixty years ago; he was the one who provided the key to open the lantern... on *both* occasions! It was Larry and the Demon of Daric who constructed Jonathan's secret portal.'

Larry had given up trying to wriggle his way free of Mokwug physically.

He resorted to attempting to talk his way out of it.

'It's not true; he's lying to you, Mokwug! You know humans can't be trusted. *Indeed*, it's Harlem who is betraying you. He helped Jonathan North; I even saw him rescuing him as the walls collapsed. Come on, Mokwug, you see through him, don't you? His actions had us all placed in danger!'

Mokwug listened, and from outside appearances, she appeared to agree; she put Larry down and then growled at Harlem.

She turned and leaned inwards to lay a fist on the chin of her intended target.

Mokwug's fist made heavy contact with Larry's jaw; he whizzed across the floor and landed in a heap. Larry wouldn't be waking up for several hours, possibly even several days.

'Back to my office... my office...right now! *This instant and right away*... right... away!' demanded Herrifurus.

Mokwug didn't release her stiff grip on Jonathan. She grabbed the anaesthetised Larry by his hair and lugged him savagely to the office with her other hand.

Herrifurus sank into his desk chair, opened his drawer, and fidgeted within its hidden depths until he finally grasped what he desired.

Herrifurus hastily opened the hatch of an orange and blue child's toy rocket, which then expanded to the size of a standard microwave. Mokwug expeditiously crammed Larry inside and firmly replaced the hatch.

'Harlem, have you... have... you... ever seen a shooting star... a... shooting star?'

'*No*,' answered Harlem, bewildered.

'Well, you shall right now... right now... come out into the field... into the field!'

Out in the field of Motherhood, the rocket inexplicably whooshed off into the sky at a terrific rate.

'Harlem, there is no such... no such thing as shooting stars. It's just an intergalactic messaging service to fool humanity. This one is too important to wait for nightfall. I have sent Larry back to Mars; the authorities there will deal with him. Mark my words; he will be dealt with, that is a certainty, mark… mark… my words!'

On returning to the office, Harlem was hugged firmly by his proud grandmother. But the answer as to why Enduring Crave hadn't fractured was yet to be determined. Monocle Sway was itching to know the details.

'Inform us, my fine fellow. You must enlighten everyone about what transpired in the ballroom! It would be awfully decent of you, old chap,' he begged.

'It wasn't the real ballroom,' replied Harlem. 'I remembered watching Dirk Hader, where prototypes didn't work in the real world. It gave me the idea of a fake ballroom with a fake lantern. Jonathan never touched the real lantern. I mimicked the true ballroom and everything inside. The other evening, when Larry was comatose after being walloped by Mokwug, it was my opportunity to steal the improbable pockets, replacing them with a lookalike, defunct pair, from within the improbable pockets themselves… Larry never knew. I obtained the hovercraft and all the other gizmos from these pockets. I realised Jonathan couldn't be trusted, and I understood there would be a final showdown; Jonathan would never see beyond the handkerchief. He had no answer, so he would run to the lantern. It was odd that Jonathan knew where the lantern was loosely hidden. How did he find out about the Eight Curators running out of patience? Larry had been in the room with us, invisible and spying with prying ears… After all, I never went to the little boy's room; I was busy creating my greatest illusion, all with the help of the improbable pockets. I pulled out a slightly miniature version of the ballroom, a fake with everything within it, an exact dummy. I stood at the doors of Red Envy and watched this wonder expand until the trick was ready to pull off. Jonathan's utter confusion would be when the wishes from the fraudulent lantern absconded him.'

Herrifurus began tap dancing in celebration.

'*Right, Johnny Rotter*, there must be acceptance... acceptance... in the notion that the Demon of Daric killed your parents to corrupt you. Who better to deceive... to deceive... than one who already had permission to Enduring Crave? Bump off your folks... and convince... and convince you into believing you could manipulate time with a granted wish. When this wasn't to be, you were inculcated... yes... inculcated... into stealing wishes and destroying us in the... in the process... The demon and Larry sensed... sensed the anger you would carry after your parents' deaths. But alas, you constructed your own plan, didn't you... didn't you? You, Jonathan North, concocted the cobbles' demise and the Grottlers' rise. The demon has played... has played you all along. This entity cares not one jot about you, only that you destroy the worlds. *You have both failed!*'

'What are we going to do with him?' snapped Mokwug. 'Let me tear him limb from limb!'

'If I may interject, I may have a solution,' reasoned Grandma. 'Herrifurus, under the grand scheme of things, it was my wish that saw Jonathan stuck in school for sixty years.'

'Go on... go on,' responded Herrifurus inquisitively.

'I wish Jonathan could be locked inside the school for another sixty years,' continued Grandma. 'Only this time I want to be trapped with him, to keep a close eye on him.'

'I think… I think under the grand scheme of things, I can… I… can accommodate this and add… and add some concessions…' confirmed Herrifurus.

'Harlem, I hope you understand,' pleaded Grandma. 'Please don't say anything to your mother. I shall make my presence known to her in school! Come and hug me, but remember, you must wake up your parents!'

Herrifurus granted Grandma's wish, and with some extra tinkering, he made Grandma twelve years old again. Grandma held Jonathan's hands. He was happy to have his sister back; it meant a great deal to him. The two slowly faded away within a fiery ball of crimson, magnetic energy.

'*Right*, I suppose I'd better clean up Operation Flog a Dead Horse,' groaned Mokwug. 'No one else is going to do it!'

Harlem and Herrifurus agreed to take a trip to the Whitewash Woodland. It was upsetting to see the damage and disruption, and with four billion lost Grottlers, a monumental part of the natural environment had disappeared. That horrible sticky sludge was unpleasantly widespread throughout the forest.

Both visitors sat dejectedly on a garden bench, their facial expressions dismal. Herrifurus stared at his hands whilst shaking his head in sorrow.

'It will take me forever… forever… to carve four billion blighters. *I had better get to work, and fast…* and fast!'

'Herrifurus, please tell me what happened to all the wishes we witnessed at the zoo. What became of them? Were they destroyed? The footballer, the lady in church, and the lady with the poorly child?'

'Harlem, I am relieved... relieved... to say... to... say those wishes were spared. *Fate allows them to endure... to endure!*'

The nagging feeling that all was not over would not escape Harlem. The demon who had created the first batch of witches from Gradun was the same demon who had orchestrated the Jonathan North wars. The Demon of Daric had somehow coaxed the Eight Curators into almost giving up on humankind.

Harlem knew that the Demon of Daric would one day send the BinBags to finish off their previously failed missions. Harlem acknowledged that this demon was responsible for the disappearance of the missing wish and that the next battle would pit him against the demon.

A new monstrous plot would soon unfold, and it would be Merkle's Dawn.

The following evening, Harlem stretched on the sofa, watching television. (One more night of sleeping parents wouldn't hurt.) Now that humans had found hope again, they quickly forgot about the riots, destruction, chaos, and the looming threat of war. That is the problem with Sapiens: give someone hope, and they forget what it was like to have none.

'Welcome to the news at ten; with me, Noah All. The headlines tonight: horologists have stunned the scientific community by confirming a breakdown and loss of time. Recent worldwide studies confirm that a minute now consists of only fifty-nine seconds. The horology community can provide no explanation.'

Harlem sat up, taking note. A breakdown and loss of time! Where *was* Vincent Garrison?

Printed in Dunstable, United Kingdom